Astrid blinked. The fire's glow licked at his shadowed face as he stared down at her, concern etched in the hard lines.

"You're safe now," he murmured, brushing a lock of hair from her forehead. "You're safe," he repeated; the tips of his fingers brushing her forehead, tenderly, gently.

Her eyes locked with his, drowning in the pale blue of his eyes. Tearing her gaze away, she looked around her, noticing for the first time that they shared the tarp and blanket. Some time during the night he had joined her. The air caught in her chest. A space no more than an inch separated their bodies. Her lungs tightened.

But even that space was suddenly too much. . .
She had to be closer.

Other **AVON ROMANCES**

Coming Soon

And Don't Miss These
ROMANTIC TREASURES
from Avon Books

Surrender To Me

SOPHIE JORDAN

AVON

An Imprint of HarperCollins*Publishers*

AVON BOOKS
An Imprint of HarperCollins*Publishers*
10 East 53rd Street
New York, New York 10022-5299

First Avon Books paperback printing: August 2008

Avon Trademark Reg. U.S. Pat. Off. and in Other Countries, Marca Registrada, Hecho en U.S.A.
HarperCollins® is a registered trademark of HarperCollins Publishers.

Printed in the U.S.A.

10 9 8 7 6 5 4 3 2 1

For Rosanne
Thank you for all the love and time
you so generously give.
Your heart knows no bounds.

Surrender To Me

Chapter 1

After nearly an hour in the Countess of St. Claire's drawing room, the long-suppressed words finally stumbled past the Duchess of Derring's lips. "He's alive."

Conversation halted and all heads swiveled to gape at her. Astrid smoothed a trembling hand over her faded muslin skirts and suffered the wide-eyed stares, wondering if there might have been a more prudent way to introduce the topic that had burned on her mind and left her staring into the dark long after she retired to bed last night.

"Bertram," she clarified, pausing to clear her throat. "Bertram is alive."

The room's other occupants—the Dowager Duchess of Shillington and Lord and Lady St. Claire—continued to stare at her as if she had sprouted a second head. Only Lord and Lady St.

SOPHIE JORDAN

Claire's baby, bundled on the lap of her mother, appeared unaffected by the announcement, letting loose several happy shrieks, incongruous to the charged silence.

Lady St. Claire was the first to gain her voice. "Bertram lives?"

Astrid nodded to Jane as she bit into a savory tart. If she dined now, she would not need to eat later, which meant more food for the servants.

Cheeks full, she chewed slowly, the flaky crust and burst of pungent truffles and minced onion resembling dust on her tongue. Unfortunate that she could not appreciate the fine fare. Her own cook was good, but she could only do so much with the paltry sum Astrid gave her for market every week. Astrid shook off the thought. *No sense worrying over what could not be helped.*

"Bertram?" Lord St. Claire echoed beside his wife, his expression politely inquiring.

Jane smoothed her hand over his larger one, the gesture intimate and loving in a way that made Astrid squirm in her seat. Likely it was the strangeness and unfamiliarity of it that disturbed her so. Sentimentality, genuine affection between a man and a woman, struck her as . . . odd.

"Astrid's husband, dear," Jane explained in a hushed voice, looking Astrid's way almost apologetically—as if she knew how much that particular truth aggrieved her.

Husband. Unfortunately, she could not deny it. She was in fact married, no matter that some days she managed to forget . . . managed to pretend she was not.

Perhaps it was insensitive, but she found it easier to believe Bertram dead than the cold truth of the matter—that he lived his life blithely unconcerned of her and the family he left behind.

Only a part of her always knew he lived. And now she possessed a letter indicating her instincts were correct.

"How do you know he's alive?" Lucy, the Duchess of Shillington, asked. "It's been a long time—"

"Five years," Astrid quickly replied, the number embedded in her mind as sharply as her own name. Five long years she had waited. Even knowing he would never return. Not for her. Not for his responsibilities. And certainly not for the hangman's noose that faced anyone found guilty of forgery.

She had waited, clinging to a thin thread of hope. The hope that perhaps homesickness, at the very least, would seize him and bring him back to face his crimes . . . and set matters right.

With shaking fingers, she loosened the tattered

strings of her reticule and removed the anonymous letter she had read countless times since its delivery yesterday. Without a word, she handed it to Jane, then reached for another biscuit.

Jane accepted the letter, transferring baby Olivia to Lord St. Claire's arms. He tickled one of the rolls beneath the infant's chin and she made a gurgling sound, halfway between a coo and giggle. The sound was bittersweet. Astrid closed her eyes against it, against the reminder of all her life might have been. At nine and twenty, the prospect of hearing her own children's laughter winked dully, a gem without life or luster.

She opened her eyes and schooled her features into the familiar mask she had mastered over the years. Even before she had married Bertram, she'd made impassivity an art form. Duty and forbearance. Chin high. Eyes straight ahead. Keep the emotion out. With good reason. Emotion led people astray and ruined lives. A lesson learned well when her mother abandoned her for the arms of Mr. Welles, Astrid's dancing instructor.

Hiding had become as natural as breathing. A vague smile, a cool look, all calculated to reveal absolutely . . . nothing. A Drury Lane actress could give no better performance.

"No," Jane gasped, her hazel-gray eyes wide

as they lifted from the missive. "Bertram's in Scotland?"

First Astrid gave a single nod, swallowing the last bit of her biscuit. The emptiness in her belly still there, she plucked another tart from the tray. Taking an indelicate bite, she chewed as Jane passed the letter around, permitting her husband and Lucy to read the words that had reverberated through her head since yesterday.

"Engaged!" Lucy cried in affronted tones. "That—that wretch! He's wedding an heiress under an *assumed identity*?"

"A Sir Edmond Powell," Astrid supplied. Having already investigated the man, she elaborated, "A prosperous gentleman in possession of quite a bit of land in Cornwall. Coal mines. He spends most of his time abroad. It appears he has not stepped foot on English soil in quite some time."

"A prime identity to assume," Lord St. Claire murmured dryly. "No one likely recalls the fellow's face."

"He must be stopped," Jane announced, stabbing an elegant finger in the direction of the letter.

Astrid dabbed at her lips with a napkin. "I agree," she murmured, carefully wrapping herself in a mantle of calm lest she become swept away on the tide of her friends' burning indignation. "If

5

in fact Bertram is this Powell fellow. That must be the first matter established."

"How can you be so self-possessed?" Lucy asked with a shake of her head. "I would be an utter wreck."

Because I've been an utter wreck before.

When Bertram left she had surrendered to emotion. She had let herself *feel*. Dark roiling emotions: rage, betrayal, desperation, *fear*. She had lost her head. And committed an unforgivable act. Sucking a deep breath into her lungs, she shoved the memory back down, the taste bile in her throat.

Lord St. Claire lowered the letter and gazed at her with unflinching intensity. "When do you leave?"

She inclined her head, respecting his ability to know her mind. Likely because an honorable man such as he would not let such an affront slide past.

"Tomorrow morning."

"You mean you intend to go to Scotland?" Lucy blinked.

"Naturally. I have to see for myself if it is Bertram." She inclined her head slightly. "And if so, I've a wedding to stop."

"B-but how?" Lucy asked. "You—" Her mouth shut with a snap as color flooded her cheeks.

"Haven't any money?" Astrid supplied, smiling thinly. Five years and Lucy still tiptoed around the subject of her insolvency.

Astrid had stoutly turned down her friends' offers of money. The idea of taking money from Jane or Lucy turned her stomach. They were the only *good* in her world. She would not use them. Her friendship with them would remain untarnished.

Lucy examined the letter again. "Where is this Dubhlagan?"

"Just north of Inverness," Astrid answered, having already researched a map of Scotland.

"Good God," Lucy muttered. "The very ends of the earth. However will you manage to travel there?"

"I'll take the train to Edinburgh. From there I'll take the mail coach."

"Mail coach?" Jane snorted, then sobered when she met Astrid's solemn expression. "Good Heavens, you're serious."

"Take one of our coaches," Lord St. Claire offered. "My man John is a crack driver and you'll get there in half the time." He frowned. "Although you really should have an escort."

"My maid will suffice."

"I was thinking more along the lines of a man."

Astrid shook her head. Her father had passed away shortly after her marriage to Bertram. Yet even if he had not, she could not imagine him accompanying her on such an errand. He had not chased after his own wife when she left him, nor welcomed her back when the chance arose. Why would he have supported Astrid in going after her errant husband? He would have advised her to leave well enough alone. That it was Bertram's shame . . . as it had been her mother's. That she should stay put and forbear. *Duty and forbearance.* The noble, dignified path.

Lord St. Claire reached beside him for his wife's hand. Astrid watched as he folded Jane's slim fingers into his own, her throat thickening at the display, at how things *could* be between a husband and wife.

"I would accompany you myself, but I cannot leave Jane," he explained.

"Of course not," Astrid agreed, clearing her throat with a swallow. Her heart tightened at the idea of a man so devoted to his wife that he would not leave her during her confinement. "I am capable of going alone."

"Astrid, are you certain—"

"That I wish to confirm whether Bertram is posing as another man? Do I want to stop him from marrying another woman?" Astrid looked starkly into Jane's eyes and nodded firmly, cold determination sealing her heart. "Positively."

If she could save another woman from Bertram, perhaps she could gain a small measure of redemption.

Perhaps she could look herself in the mirror again and see a person worthy of respect.

After all, how difficult could such a journey be? A quick jaunt to Scotland, a few words with Bertram—and, if need be, the father of the girl to whom he was betrothed—and she could return home a new woman, duty satisfied.

Chapter 2

Astrid stared down the unwavering barrel of a pistol as she stepped from the carriage into the cold, buffeting wind and wondered precisely when her journey had detoured directly to hell.

"That's it. Nice and easy with you." The highwaymen motioned for her to stand beside Lord St. Claire's coachman.

Her maid followed closely, clinging to her hips as though they were handholds.

Astrid struggled to keep her footing on the rutted and uneven road that had so abused her for the last several days of the journey, culminating in this final indignity. Robbery. And just when they were so close to their destination.

With the coach at their backs and the three highwaymen before them, Astrid, her maid, and the coachman were effectively caged. Not that there was anywhere to run in the rocky gulley that rose up on either side of them.

Her nose wrinkled as the blackguards drew closer. Their odor reminded her of the way her father's hounds had smelled, wet and muddy after the hunt. The unkempt trio wore soiled tartan and leered at her from long scraggly strands of hair.

They were not the first Highlanders she had seen since crossing into Scotland, but they were by far the filthiest. And most imposing. Desperate men. And she knew from experience that a desperate man could do just about anything. Indeed. She knew that fact well.

Their eyes darted and assessed with rapacious speed, wild animals honing in on their prey. They snatched her reticule from her wrist. She watched in bleak frustration as one of the louts pulled open the strings and dumped the paltry few coins into his grimy palm.

"This all you have?" he barked in a thick burr.

"Yes," she lied. A few shillings remained, sewn into the hem of her cloak.

She may have agreed to borrow Jane's carriage and coachman, but she had refused offers of money. Pride insisted she could fund the journey herself. Over the years, she had learned how to economize, selling off everything she possibly could. Anything that wasn't entailed. Any item of value that Bertram had not taken with him when he fled. She estimated she could journey to Scotland and back on her own resources. Just barely. But not if these ruffians confiscated what she hid in her cloak.

The highwaymen frowned over the meager sum, exchanging questioning looks. Clearly they expected to find more plunder from the occupants of such a fine carriage. They snapped at one another in Gaelic, motioning to her as they did so.

Coral's fingers dug through Astrid's cloak and gown, bruising her hips. She reached behind and clasped one of Coral's tight fists, attempting to ease her clawlike grip.

"A dove like you," the ringleader snorted, his lips undetectable through a thick reddish beard. "Riding in such a fine carriage . . ." his voice faded as he stepped closer and pressed his pistol against her cheek. Astrid tried to scoot back, but the clinging maid prevented her.

Cocking his head, he lifted his arm high and dug the cold metal barrel against her cheek, grinding the inside of her mouth against her teeth. The coppery taste of blood flooded her tongue and a whimper of breath escaped through her nose.

Coral made a strangled sound behind her,

as if the gun were pressed on her face and not Astrid's.

"Would be a shame to ruin such a bonny face. Now be a good lass and hand over your valuables before I spill your blood all over this road."

"The carriage belongs to a friend," Astrid gritted through clenched teeth. "I haven't anything else." She lifted her hands and splayed her fingers wide. "Do you see any jewels?"

"Nay," he said slowly, his gaze moving from her hands back to her face. "No jewels."

He scoured her from head to toe then, his eyes hard and considering beneath thick brows. "You have something else, though."

"What would that be?" she asked breathlessly, the air seizing in her too-tight chest, afraid she already knew his answer.

One side of his ratty mustache twitched in a semblance of a smile. "What women have bartered since time began."

His free hand lifted, a great paw moving toward her.

She watched that hand with dirt-encrusted nails moving, drifting closer. He grabbed the collar of her cloak and, with no care that it was tied at her throat, yanked brutally, attempting to tear it free.

13

"Now see here." The coachman, a grandfatherly sort that had been with the Earl of St. Claire's family for years, stepped forward in objection.

One of the highwaymen brought his pistol down against his head in a swift arc. Astrid watched in horror as John crumpled to the road. Still. Lifeless. No help to her or himself.

Everything happened quickly then.

One of the men yanked Coral from behind Astrid. The girl screamed, the sound shrill and terrified, echoing through the gully that sheltered them, sending the birds from the treetops in a flap of wings and startled squawks.

Heart hammering fiercely in her chest, Astrid watched their fluttering wings take them far into the gray sky with a strange sort of detachment, wishing she, too, could take to the skies and flee with such ease.

Instead, she felt the ties cutting into the tender flesh of her throat finally give and snap as she was flung down.

Griffin Shaw turned his face to the skies and shivered at the bite of cold in the air. The clouds moved swiftly overhead, patches of dirty wool drifting through the sky. With a curse, he pulled up the collar of his jacket. No wonder his parents had emigrated. The damnable weather was reason enough.

Soon he would be home, he reminded himself, even as he tried not to think too hard on what had brought him halfway across the world—the foolish urge that had seized him following his father's recent death to investigate the deathbed ramblings of his mother three years past.

His horse blew heavily against the fierce wind, pulling him from thoughts and questions he could never quite answer . . . a gut need that drew him to Scotland he could not understand.

He scanned the craggy horizon. Unremitting rock, broken up by wild gorse, heather, and leafless trees that shook in the wind like naked gnarled old men, stared back starkly.

Reaching down, he patted his horse's neck. "Beats the heat back home, Waya," he offered. Griffin would take a little chill over the sweltering heat of south Texas any day.

Waya blew out harshly through his nose, his breath a frothy cloud on the air, and Griffin wasn't certain whether to take that as agreement or not from the Appaloosa.

At that moment another sound pierced the graying skies. Shrill. Chilling. The hairs on his arms tingled.

Waya's ears flattened and he neighed in agitation, dancing sideways at the sound. A woman's screams strongly resembled the cry of a mountain lion.

Griffin slid his rifle free of his saddle and urged his mount ahead with a squeeze of his thighs and dig of his heels. His parents had instilled a streak of chivalry in him that even good sense could not suppress. If a woman was in jeopardy, he could not stop from investigating, and helping, if need be.

Rounding the bend, his eyes surveyed the scene at once: the idle carriage, the man crumpled in the road, the two females fighting off an unsavory-looking pair of men while a third watched, cheering on his cohorts and shouting lewd suggestions.

Highwaymen.

He'd been warned of their prevalence. Especially with Scotland caught in the throes of a famine. Desperate times brought out the worst in men. He knew this firsthand. A grassy blood-soaked plain flashed across his mind as testament to that.

A shrieking, dark-haired woman flailed in the mud as one of the bastards cut open her dress and hacked at her corset with an ugly-looking blade.

16

Intent on their foul business, none took note of his approach.

Griffin lifted the rifle to his shoulder, closed one eye, and fired. He watched in grim satisfaction as the man collapsed atop the dark-haired girl. Her shrieks only increased as she fumbled beneath the dead man's weight.

Wincing over the racket, he turned his attention to the remaining two men.

A grisly red-bearded Scot whirled off the other female, one as fair as her companion was dark.

In a blur of movement, her attacker flung a blade through the air, sending it whistling on the wind in Griffin's direction.

He dodged to the side, missing what would have been a clean hit to the heart.

"Shit," he swore as he righted himself back in his saddle.

Lifting his rifle with one hand, he propped it against his shoulder, and squeezed the trigger. Red-beard fell back into the road, his expression forever locked in shock.

The third Scot grappled for his pistol and raised it the precise moment Griffin swung his rifle in his direction.

Everything slowed then.

The squeeze of his finger on the trigger felt like

an eternity. Out of the corner of his eye, he noticed movement, a flash of color in the otherwise brown landscape.

It was the girl. The fair-haired one.

She flung herself at the man, shoving him off balance. He went down with a burning oath, struggling in the road for his fallen pistol. But it was enough. All the time Griffin needed.

He squeezed the trigger.

The Scot jerked once. And yet his hand still grappled in the road, foraging for some type of weapon. His fingers closed around a large rock littering the road. Too late, Griffin realized his intent.

Pain exploded in his head. His hands tightened on his reins to keep from sliding off his mount. His vision blurred, and he brought one hand to his forehead, feeling the slipperiness of his own blood on his fingertips.

Blood pouring from the wound in his chest, the Scot fell back in the road, a damn fool grin of triumph on his face as he expired, his life's blood feeding the earth.

The woman rose to her feet, staring down at the fallen highwayman, her posture stiff and dignified despite her mussed appearance. A long pale strand of hair hung in her face that several swipes of her hand did nothing to remedy.

The sleeve of her dress was torn from elbow to wrist, revealing a strip of creamy flesh, a stark contrast to the dark blue of her gown that covered her from hem to neck.

Blood marked her mouth, vivid and obscene on rose-pink lips. That mouth was the only hint of softness in her rather severe appearance. The blood there seemed wrong, upsetting and offensive somehow. Another face flashed across his mind. Another woman with dark, obsidian eyes, whose blood ran freely. A woman he failed to save. The years could not chase her memory from his head . . . or rid him of his guilt.

A deep, primitive satisfaction swelled inside Griffin that the men who harmed this woman were dead. That he had managed to save *her*.

She broke from her trancelike state with a ragged breath. Her gaze lifted from the dead man and caught his.

Pressing a hand to his throbbing skull, he nodded once in acknowledgment. He never would have thought a wisp of a woman, one who looked as though she could use an extra meal or two, could possess the mettle to save his life.

She stared at him with dark brown eyes, an unusual contrast against her fair hair. Her mouth firmed into a hard line, until all softness vanished from those lips. She returned his nod with a brisk one of her own. And instantly he knew she rarely smiled, rarely surrendered to emotion. While the other female wailed on the ground three feet from her, she stood composed, remote as a queen, as if the ugliness that had just occurred failed to touch her.

She wiped the blood from her lip with the back of her hand, and it was as if that motion alone freed her of the day's events.

God, she was a cool one.

Those dark enigmatic eyes moved to his head. "Are you all right?" she asked, shoving at that strand of hair again.

"Fine," he replied even as a languid sensation stole over him, like he was perhaps slipping away from himself, drowning, sinking.

She pointed a slim finger to his face just as a slow dribble of blood trickled past his eyebrow into his eye. "You're bleeding."

He nodded. The movement added to his lightheadedness, making him feel suddenly, damnably ill.

Waya danced sideways, no doubt scenting his blood.

Griffin swayed in the saddle. One of his hands dove to his pommel for support. A hiss of air escaped him as he fought against an increasing wave of dizziness.

The edges of his vision blurred and he heard himself curse again, but to his ears his voice sounded disembodied, as if it belonged to some-one else.

"Sir?" He heard her feminine voice ask, refined, clipped and soft, like rum swirling in his stomach, in his blood. "Sir, are you all right?"

Leaning forward, he slid his hands along Waya's neck, tangling his fingers in the coarse mane of hair, knowing he was dangerously close to losing consciousness.

His gaze narrowed on the face looking up at him, on the expression both concerned and imposing, as if his *not* being well was strictly forbidden.

Bones and muscle suddenly fluid as water, he pitched forward off his mount and fell with a hard thud to the ground.

"Hell," he muttered, staring up at the gray clouds moving overhead. Felled by a rock. It was damn humiliating.

Again, her face emerged, looming over him and blocking out the sky. That pale lock of hair fluttered in the wind and, absurdly, he wondered if it felt as soft as it looked.

Her lips moved quickly, speaking. And yet he could hear nothing beyond the roaring in his head, the pulse of cold unyielding earth beneath his back.

She might have been an angel with her flawless skin and fair hair. And yet those demon dark eyes void of emotion, and her hard unforgiving mouth, proclaimed the opposite.

A fallen angel, he mused.

One of God's banished.

And he was at her mercy.

Chapter 3

Astrid studied the man at her feet, cringing as a knot the size of an egg swelled upon his forehead. Biting her lip, she considered her options. A quick glance around her revealed what she already knew.

Three Scotsmen lay dead—and for that she could not summon a scrap of remorse, not even for the human lives lost. She still tasted the fetid kiss Red-beard had forced on her, felt the coppery tang of her own blood as his teeth mashed against her own, felt his filthy hands foraging at her skirts. A shudder rushed through her. She could not regret the end to his life if it meant saving her from the depravity he would have forced on her.

John still did not move from where he had fallen. Coral, whose screams had now ebbed into pitiful moans and sniffles, leaned against the side of the carriage and mopped at her face with a handkerchief. Useless as ever. The clouds thickened overhead. A threatening nip of snow rose on the air. All in all, a rather dire state of affairs.

She glanced down at the unconscious man at her feet again. His wide-brimmed hat lay several feet away. His brown hair, unfashionably long, flowed into the earth, nearly as dark as the trickle of blood running from his forehead.

Squatting, she assessed the injury, pressing her fingers gently to the goose-egg knot, wincing at his low moan. Blood oozed slowly from the short, jagged tear at the center of the fast-forming lump.

Clucking her tongue, she reached under her skirt and ripped several long strips off her petticoat. Carefully, she lifted his head and snugly wound the strips around his head, hoping to impede the flow of blood altogether.

She gave a gentle pat to his chest, the fabric of his fleece-lined jacket remarkably soft beneath her palm, unlike anything she had ever felt before.

"Coral," she called.

When the girl failed to respond, she looked up and spoke sharply, "Coral, come here."

Still sniffling, the girl approached, pulling the tatters of her dress over her corset.

"You take his feet," she directed. "I'll take his shoulders. We need to move him inside the carriage."

"W-what?" Coral stammered, looking from the man to Astrid.

"You heard me, take his feet—"

"But my lady," Coral objected, eyes wide, "we know nothing of him. He looks little better than the vermin who attacked us."

"Only he is *not* one of them," Astrid reminded her. "Not even close. He saved us."

"It isn't fitting that we should—"

"He saved my life . . . and yours," Astrid emphasized with a wave at Coral's person. "Now bite your tongue and take his feet."

Coral reluctantly moved to his feet. With a grunt, she lifted his boots.

Astrid hauled him up by the shoulders. His head fell back to rest against her chest. With several grunts of exertion, they half carried, half dragged his considerable weight toward the carriage, stopping when they reached the door.

"How are we going to get him inside?" Coral panted, unceremoniously dropping his feet. Propping a hand on her slim hip, she scratched the back of her head with no thought that she left Astrid struggling with the weight of his upper body.

Trying not to feel disconcerted from his head resting snugly between her breasts, she carefully lowered him down to the ground, only noticing then that his horse had followed them. A peculiar-looking beast—white with brown spots lightly scattering his neck, increasing in number on his rump. Handsome, she admitted. Her father would have paid through the nose to purchase such a stallion. The creature stood near, watching them almost suspiciously from large brown eyes.

Shaking off her uneasiness at being evaluated by a horse—and judged lacking—Astrid positioned one foot on either side of her rescuer. Wrapping her arms around his chest, she hefted him up with a deep exhalation.

"Grab his legs," she wheezed, her nose buried in his hard chest, fingers laced tightly behind his back.

For once, Coral scrambled to obey.

The stranger's chest purred against her face, his breathing deep and shallow. The rough texture of his vest made her nose itch.

With much huffing and puffing they guided him inside the carriage. With Coral shoving him from behind, Astrid managed to pull him in after her.

Exhausted, Astrid collapsed on the seat, the stranger sprawled atop her, a dead weight wedged between her legs. Her chest heaved beneath the hard press of his body, the smell of him swirling around her, a heady mix of man, wind, and horse.

The indignity of the position struck her at once, prompting her to squirm against the velvet squabs in an effort to free herself. Heat licked at her face. With a squeak, she slid from beneath him and landed on her knees on the floor of the coach.

Leaning forward, she watched as his eyes flickered open, their blue color startling against his swarthy skin. His too-long hair framed the sharp planes of his face, the dark locks in desperate need of cutting.

He gave her a quizzical, not quite lucid look. "What are you doing to me, woman?" he drawled in that strange accent of his, his voice warm as honey sliding though her and curling in the pit of her belly—even if his words rang out with a decided lack of charm.

"You're wounded. We're going to find a physician, of course."

Pulling herself up off the floor, she fell back on the seat across from him and eyed him, still as

27

death on the squabs, his booted feet still jutting out the door. His eyelids fell shut, lashes fanning his swarthy cheeks, dark as soot.

Chest rising and falling, she permitted herself to look her fill, her gaze lowering to his mouth. *Lovely. Full, wide, kissable lips.* Her lips began to tingle the longer she stared. Appalled for noticing a man's mouth, she sighed and dragged a hand over her face as if she could wipe the inappropriate musings from her mind.

She had been propositioned over the years. Since Bertram had abandoned her. Her swift change of fortune had made her prime pickings for rakes and libertines.

And yet she had never accepted an offer. Even when to do so would have provided her with more comfort in life. The idea of another man filled her with distaste. Her father, her husband, even Mr. Welles . . . they had brought her nothing but grief.

Coral stuck her head in the carriage. "Is he dead?"

"No." Astrid shook her head, brushing her fingers over lips that still hummed from the direction of her thoughts.

The man would probably be disgusted to learn that his mouth had become a subject of fascination. He had proven himself an honorable sort or he would not have risked his neck to save them.

Dropping down from the carriage, she turned to John, relieved to see he was sitting up, his expression only mildly dazed. Astrid and Coral each took an arm and assisted him inside the carriage.

With both men secured, Astrid propped her hands on her hips and faced the carriage, head falling back to eye the driver's perch.

"Coral," she began.

"No, my lady," the maid rushed to say, following Astrid's gaze. "I simply couldn't. Never. I wouldn't know how to drive this contraption."

Sighing, Astrid approached the stranger's stallion, eyeing him warily. The beast eyed her in turn, and yet permitted her to take his reins and tie him to the back of the coach.

Snatching her cloak from the road, she reclaimed her reticule and then clambered up to the driver's seat.

Looking down at Coral standing in the middle of the road, a dubious expression on her birdlike face, she advised, "Secure yourself within and keep an eye on the men." With more assurance than she felt, she added, "I've driven a gig. Many times."

Although not in years. And never on a road that looked like something a team of oxen traversed in biblical times. And a gig was certainly not as large as this four-teamed carriage.

Grasping the reins, she drew a steadying breath and reminded herself that the next village wasn't far. *And Bertram.* She inhaled deeply, fingers tightening around the leather.

She would have her say at last. If in fact Bertram was in Dubhlagan, posing as the prosperous Sir Edmond Powell of Cornwall. For some reason, she knew he was there. She could not explain it, but she *knew* she would find him in Dubhlagan. She *knew.* She would confront him and have her say. And stop him from ruining another woman's life.

With a snap of the reins, the impatient team surged forward, throwing her back on the seat. Balancing herself, her thoughts turned to the man inside the carriage. Again, her lips tingled.

She wondered at him. *What manner of man is he? With his strange speech and appearance? With his unusual speed and dexterity with firearms?*

Astrid shrugged. It mattered naught. She would never know. She would see to his care—it was the least she owed him—and move on. He bore no consequence and she would do well to remember that.

"Here you are." Molly, a serving maid at the Black Hart Inn, set a basin of warm water on the bedside table. Plopping a pile of linens down, she faced Astrid with an expectant arch of her brow. "Shall I help you undress him, then?"

Astrid blinked at the servant from where she stood several feet from the bed, keeping a proper distance from the man who lay there. "Me?"

Molly nodded. "Of course. The doctor will want to examine him when he arrives." The older woman's lip curled. "I don't think that girl of yours will be much help. She's downstairs now asking after the next coach."

"Yes. Of course," Astrid agreed as if it were commonplace for her to undress a strange man.

And yet she found herself unable to move as Molly set to work, removing first one heavy boot and then another, each dropping to the inn's wood floor with a thud. She stared at the man's bare feet against the stark white linens.

Surprisingly attractive feet. Long with clean lines.

Molly cleared her throat. "Are you going to help or just stare?"

Mumbling, Astrid stepped forward. With Molly's help, they forced him into a sitting position and removed his buttery-soft jacket from broad shoulders. She winced at his low groan. She hated that he was in pain, that he suffered . . . all because of her. She blinked, alarmed at the sentiment. Unusual of her. This *caring* for a stranger. Even if he had helped her, she did not know him. Why should she care so much?

"There, love," Molly crooned, humming as they stripped him of his wool vest and shirt, lowering him to the bed, leaving him bare from the waist up.

Astrid's throat tightened at the sight of so much bronzed skin.

"Lovely man you've got here," Molly praised with a wink, trailing a chapped, work-worn hand down the hard muscles of his chest to the flat, sculpted plane of his belly.

"He's not *my* man," Astrid quickly corrected, heat firing her cheeks.

"No?" Molly cocked her head to the side. "Would that I were twenty years younger." She winked at Astrid again, her hands moving to the man's trousers with decided enthusiasm.

"I was something to look at in those days," she continued. "Every man in my clan vied to have me in his bed. Even the Laird MacFadden himself . . . before he got himself wed." Her eyes slid over Astrid critically, and her voice lowered to a conspiratorial whisper. "Course I knew a thing or two about showing off my assets."

Astrid opened her mouth, and then completely forgot what she was going to say when the maid began tugging those breeches down narrow hips. One fierce yank and his trousers came to a stop at the middle of his muscled thighs.

Fire lit her cheeks.

"Oh, my." Molly chuckled, eyes wide in her lined face. "He's a brute of a man, isn't he? Lovely."

Astrid had not even occupied a room with an undressed man in years. She never thought the male form could be beautiful. Or particularly daunting. But then she had never seen a man like him before. Bertram only ever visited her room in the dark of night, arriving silent as a thief.

Swallowing past her suddenly tight throat, she forced her gaze away as Molly pulled his trousers down his legs.

The maid covered him with a blanket from the waist down, shaking her head sadly. "Shame to lose sight of that," she mumbled just as a knock sounded at the door.

Grateful for the distraction, Astrid opened the door to reveal a florid-faced gentleman who stood no higher than her shoulder. He nodded in greeting. "Afternoon, ma'am. I'm Dr. Ferguson. The innkeeper sent for me."

Astrid waved him in, standing back as he moved to the bed, wasting no time inspecting the man lying there, prodding at the knot on his head until it bled freshly. Pausing, he frowned and glanced at Astrid. "How long has he been unconscious?

"Perhaps two hours," she answered, seeing the stranger in her mind as he shot the highwaymen from atop his mount, reminding her of a warrior from old. A barbarian. Nothing like the proper gentlemen that pervaded her world back in Town.

Molly moved beside her and together they watched as the doctor grunted in what could have been disapproval. Standing back, he shed his coat and rolled up his sleeves.

Picking up a damp cloth, he set to work cleaning the gash with swipes that could hardly be considered gentle. "He's lucky. A little lower and he might have lost his eye. Highwaymen, I take it?"

Astrid nodded.

"They've been a plague in these parts lately. Damned famine . . ." his voice faded and he shook his head. "Most crofters in these parts have been evicted to roam the countryside . . . the rest are living off oat rations that wouldn't keep a goat alive through winter," he muttered. "How can a man survive, I ask you?"

Astrid shook her head, saying nothing. No comment was needed. The frequent aches of her own belly had taught her a thing or two about hunger.

With quick movements, the doctor rummaged through his satchel, soon settling back with a needle and thread. "A few stitches should set him to rights."

Astrid watched for only a moment before turning away and moving to the window facing the yard. The flash of the needle before it plunged through flesh turned her stomach.

"He should be his old self in no time," the doctor murmured as he worked, his voice carrying to her where she stood. "Assuming infection doesn't set in."

Astrid prayed it did not. She did not want this man's death on her head. Her conscience was already burdened enough. It could not endure more.

"There now," the doctor announced, rising to his feet.

Astrid returned her attention to the man asleep

on the narrow bed, wrapping her arms around her middle.

Some of the color had fled his skin. The physician finished securing a stark white bandage to his head. A small stain of blood already spotted it.

"Change his bandages periodically, and keep the wound clean." He set two small vials on the wood-scarred bedside table. Moving his hand from one jar to the other, he explained, "A salve for the wound and laudanum for the pain. Administer the laudanum with care. See he gets no more than a few drops a day."

Dr. Ferguson looked directly at her as he spoke. "If infection sets in, send for me."

"And how will I know if it does?" she asked.

"If the wound turns foul or a fever arises"—his mouth set in a grim line—"you'll know."

She glanced down at the man who had somehow fallen under her care, frowning at that irony. She did not possess a nurturing instinct. Not like other ladies—friends included—that cooed over kittens and babies in prams.

"He's strong." The physician's voice broke through her musings as he shrugged back into his black wool coat, pulling up the thick collar in preparation for the cold. "I suspect your husband will pull through."

She opened her mouth to correct him, but his next comment froze her, flooding her mouth with a sour taste.

"Now, my fee . . ."

Reluctantly, she walked to her reticule lying on the table, thinking how quickly her funds were dwindling. She had not taken unforeseeable possibilities into consideration.

She fought back a cringe as she handed a coin to the man. He waggled his fingers, indicating more. Sighing, she added another.

At least she was close to her destination. According to the innkeeper, Dubhlagan loomed only a day's ride ahead. At the first opportunity, she would reach the village and learn where Bertram took lodgings. Hopefully he did not reside with his heiress's family. She had no wish to arrive on the doorstep of some young woman's home and put her to shame with the announcement that she was Sir Edmond Powell's wife—that her beloved fiancé was in fact the Duke of Derring, imposter and fugitive from law.

Astrid cringed, imagining the ugly scene. She merely wished to stop Bertram's farcical wedding, to speak her peace. Then she could return to her life. One that did not particularly fill her with happiness, but she had settled into an easy sort of routine nonetheless. Tea with Jane and Lucy. Juggling account ledgers with a negative balance. Attending select *ton* galas so that she might eat.

She deserved no better. On those rare occasions when she had been granted choices, she had failed. *Herself and others.* Astrid grimaced at the familiar pinch near her heart. It was the failing of others that stung. That remained her cross to bear.

"Thank you for coming so quickly." Astrid held the door for the physician.

"I'll see these are cleaned and bring you a bite to eat," Molly said, following him out, arms full of the man's garments.

"Thank you," Astrid murmured, shutting the door behind them, her stomach clenching at the mention of food.

She had not eaten since earlier that morning, and then only tea and toast—the cheapest fare to be had at the inn where they stayed the night. But then she was accustomed to skipping a meal here and there.

A brisk knock sounded at the door. Astrid hurried to open it, knowing it was too soon for Molly to return, but hopeful that another servant had been sent ahead with a tray.

"Coral," she acknowledged upon opening the door.

Her maid entered the room, glancing at the man on the bed as if he were some dangerous animal that might waken any moment. "A coach is heading south within a few hours."

Astrid blinked at the young girl. "What has that to do with us? I cannot leave yet."

Her gaze strayed to the man who lay naked beneath the blankets. She winced. Her first thought should not have been for him. A stranger. Her thoughts should be on Bertram—her *husband*. On stopping him and setting matters to rights. That alone should be her primary reason for remaining.

Coral's thin nose lifted a notch. "Then I insist you pay my fare and send me home."

Astrid waved to the motionless man on the bed. His muscled chest lifted distractingly above the blanket's edge. "And what of him? Shall we leave him unattended? To say nothing of the business that brought me to Scotland in the first place. We are only a day's ride from Dubhlagan."

Coral shrugged. "Let the innkeeper see to him. He is not our concern."

"And yet he certainly made us his concern," she countered. "I would think a little appreciation would be in order."

39

"I've had my fill of this inhospitable country." Coral wrapped her arms about her as if she still wore her ravaged gown and sought to shield herself.

They had both changed clothes upon arriving at the inn. Even though Astrid's dress hadn't suffered the damage of Coral's, she too had felt the need to don grime-free clothes—to put distance from the day's sordid events. "Just another day. Perhaps two," she appealed.

"I'm going home. With or without you."

Astrid nodded grimly, once again moving across the room to her reticule. Returning, she placed several coins into Coral's hand. "Without, then."

Coral shook her dark head. "Very well. I will return to Town alone."

"Do what you must." As would she.

"I trust you will still grant me character letters."

Astrid smiled tightly. "Naturally."

"I fear you're making a grave mistake in staying, my lady," Coral announced. "I hope you don't come to regret it." With that, she departed the room in a flurry of skirts.

The only mistake Astrid feared she had made was in selecting Coral to accompany her. Not that she had much choice. It was either Coral or Cook. The other three servants she had managed to retain over the years were all elderly men. Astrid had bowed to propriety in selecting Coral. And yet she was no fool. She knew the former scullery maid only used her, accepting a paltry wage, exploiting her situation as lady's maid to a duchess—even an insolvent one—in hopes of one day securing a better position.

She would have been better off with Cook, old as she was, or one of the men.

Her gaze flitted to the man on the bed.

Now she would be sharing a room with him. And without Coral to act as chaperone. A man whose name she did not even know, yet whose lips, wide and almost too lovely to belong to any of his gender, made her mouth tingle. No matter how unwanted or inappropriate, she yearned to touch them, to feel for herself. A wholly intolerable impulse.

Each day she woke to the unwelcome fact that she was the Duke of Derring's wife. A married woman. Even if *he* had forgotten, she had not. Could not.

Moving to the corner, she removed her shoes and lowered herself to the hard-backed, utilitarian chair that overlooked the inn's yard. From her vantage point, she wriggled her stiff toes and watched Coral stride across the yard, never once looking back. And why should she? She had met her goal to further her credentials.

On the other side of the busy yard, John talked to a cluster of men near the stables, motioning to his head, no doubt diverting them with his tale of near death at the hands of highwaymen.

Astrid rubbed her forehead tiredly, easing the worry lines with her fingers. At least the innkeeper was letting John bed down in the stables at no cost. Perhaps not the most comfortable arrangement for the coachman, but one less worry for her. And his bed of hay was doubtlessly better than the chair in which she would sleep.

She glanced across the room to her rescuer, eyeing the steady rise and fall of his muscled chest, the dark stain of his hair on the white pillow . . . helpless against the quickening of her pulse. The virile sight of him certainly bore no resemblance to the properly dignified gentlemen in Town. Astrid's lips twisted. But then she knew most of those gentlemen to be anything but proper or dignified.

She shifted on her seat, searching for a comfortable position. Finding that elusive, she gave up. A long night loomed ahead.

The man on the bed moaned and shifted restlessly. The blanket slipped lower, revealing a glimpse of lean hip and a dark line of hair trailing down his navel.

Definitely a long night.

Chapter 4

Astrid woke with a jerk, lurching upright in her chair. Her body protested from the sudden change in position. Pain lanced her neck, shooting down her spine. Rubbing at the painful crick, she blinked against the gloom, wondering if the floor might not have been more comfortable.

Scrubbing her eyes with the base of her palm, she surveyed the darkened room. The tray Molly had brought sat where she had left it on the bedside table, not so much as a crumb littering the dishware. Astrid had devoured the tasty soup and bread, falling asleep shortly after.

The lamp had burned out sometime during the night and the coals in the grate smoldered low. Moonlight spilled through the mullioned window, making the hardwood floor gleam as if it had actually been cleaned in the course of the year.

It soon became clear what woke her. Her patient

thrashed on the small bed, moaning unintelligible words. Rising, she drew closer, the hardwood floor cold and gritty against her stocking-covered feet.

Peering down at him, she hesitated before finally pressing a hand to his brow, frowning. The late winter chill permeated the room, enough to keep one from feeling so warm. Yet his skin roasted her palm.

She trailed her fingers down the plane of his cheek, over the dark bristle, telling herself that the texture of his flesh, so unlike hers, did not intrigue her in the least . . . that the *man* did not. Her nails gently scoured the stubble over his hard jaw, enjoying the sensation.

"No!" His sudden hoarse cry caused her to jerk her hand back.

"Stop!" he shouted. "Not her! Leave her be!" With his eyes still closed, his head tossed wildly against the pillow. "Sorry," he muttered, his voice quieter, smaller, almost like that of a child. "So sorry."

Astrid felt his despair as keenly as a blade to her skin, could not stop herself from reaching down to stroke his burning brow.

His hand flashed out with the speed of wind, ripping a cry from her throat. Hard fingers locked around her wrist, the pressure excruciat-

45

ing. With a tug, he brought her tumbling over his chest.

With a cry, she pushed against the feather mattress on either side of him, arching her back, staring down into eyes that glowed through the room's gloom, lucid and awake, a pale blue, frosty as ice-covered water. Clearly, he had escaped whatever nightmare had held him in its grip.

Inhaling through her nose, she grasped for the composure that always carried her through. Of course she had never found herself in a situation like this before. Since Bertram, she had been careful to keep men at arm's length. Her life was difficult enough without adding a man into the fray.

"Who the hell are you?" he demanded in that velvet voice, the deep, guttural incantation unidentifiable to her ears.

His gaze skipped beyond her, assessing their surroundings. "Where am I?"

"You don't remember?" Astrid asked, her voice a breathless croak. "Earlier today? The highwaymen on the road?"

"Highwaymen?" he echoed, scowling, dark brows drawing tightly over his eyes.

She studied him carefully. Sweat beaded his upper lip, and his eyes seemed to look through her. Grimly, she acknowledged that he was in the grip of fever.

Adopting the voice she heard Jane use when talking to Olivia, she said gently, "You're ill. Release me, so I can tend to you."

His brow furrowed as if trying to decipher her words.

"Release me," she repeated, "and I can help you."

His fingers came up to her arms, flexing into her flesh, and for a moment she thought he would hold her all night.

"Please," she added, her voice a ragged whisper. His hands loosened, dropping to the bed.

Clambering off him, she relit the lamp on the small dresser and slid her boots from underneath the chair. Sitting, she slipped them back on her chilled feet.

With one last glance at the man lying on the bed, head moving listlessly on the pillow, she slipped from the room in search of Molly.

The inn was quiet as she made her way down the worn wood steps. In the taproom, a few men lingered over tankards, huddled in their cloaks and tartans, tossing her speculative looks as her gaze searched the room.

Failing to spot Molly, she moved on until she

discovered a set of stairs leading down into the kitchen. She descended the steps to a toasty room that smelled of grease, yeast, and sweat.

Two maids slept on pallets near the fire, shadows dancing over their still forms, the outline of their bodies like shadowed hills in a distant horizon.

"Molly," she whispered, recognizing the dark braid over one of the women's wool blankets. Creeping closer, she shook the servant awake. Molly sat up with a startled snort.

"I need your help."

The groggy-eyed maid nodded and slipped on the shoes waiting for her beside the hearth.

Following Astrid back up the steps, she grumbled over the loss of her warm pallet as they made their way to the second floor.

Once in the room, Molly leaned over the man, pressing both hands to his face. He opened his eyes and looked up at her with a wild unseeing gaze.

"I know, love," she cooed in her thick burr. Glancing to Astrid, she said, "He's feverish."

"Should we send for the physician again?"

"If you want to waste good coin for him to tell you what I already know."

"What do we do, then?"

"We need to bring down his fever," Molly replied, undoing the buttons at her cuffs and pushing her sleeves up to reveal brawny forearms. "And clean the wound," she said as she peeled back the bandage to inspect his injury. Whatever she saw had her shaking her head. "I'll fetch some water. You'll need to help me bathe him."

Astrid stared after Molly long after she left the room. Undressing him had been bad enough. Now she must bathe him?

She approached the bed. Biting her bottom lip, she stared down at him—at the bronzed muscles waiting for her ministrations. Her palms tingled and her fingers twitched at her sides.

Familiar self-loathing rose up to choke her. She was a married woman. One of the few things left to her was the fact that she had remained faithful to her vows. She had not caved to any of the propositions put to her these many years, even when it had been clear that to do so—to say yes— could help restore her funds and save her from the sneers of the *ton*'s dames when she passed by them in a gown four seasons old. The tremor of anticipation now coursing through her was just another strike to her self-respect. She was above base desire for a man not her husband.

"Here we are," Molly announced, arriving back

in the room, several linens tucked beneath one arm and a basin of fresh water in her hands. Setting the basin on the side table, she dipped one of the cloths within. Wringing it dry, she laid it on one side of his wide chest.

"Straight from the well," she murmured in a soothing voice. "There you are, lad. Nice and cold for you. Doesn't that feel better?"

Nodding, she instructed Astrid, "Pull the blanket off him."

The command gave her a jolt, but she obeyed, baring the man before them and schooling her expression into the neutral mask that had become second nature.

Molly soaked another cloth for his chest.

Astrid followed suit, gasping as her hands met the cold water. She pressed the wet linen to his face, wiping the beads of sweat away.

He moaned and turned his face into the linen.

Her belly tightened at the sound, low and primal. The image of his big body, hot and naked—like now—tangling with hers amid the sheets flashed through her mind.

"Och," the maid tsked, spreading a dry linen towel over his hips and groin area. "Even cold, he's impressive to behold." She winked at Astrid. "No diminishing this man, that's for certain."

With a disdainful sniff, Astrid continued her ministrations, moving on to his neck, reminding herself that she was no green girl fresh out of the schoolroom but a married woman. She should not be affected by the mere sight of a man's body.

The maid chuckled. "You're an icy one. Likely not had a proper bedding."

"I'm a married woman."

"What's that to do with it? If you ever had a man plow you good and well, you wouldn't look at this one with such cool eyes," Molly chuckled roughly, adding, "Let's roll him over now."

They rolled him onto his side, paying special heed to his injured head.

Her chest grew heavy and tight. Molly's coarse words played over in her head. *Likely not had a proper bedding.* Astrid supposed she hadn't. Or else she had forgotten. But then she suspected that was the sort of thing one never forgot.

Molly slapped another damp linen over his impossibly broad back, the skin smooth and flawless save one crescent-shaped birthmark. Suddenly, Molly paused with a stillness that Astrid found uncustomary in the woman, even in their short acquaintance.

"What is it?" Astrid queried, looking back and forth between Molly and his naked back.

Molly traced the small birthmark that rested high on his shoulder, an odd expression on her face.

"N-nothing," the maid murmured, her gaze dipping to study the man's profile with an intensity that made the hairs on the back of Astrid's neck prickle.

She, too, studied his face as if she should see something there. Something beyond the handsome man that made her feel things she had no business feeling.

"Nothing at all," the maid repeated and fell into a silence that lasted for the remainder of the night. They placed cloth after cooling cloth over his big body, cleaning his wound several times and reapplying the salve Dr. Ferguson had left.

When dawn broke, its misty light peeking through the mullioned window, she felt certain she knew his body, every ridge and hollow, every scar, every muscle and sinew, better than her own. Even his smell—wind and man—seemed imprinted in her nose.

Astrid glanced to the silent maid as she gathered the heap of damp linens, piling them on a tray before moving to the door.

"I'll send breakfast up shortly. See that you eat.

Doesn't look like there's much to you beside bones, and he'll be in need of your care." Her gaze fell on the man and that strange, intense look came into her eyes again. "We can't have anything happen to him."

Then she left the room. Astrid stared after her, wondering at that parting remark. It sounded almost like Molly had a personal interest in his survival.

Bone-tired, Astrid shook her head and dragged the chair from the window to the bed. After tending to him through the long hours of the night, it seemed natural to stay close, to feast her eyes on him, to perhaps even hold his hand while he slept. . .

She snorted lightly and pushed that mad impulse from her head. Foolish sentiment. And so unlike her.

He seemed less restless. Almost as if he truly slept. Leaning over the bedside table, she blew out the lamp, allowing the dim gray of dawn to light the room.

Settling back in the stiff wooden chair, she laced her fingers over her stomach. Eyes achy and heavy from lack of sleep, she cocked her head, studying the steady rise and fall of his chest through slit eyes, wondering what had motivated him to stop and help her today. To put himself at risk for strangers.

Her father would not have done so, would have considered it beneath him to assist a pair of unknown women. He had not even helped Astrid's mother when she sent word, pleading for his help to come home after she had run away with her lover.

Bertram would certainly not have stopped to lend aid to them either. Not at risk to himself.

Sighing, she closed her eyes and tried to sleep.

Tried to forget.

Only the years had taught her she could never forget. The past could never be outrun.

Chapter 5

She woke with her cheek cushioned against a silky hardness that was at once strange and comforting. Opening her eyes, she stared into a pair of startling blue ones.

"Morning, sweetheart," he drawled, his deep voice rumbling beneath her cheek. Warm fingers brushed tendrils of hair from her face. "Usually I know the names of the women who use my chest for a pillow."

Astrid surged up from his chest. Glancing around, she found herself still sitting in the chair. Apparently she had succumbed to exhaustion and fallen forward, using his chest as the pillow.

Straightening her stiff spine, she tucked stray tendrils of hair behind her ears. "G-good morning. How are you feeling?"

A smile tugged at his mouth. "Like a stampede ran over me."

Before she could think better of it, she reached out and felt his brow with her fingers, her familiarity with his body temporarily blinding her to the fact that the virile man she had admired and touched so intimately was now awake and no longer unaware of her attentions.

And he was aware. His pale blue gaze fixed on her with an intensity that made her snatch back her hand.

He stopped her, catching her wrist and pressing her hand back against his face.

"You stayed with me?" he asked, clearly having no difficulty remembering the events of yesterday now. He glanced about the room. "You brought me here?"

"Of course. I couldn't have left you bleeding to death on the roadside, could I?"

"Oh, you could have," he countered, silver lights glinting in the pale blue of his eyes. "Others would.

"Well, *I* couldn't have."

"Well, then you're very kind."

Kind? She winced. No one had ever described her as kind before. With good reason.

"No," she replied, her voice more of a reprimand than she intended. "I am not."

He seemed to stare at her even harder then, his fingers tightening around her hand.

Amending her tone, she explained, "Fair recompense, I should think." She curled her fingers against his cheek to keep her palm from caressing his flesh, warm and supple beneath her hand, the gritty growth of a beard tickling the backs of her fingers. "The least I could do for you after you came to my aid."

He grinned, a disarming smile that revealed a flash of white teeth in his bronzed face. A smile that would curl any female's toes. Only Astrid was not *any* female.

Bertram had possessed his fair share of charm and endearing grins. Her heart had fluttered on more than one occasion in the course of their courtship. And yet that all ended after they were married and he had obtained what he sought— her dowry to spend. And spend he did, running through it in record time.

Never again. A charming smile would not worm its way past her defenses. She was dead to such things. Nothing like her mother, so easily charmed and lured by a man.

"Ah, then. I'm not in your debt?" His eyes twinkled with a lively light and she marveled that anyone should be in such good spirits while suffering from a nasty knock to the head. She could not fathom him at all.

Bertram would have gone to bed for a month, every servant in the house put to use attending him. The man had been fractious when he came down with a mild cold.

"Of course not," she replied briskly, attempting to slide her hand free again. "I merely brought you here and played at the role of nurse . . . and not very well, mind you." She gave her hand another tug, uneasy beneath the gleam of his light blue stare. "If anything, I'm still very much indebted to you and your heroic efforts."

He cocked a dark brow. "Oh? Interesting. And how might you repay me?" His eyes skimmed over her suggestively, his mouth curving in that beguiling grin again. Oh, he was a wicked charmer. His thumb moved in small circles over the sensitive inside of her wrist. Tingles shot up her arm.

Cheeks burning, she yanked her hand free with a disgusted sniff. "A *gentleman* would not require a lady to repay him." She rubbed her wrist, the imprint of his hand burning like a brand.

Rising, she poured a glass of water from the pitcher on the bedside table and offered it to him. He accepted the glass. She watched, transfixed at the play of his throat as he drank thirstily.

"Easy," she cautioned.

He handed back the glass with a satisfied sigh

and folded an arm behind his head, revealing the paler skin beneath his nicely sculpted bicep. Even the tuft of hair beneath his arm drew her eye, the sight so male, so . . . primal.

"Not even a small token, then?" he asked. "I believe knights of old accepted tokens from ladies in payment for services given."

"An antiquated custom no longer in practice, to be sure."

"But not without some sense." His blue eyes warmed. "And appeal."

Her mouth twisted with disdain. "Such tokens, I believe, were freely given and not coerced." Were men everywhere alike? Grasping, devious opportunists doing all they could to get what they felt they deserved? "What would you have me give, sir?"

"Call me Griffin."

She arched a brow. "What would you have me give, Mr. Griffin?"

"The name is Griffin Shaw, but I think we have crossed the line where we may use our Christian names."

Folding her hands neatly in her lap, she repeated her question. "*Mr. Shaw,* what would you have me give?"

He chuckled, shaking his head. "You are a

chilly one. Are all British ladies like you?" Without waiting for her response, he reached out and reclaimed her hand, tugging her nearer. "I wonder what I could possibly want from such an attractive lady?"

She permitted him to pull her close, watched his well-carved lips move, hugging every word as he spoke. *The rake.*

Lips a hairsbreadth from her own, she heard herself ask in her starchiest tone the one question most likely to gain a reaction, "Tell me, Mr. Shaw. Are you in the habit of kissing married women?" She held her breath, waiting to see what kind of man he was—how deep his honor ran.

He paused, the whole of him tensing beneath her.

"Married?" His eyes dropped to her ring finger. "You wear no ring."

"I left it behind lest some person of dubious morals decide to relieve me of it," she lied. The ring had vanished in the night with Bertram years ago. Along with the rest of her jewelry.

"Shit." He released her as if he suddenly held a viper in his grasp. His pale blue eyes roved over her regretfully. "Pity."

She had so few dealings with truly honorable

men that she did not quite know what to say at his immediate release of her. She knew Bertram considered married women fair play. As did most gentlemen of the *ton*. It would not have stopped them. Not as it stopped Griffin Shaw.

"And where is this husband?" His gaze flicked about the room as if he would find Bertram tucked away in some corner.

"I'm to meet him in Dubhlagan," she replied, hoping he did not pry further, that he did not ask for answers she was unprepared to give.

"Ah, my destination as well." He nodded slowly. "Perhaps you would allow me to escort you and your companion? I feel obliged to see you reach your destination safely." He sat up higher on the bed.

"My companion?" She felt her brow wrinkle. "Oh, you mean Coral. She resigned her post. It appears she lacks the constitution for Scottish . . . weather." Her mouth twisted at the wholly inaccurate euphemism.

"Weather? The girl seemed hardy enough. She had a strong set of lungs on her as I recall." He lifted a dark brow in skepticism.

Astrid felt her lips twitch.

"So she left you here alone, then?" he asked. "Rather cowardly of her."

Astrid shrugged. "I still have my driver. So you needn't feel obliged to see me to my destination."

"But I do," he countered. "You've already sampled the dangers of this—"

"It's unnecessary," she insisted.

He studied her a long moment before replying. "Where I come from Indians believe that once you save a person's life, you are forever bound."

Their eyes held for a long moment. Longer than appropriate. Longer than comfortable.

"And what if one has no wish to be bound?" she asked, her voice a treacherous shiver on the air.

"One cannot simply decide to be freed." His eyes roamed her face, searching. Looking deeply at her . . . in a way no one had ever looked at her before. Almost as though he saw her. Truly saw her. "In our case, we saved each other. I suppose that makes us doubly bound to one another."

Bound. To him. A stranger? Another man.

She was already bound to one man she did not want. Must she suffer ties to another? Even one as enticing as him? Would she never be free?

With a small shake of her head, she dismissed the foolish thought. *Of course not.* He was being fanciful. Likely toying with her. They were not bound because they helped each other out of a sticky situation. *Stuff and nonsense.*

Her gaze drifted from his watchful eyes to his bandaged forehead. "Well, I don't think you are fit to travel anywhere. Not for a good while."

He brushed his fingers over his bandaged forehead. "What? This? Merely a scrape."

Unable to stop herself, her gaze dipped, roaming the expanse of his chest, skimming the many scars on his sculpted muscles, staring overly long at the flat copper-brown nipples so unlike her own. Heat swarmed her face at the unbidden thought and she quickly looked away. "I see you're accustomed to such misuse."

From the corner of her eye, she saw him lift one shoulder in a shrug. She allowed her curiosity to get the better of her and faced him again, waving at the scars and asking the rather impertinent question, "Where did you get those?

He smiled, his teeth a blinding flash of white in his tanned face. But the smile was somehow empty, guarded. A distracting flash intended only to . . . well, distract. "Can't remember the origins for half of them."

She pointed to the largest one, a dark, jagged scar that spanned his ribs. "You can't remember *that*?"

His smile slipped. A shadow fell over his eyes, darkening the pale blue to a deep indigo, murky as stormy waters. "That prize came from a Mexican bayonet at San Jacinto."

"San Jacinto?" she echoed.

"You've never heard of the battle of San Jacinto?" He frowned. "Let's try something bigger. How about the revolution for Texas independence?"

She shook her head, feeling rather stupid . . . and angered at the mockery of his voice. Who was he to judge her?

"It was a long time ago, I suppose." His top lip curled. "I don't suppose a nasty little revolution so far from your shores would attract the notice of a lady like you. Too many balls to occupy your time. I imagine you have never even picked up a newspaper."

In truth, she had not. Not until she married and left her father's house. Her father claimed newspapers accounted the world affairs of men and were unfit for a lady's eyes. And, truthfully, balls had occupied a great deal of her time. At her father's behest. How else would she have attracted a husband for Papa to select for her—without thought to her preferences?

Shoving such thoughts away before she let her emotions get the best of her—emotions she had always been so careful to suppress—she continued, her voice composed and neutral as ever, "Texas, then? That is where you are from?"

"Yes," he replied, "And what of you, Mrs. . . ." his voice faded and he lifted a dark brow.

"Lady Astrid, Duchess of Derring," she supplied.

"*Lady*, is it?" His lips twitched as if amused. "A *duchess*. You mean I've met my first blueblood?" He raked her with that potent blue stare of his. "Somehow I'm not surprised."

She bristled, somehow certain she should not feel complimented.

"What brings you to the Highlands?" His brow furrowed. "Not exactly Paris, is it?"

She turned her attention to his wool blanket, suddenly feigning interest in smoothing its wrinkles and folds along the edge of the bed, careful to avoid touching him as she did so.

She felt his stare on her face and knew he waited for some kind of explanation. "A wedding," she answered, blurting the first thing to come into her mind. Not precisely a lie.

"I see," he replied, and she could tell that he did not. He was either too polite or simply did not care enough to press her with more questions. "Well, I feel obliged to escort you the rest of the way. This is dangerous country as you yourself know," he murmured. "It will put my mind at ease to deliver you safely into the care of your husband."

The thought of him escorting her into Bertram's dubious care made her stomach knot with discomfort . . . and a familiar shame.

Griffin Shaw was a stranger. She should not care what he thought of her, but the idea of him knowing that Bertram had *abandoned* her, that she had not seen him in almost six years, that she journeyed to Scotland to stop him from marrying another woman. It was too mortifying.

Such a confession made her chest tighten. Humiliating heat swept over her. Dragging a steadying breath into her lungs, she ruthlessly shoved the sensations back.

Resolve gleamed in his pale blue eyes, and she knew she would not be able to sway him from his chivalrous impulse. For whatever reason, he was committed to assisting her. Perhaps he truly believed that nonsense of them being *bound* now. Perhaps. But there was more to it. Another reason lurked in his ever-shifting gaze. And it made her skin prickle.

Instead of protesting, she nodded, smiled tightly, and feigned acquiescence. "Very well. I would appreciate that, Mr. Shaw. We may depart as soon as you're fit for travel."

"We can leave this very morning."

"I don't think so."

"Then tomorrow," he declared with an easy smile.

"We shall see," she murmured, thinking she would certainly be well gone by tomorrow. Without him.

The day passed slowly, the howling wind outside making her glad for the cozy warmth of their room.

Griffin Shaw might deem himself ready to travel, but his injury clearly still plagued him. Even without the laudanum she offered him—and which he declined—he slept off and on throughout the day, waking only when she roused him to change his bandage and at the arrival of their meals. The piping-hot smell of yeasty bread instantly worked to revive him.

He ate heartily, using his bread to sop up the remains of his thick stew. She couldn't help but stare as he licked the juice off his thumb, reminded afresh of his primitive nature and oddly intrigued. Even when he licked his thumb, he managed to look . . . handsome. Unnervingly so.

"You're finished?" he asked, looking up and eyeing her empty bowl.

She nodded, as always wishing there had been more. And yet accustomed to the lingering pangs of hunger.

She ate well when at Jane's or Lucy's. Or when she braved the sneers and speculation and attended a party or ball. Something she only did when the pantries at home were woefully bare and she did not want to take food from the mouths of Cook or the others. An occasional evening on the Town could be tolerated for them.

He craned his neck to peer inside her bowl. "I've never met a female who could eat faster than me."

Standing, she gathered their trays, annoyed with herself. Hunger. A weakness she couldn't banish. The gnawing ache never seemed satisfied.

They spoke little the rest of the day. When night fell and a new serving girl—it appeared the garrulous Molly had been called away on some family matter—cleared their dinner trays, Astrid bided her time, waiting for him to drop asleep again.

She had contemplated adding a dose of laudanum to his drink, but the prospect reminded her of another night long ago when she had doctored someone else's drink . . . and lost herself in the process. A shiver trembled down her spine.

She couldn't bring herself to do such a thing again. She regretted that she ever had.

She waited, sitting stiffly in the chair she had once again moved back to the window, needing the distance now more than ever considering that he was no longer mindless with fever but a vital, virile man.

When he at last surrendered to sleep, she rose from her chair and moved about the room silently, scarcely breathing, keeping one eye on him as she gathered her things to leave.

Slipping out the door, she resisted the overwhelming urge to look over her shoulder, to sneak a lingering glance.

Looking back never made sense. Only sentimental fools looked back, longing for what could never be and what never was.

Chapter 6

Her heart beat hard against her rib cage as she took step after slow step up the creaking stairs of the boardinghouse. She wore her hood low over her face even though she had left the worst of the chill outside. Several eyes watched her ascent, prompting her to shrink deeper into the confines of her cloak. Why she bothered to hide she could not be certain. No one in Dubhlagan knew her. No one would take special note of her arrival or departure.

At the top floor, she counted the doors on her right, stopping when she reached the third. John had spent half the day tracking down Bertram to this lodging house, to this very room. She had waited at an inn, her thoughts, strangely enough, on the stranger she had left behind rather than her long-awaited reunion with her husband.

Griffin Shaw. A strange breed of man, to be

certain. A man with honor. A man that stirred emotions within her that she had no business feeling. For some reason, in his presence, she had felt like a woman again. She hadn't felt that way in years.

An odd sense of guilt plagued her for leaving him the way she had. Almost as though she had abandoned him. Silly, she knew. He was plainly equipped to care for himself. And yet she felt like a thief stealing away in the night. It was almost as though they had been *bound*. As though he had cursed her with those absurd words. And she had failed him in leaving. *Brilliant*. Another soul she felt she had failed.

Still, relief coursed through her that she had not confessed her true purpose in Scotland to him. The shame of her husband's abandonment did not rest solely with Bertram. True, he had fled prosecution for his crimes and left her to face penury and cruel gossip, but she was, quite simply, the wife he had seen fit to leave. *The abandoned wife.* That much she knew, *felt*. That much Society had made plain to her.

She would have loathed seeing pity fill Griffin Shaw's eyes. Or worse, scorn.

Facing the door, a violent urge to run, to flee, seized her. Fortunately, her determination ran stronger . . . and curiosity. Curiosity to see the husband whose memory had grown dim over the years. There were days she forgot the exact color of his eyes. She knew they were blue, but knowing and remembering were separate beasts.

At that thought, another man's eyes came to mind, a shade of blue so pale they glowed as though lit from within. She could not imagine ever forgetting them. Or him.

She knocked briskly, the sound tinny in the narrow corridor. She glanced left and right, almost expecting to see others emerge from their rooms at the sound.

A slight noise carried from the other side of the door—a tinkling of glass perhaps—before the door cracked open.

Dark blue eyes, flat as a still night sea, stared out at her.

"Yes?"

Astrid lifted her chin, letting the hood fall back. "Bertram," she greeted, glad for the evenness of her voice.

His eyes widened at the pronouncement of his name, reminding her that he went by another name. Another identity. The memory burned through her, made her fists curl at her sides.

Thrusting his head out into the hall, he looked

left and right before snatching her by the arm and dragging her into the room.

"What the devil are you doing here?"

Tugging her arm free, she surveyed him from head to foot, murmuring coolly, "And good evening to you, too. You look well. A little older, but I suppose that is what time does. What the years will bring." Her gaze lingered on his prominent paunch. "You look . . . hearty." For some reason that fact provoked her ire. "I cannot convey my relief to know you haven't suffered hunger like I have these many years, *husband*." She stressed the final word, letting it hang in the air.

His face reddened and a muscle near his eye twitched. He ran a finger over the flesh there, rubbing it fiercely. "Have a care what you say. The walls are thin."

"Indeed."

She moved farther into the room, undoubtedly the most lavish accommodations in the establishment if the four-post bed with its brocade counterpane and wood-carved fireplace were any indication. She wouldn't have guessed such a room existed in the provincial town.

Her gaze flicked back to Bertram, eyeing his green silk dressing robe. "It appears you've done well for yourself."

He crossed his arms over his chest, his gaze skeptical. "And you haven't, I presume?" His tone rang out with a petulance she remembered—had heard him assume when his grandmother rebuked him for his lack of responsibility. Astrid had forgotten how very much like a child he could be. Moody and difficult, given to tantrums and pouts when life failed to meet his expectations. Scarcely a man, she realized. Certainly not a husband to mourn.

"You left me with nothing," she reminded him, drawing air through her nostrils, fighting to maintain her composure when she wished for nothing more than to bring her palm violently against his face. For all he had done. For all he failed to regret doing. "Nothing bar scandal of course."

His eyes assessed her with bitter appreciation. "You mean to say you found no protector during my absence? No one to feed and outfit you in proper fashion?"

"No," she spit the word out, marveling that he knew her so little he thought she would sell herself so that she might wear pretty gowns. She supposed if it came down to outright starvation, she would have done what she must. Heavens knew women before her had resorted to such measures, and she hardly considered herself stronger or in possession of more dignity than they.

"Then you're far stupider than I thought." He stared at her for a long moment before tossing back his head with harsh laughter. "Still such a prig, I see. Time hasn't altered that." He angled his head as if summoning a distant memory. "As I recall, diddling you was rather a chore. You never could figure out what to do."

She fought to suppress the stinging heat his words triggered . . . and the memory. He had made it clear she was a disappointment from their first night together. She blinked long and hard, recalling him moving over her, his actions rough and without rhythm, heedless of the pain involved in that first coupling. She could still smell the moist rush of brandy-soaked breath on her cheek. Hear the harsh grunt of his voice. *Can you not do anything besides lie there like a corpse?*

Her eyes blinked open, fighting back the memory of that long-ago wedding night—her introduction to sex and precisely what sort of husband her father had chosen for her. Thoughtless, selfish, more child than man.

Heat licked her cheeks. Emotion rose high in her chest. She fought it back, stuffing it back down where she stored other futile feelings.

"Ironic," she muttered, "I always felt it was something of a chore, too."

"Pity," he continued as if she hadn't spoken. "You could have been so much more . . . exciting." His eyes raked her with a sad sort of admiration. "Only you never relaxed, never let yourself accept pleasure."

"Yes, if I had been more like you, I might have exchanged honor in pursuit of pleasure and self-fulfillment, too."

"Always such a righteous one, weren't you? Never a misstep." Clearly, he did not miss the reference to his crime of forgery.

Astrid flushed, thinking of the many mistakes she had made in her life. "I don't claim to be a saint, but come now, Bertram." She tsked her tongue. "Stealing another's identity? Bigamy? I didn't think even you capable."

He plopped down in a plush wing chair and threw his arm along the back, unmoved to learn that she knew of his matrimonial plans.

"I'm a realist, m'dear. The monies brought from selling off your jewelry could not be expected to last forever. When opportunities fall in my lap . . . well, it was fate. Only a fool would pass up such a chance." His eyes narrowed on her. "It could be quite a profitable venture for you, too."

"How is that?"

Bertram waved about him. "My fiancée is the daughter of the heir to a prosperous and powerful clan in these parts. Why, when I became engaged to Petra, her father saw that I was moved into this room. Out of respect."

"What are you saying?"

"My good fortune can be yours," he explained, his hands fluttering with energy. "Once married to Petra, I can supply you with funds." At her silence, he continued, "And freedom." Squeezing a gold band from his finger, he tossed it to her.

She fumbled to catch it in her hand. Studying the familiar ducal crest, she murmured, "Your signet ring."

"It's been in my family for generations. Take it home with you as proof of my death. Once I'm declared dead, you are free."

Free.

Free of the constant strain of trying to keep the Derring holdings afloat—the derelict countryseat, the cavernous townhouse in Mayfair.

She could walk away from it all, wash her hands of it—of him—and let some distant cousin claim the Derring's endless yawning maw of debt. She would be free.

For a few moments, she continued to weave the

fantasy in her head, imagining herself retiring to some country cottage. Perhaps giving music lessons or providing some other genteel service in which to support herself.

A cozy home of her own. Occasional visits with Jane and Lucy. She wouldn't need much. Privacy and solitude . . . and ample food. She could raise a pig or two. Ham. Bacon. Kippers whenever she wanted. The gnawing ache in her stomach intensified and she quickly released the fantasy. For it was no more than that. A fantasy. An illusion. She would still be wed. Would still possess a rascal of a husband leading a secret life somewhere far away.

Walking stiffly to the dresser, she set the ring down with a clink that resounded in the room. "I don't think so. I cannot live the rest of my life under such a lie." *I live under dark enough clouds as it is.* "And I don't see how you can either. Bertram, someone alerted me to the fact that you were here pretending to be this Sir Powell. You can't think to get away with such a foul deed. I'm not the only one—"

"Who?" he demanded, scowling. "What busybody came prattling to you?"

Astrid shook her head. "I don't know. I received an anonymous letter."

"Then I doubt anything will come of it." He shook his head stubbornly, blue eyes hard and defiant. Desperate. "If this individual wanted to cause trouble for me, they already would have done so."

"They did," Astrid reminded, pressing a hand to her chest. "I am here."

Mirth entered his eyes. "You're hardly the trouble I mean, Astrid. I'm referring to people that actually might do something to see the Duke of Derring hang for forging bank notes. You may never have held any particular affection for me, but I don't think you wish me dead. You're softer than you let on."

She shook her head firmly. "I won't let you do this." *Not again. Not to another woman.* If she only did one decent thing in her life, it would be saving an innocent female from Bertram. Astrid swallowed and lifted her chin. "Don't force my hand on the matter, Bertram. You cannot succeed in impersonating this Powell fellow."

"Yes. I can."

The hairs on her neck tingled at the absolute certainty in which he spoke.

"Sir Powell is dead," Bertram continued in a chillingly even voice.

"How do you know this?"

"I know. Trust me. The man is dead. And no one knows. No one has seen him in years. Of this, I am certain."

She edged back a step, not liking his cool, calculated expression . . . or the dark weight of suspicion that settled in her stomach.

A knock sounded at the door just then, so sharp and firm it sent a jolt through her, shaking her from her unsettling fears.

Bertram lurched to his feet, color bleeding from his face. His eyes dilated, the dark centers nearly blacking out the blue as he looked wildly about the room. Motioning for her to remain silent, he indicated she should hide beneath the bed.

"What?" she hissed, shaking her head.

His fingers closed around her arm in a fierce vise, his hushed voice desperate in a way that made her heart race harder. "Only for a moment, Astrid. I'll get rid of whomever it is and we can discuss this further." His eyes drilled into her. "I vow we will reach an agreement on the matter that you will find satisfactory."

Astrid hesitated, doubting that he would bend enough to grant her the outcome she sought. Still, she relented with a brisk nod and eased herself under the bed.

Who else could be calling on Bertram at this late

hour? A chill feathered her skin at the prospect of coming face-to-face with his fiancée. The unfortunate female likely believed herself in love with the wretch. True, Astrid intended to stop their farcical wedding from ever occurring, but there were better ways to end the relationship than breaking some woman's heart with the appalling truth—with the direct evidence of Bertram's forgotten wife.

Under the bed, she tried not to think about creatures of an eight-legged variety that might be occupying the same space. Listening closely, she took shallow sips of air, not breathing too deeply of the dust and cobwebs surrounding her.

"Good evening," she heard Bertram say, his voice overly cheerful. She winced, hoping only she detected the edge of nervousness to his crisp accents. "This is an unexpected pleasure. Come in, come in."

"Hope you don't mind," a man's voice, thick with a Scottish burr replied. "I noticed your light."

"Not at all, not at all," Bertram replied, his voice effusive, and Astrid couldn't help wondering if he intended to repeat everything he said.

As they chatted, she fought to hold back a sneeze. Terribly sensitive to dust, she pinched her nose while her gaze followed a pair of dark booted feet. They circled Bertram, each footfall a heavy thud that vibrated against the floorboards.

At the stranger's next words, her blood turned to ice.

"I understand an Englishwoman arrived in the village this morning."

Silence filled the room, interrupted only by her quick intake of breath. She buried her face in her hands, dread heavy in her chest that the stranger had heard her.

"Indeed," Bertram finally responded, his voice small, a quivering thread on the air. "I hadn't known."

"I thought you might have had occasion to speak with her."

"And why would you think that?"

Her scalp tingled with warning.

"Aside of being a fellow countrywoman . . . she is your wife, *your grace*." The stranger's rough Scottish burr stressed the formal address, rolling the syllables for emphasis.

Astrid felt her eyes grow large. Her fingers tightened against her face, digging into the soft flesh of her cheeks as if she could stifle any sound from escaping.

"Wife?" Bertram laughed, the sound brittle.

"I'm not married." His laughter stretched thin. "Not yet any rate."

"Cease your lies. My man's been watching your room all night. I told him to come for me should she call on you. And she did. That's all the proof I need. That and the fear I see in your eyes now."

Astrid bit her knuckle, bewildered at the identity of this man, at how he had come to find out Bertram's true identity . . . and hers. Could he be the one who lured her to Scotland with the letter?

"No, you don't understand," Bertram argued. "Let me explain!"

Astrid watched the stranger's boots slide to a stop directly in front of Bertram's satin slippers.

"Did you think to keep such a thing from me?"

Bertram protested, his words garbled and choked.

"I warned you when we first met that I'm not a man to trifle with."

"Of course," Bertram babbled, "I would never—no!"

Astrid jerked at Bertram's panicked cry. A fist tightened around her heart at the sound of bone crunching bone, no doubt a fist meeting with Bertram's face.

"Taste justice," the stranger growled.

A heavy whack filled her ears. Bertram's feet staggered several steps.

She flattened her palms over the grimy floor, the tips of her fingers numb as they tunneled into the floor.

She watched in silence as two sets of feet danced and strained toward each other in struggle.

Another whack shook the air, followed by Bertram's pained grunt. Suddenly he fell back, his dressing gown flying at his bare ankles.

And then there was another sound.

Goose bumps feathered her flesh as a deep crack rent the air, like a melon splitting in half.

A thick, choking silence followed.

Bertram dropped with a loud thud to the floor, the sound like that of a sack of grain falling to the ground. Not a body. Not a man. Not a life.

Her husband lay inches away at the foot of the hearth, lips parted as though on the verge of speech, so close she could see the faint spittle on his lip.

Breathing hard, she squeezed her eyes shut as if she could escape the horrid reality of it all. She pressed her hands deeper against the floor to still their trembling but it was useless. Reopening her eyes, she stared, mouth widening on a silent scream.

Horrified, she stared into his eyes, watching the blue darken to night, watching the life ebb away and vanish to nothing.

Blood trickled from a deep gash along his temple, the wound telling its tale. Either deliberately or accidentally, he was dead, his head crushed.

Chapter 7

A hand filled Astrid's line of vision, broad and masculine, sprinkled with black hairs. She jerked, almost as if she feared it would swoop beneath the bed and snatch her from her hiding place.

Instead of reaching for her, the hand brushed the side of Bertram's neck. After several moments, a soft grunt drifted down to where she huddled beneath the bed.

The room's other occupant moved away. Her eyes remained fixed on the blood marring the pale skin of Bertram's face, so dark, nearly black. Its copper scent reached out to her, filling her nostrils.

Her gaze followed the boots as they moved about the room, stopping briefly before the dresser.

Her heart hammered in her chest, and she

issued a silent prayer that the thunderous sound reached only her ears.

He turned from the dresser, the toes of his boots facing forward, in the direction of the bed. For a panicked moment, she feared she had somehow given herself away. Made a noise.

Then those dark boots turned and exited the room, his footfalls hard and sure on the wood floor. No remorse. No regret for the life taken.

She remained where she was for a long moment, her breath coming fast and ragged as she stared at Bertram, blood seeping profusely from his head, running to the floor in a dark river, silent as the flow of wind outside the window. The blood seemed a living thing, sweeping toward her.

With a strangled cry, she slid out from beneath the opposite side of the bed and rose to her feet, wiping her grimy hands on her skirt. She came around and crouched over the body of the man she had sought, the man that she had, in the darkest shame of her soul, wished dead on more than one occasion.

She reached out a trembling hand and touched his neck as his killer had done.

Nothing. No steady thrum of life, not even the barest thread. Dropping her hand as though burned, she rose, freezing when she caught sight of the blood staining the hem of her gown. She grabbed fistfuls of her skirt and shook fiercely as if she could shake off the stain like so many crawling spiders.

With her hands fisted in her skirts, her gaze drifted down again. To Bertram. Her husband. Dead. Alive only moments ago and bartering for the chance to continue his dastardly ways without interference from her.

She could not look away from the vacant pull of his gaze. Could not stop the deep pang of remorse in her chest. Child or not. Selfish, neglectful . . . even criminal, he did not deserve such an end.

And yet somehow she had brought about that very thing. She felt responsibility for his death as keenly as the prick of a blade to her flesh.

His murderer had used her to confirm his suspicions about Bertram. How he knew her identity—or Bertram's—she hadn't a clue. Perhaps he had been the one to send the anonymous note to her? She shook her spinning head, not understanding any of it. Only that Bertram was dead. And she was a widow. But without the sense of freedom she had thought such status would carry. Pressing a palm to her cold cheek, she drew a deep breath into her lungs.

The whirling in her head did not cease. She

moved on legs heavy as lead to the door. A dull roar grew in her ears, filling her head. Stopping, remembering, she turned. Her gaze flew to the dresser, to the spot where she had set Bertram's ducal signet ring, the proof, he had said, to offer as evidence of his death.

It was gone. The dresser's surface gleamed bare in the firelight. She would not even have that item to offer his sister and grandmother.

Eager to leave, to flee the coppery tang of blood that seemed to color the air, to chase her, she turned, easing open the door and peeking her head out to survey the corridor. Finding it empty, she stepped out and quietly closed the door.

Turning, she stifled a scream when she came face-to-face with a young woman, a maid if the linens piled high in her arms were any indication.

"Ma'am," the girl greeted, her eyes moving to Bertram's door, then flicking back to her. Lips pursing in a knowing manner, she skirted past and disappeared down the hall.

Pulling the hood of her cloak low over her head, Astrid hurried down the stairs and out into the night, seeing nothing. Nothing save a pair of vacant eyes.

The sight of Bertram, his blood staining the

floor, clouded her mind as she stumbled through the chill night, past cottages that leaned slightly in the biting wind, hunkered shapes that seemed to watch her as she hastened past.

Her legs moved automatically, eager to reach the inn and the privacy of her room where she could . . .

What? Astrid shook her head. Cry? Shout? *Permit yourself to feel relief,* a small, wretched voice taunted.

All seemed useless, pathetic behavior. The mark of an inept woman.

She drew cold air into her lungs, bracing herself. When the shock ebbed. When the image of Bertram no longer filled her mind, she would dust her hands and move on from here. Like always.

She passed a tavern. Raucous voices and laughter spilled out into the night and she gave wide berth to a group of men entering the establishment, ignoring them when they called out suggestive comments.

Ducking deeper inside the hood of her cloak, she increased her pace, passing the building and turning left—and running directly into a large wall of a body.

"Whoa there." A familiar drawl filled her ears.

Hard hands came up to grasp her arms, steadying her.

Her eyes snapped to his face, to the eyes she knew she would see. Even in the dark, his pale blue eyes flared brightly in recognition . . . and anger.

"*You,*" he growled.

She opened her mouth but no sound fell as she stared up into Griffin Shaw's glowering face. Moonlight limned the lines of his face, making them appear harsh as rough-hewn granite.

"I thought we were to travel here together?" His fingers flexed on her arm, singeing her through her cloak. "What? Can you not speak? Or would I hear only more falsehoods?"

A strange little mewl escaped her and her legs suddenly went from lead to jam. His hands tightened, supporting her.

"What is it? Are you hurt?" His hard gaze skimmed her, then moved beyond her shoulder, as if suddenly remembering her purpose in traveling to Dubhlagan. "Where is your husband?"

"Husband," she echoed, shaking her head slowly, as if she had never heard such a word before, as if its meaning escaped her entirely.

"Astrid," he urged, saying her name as if he possessed the right to do so. And strangely, the sound of her name sounded *right* falling from his lips. Comforting.

"Dead," she managed to get out . . . and not fall apart at the declaration. Squeezing her eyes, she pushed the image of Bertram lying motionless on the floor from her mind.

Griffin Shaw's eyes drilled into her with a burning intensity, thawing some of the numbness. He drew her close, his heat solace against the night air.

Wrapping an arm around her, he led her to the inn at the end of the lane. "Come," he encouraged. "Let's get out of the cold."

Nodding, she allowed him to lead her inside and up the stairs.

"You're staying here?" she asked.

He nodded. "And you?"

"Yes," she murmured, thinking that perhaps their paths had been destined to cross again. Whether she willed it or not.

She didn't protest as he led her to his room, coincidentally, only two doors from the room she occupied. She hesitated for a bare second at the door. It seemed a little late for a sense of propriety to seize her now.

His room was almost identical to hers with its single bed and a utilitarian dresser, table and chairs. He guided her to the table and seated her with care, as if she were some fragile piece of crystal. She almost gave in to laughter. There was nothing soft or delicate about her. Not after tonight. Hell, not after the last five years.

"What happened?" he asked, sitting and pulling his chair close.

She carefully lowered her hood, her fingers playing with the worn edges before splaying on the table's scarred surface. She frowned at the way they trembled, reprimanding herself to gain control of herself, to fight the distress that threatened to break free.

Sucking in a deep breath, she began to speak, confiding the very shame that she had wanted to keep from him before. That her husband had abandoned her years before. That he thought to marry another as if she did not exist. Tight laughter bubbled up in her chest. Now he knew.

"You tracked him here?" Griffin asked.

"Yes. I confronted him and demanded he end the betrothal." She shook her head. "He showed no remorse. Offered to buy my silence if I returned to England." At this she did laugh, the sound ringing hollowly through the room.

"Bastard."

Her eyes widened at this harsh pronouncement, at his grim expression.

She shook her head, her jaw tightening. "Don't say that." God knew she had said it to herself over the years, but now she could not stomach the thought— or sound—of a deprecation against Bertram. Not while his life's blood stained the hem of her skirts.

"Astrid," the low rumble of his voice pulled her gaze to his face. He took her hands from the table. His eyes drilled into her, probing, demanding the truth. "You said he's dead. Did you . . ." his voice faded, leaving the question in his eyes for her to interpret.

"No!" she cried, pulling her hands free of his, horrified that he would suspect such a thing of her. True, she was no saint. She had made mistakes in her life. But murder her husband? "God, no!"

He caught her hands again, holding tight and staring intently into her eyes. "I had to ask. You had every reason to want him dead—"

"I didn't kill him," she hissed, indignation sweeping through her. And yet deep in the shadows of her heart, there had been times, in the dark of night, in the privacy of her room, when she had burrowed deep into her bed and wished him dead.

The bitter realization only confirmed that she was utterly and completely irredeemable. And she had thought stopping Bertram from marrying some unsuspecting woman would be a form of atonement. Instead her arrival appeared to have brought about his death.

"Go on. Finish telling me what happened."

Swallowing, she inhaled and told him everything, her voice rushing out as if the speed in which she spoke would make it somehow less real.

His eyes skimmed over her soiled skirts, and his thumbs rubbed the smudges of dirt on her hands.

"Did anyone see you leave the lodging house?"

Astrid blinked at the sudden question. "Yes. A maid."

Releasing her hands, he paced the length of the room once, stopping at the window and looking down onto the dark yard. After a few moments, he glanced back at her, eyes pale chips of blue beneath his dark brows. "I recommend you leave at first light. Before even."

She tucked her hands beneath her skirts, feeling the corners of her mouth pull into a frown.

"You're a stranger in these parts," he continued. "An Englishwoman who was last seen coming out of a dead man's room."

"You're saying suspicion will fall on me?" she queried, shocked despite the logic of his reasoning.

"Where's your driver?" he asked.

"He bedded down in the stables for the night."

"I suggest you rise early and join him there. Depart before anyone even has a chance to realize your husband is dead."

As his cold, matter-of-fact words sank in, she realized he dispensed sound advice.

"Very well," she agreed. There was no reason to dally in Scotland after all. No reason to linger. Bertram brought her here. And Bertram was gone.

Even if she did not relish the world she inhabited in Town, it was her world nonetheless. She needed to return to her place in it . . . and begin the messy business of proving her husband's death.

"Let's get you to your room."

At his brusque tone, she nodded numbly, allowing him to lead her down the hall to her room, the slight pressure of his hand on her elbow comforting.

At her door, they both stood for some moments, an awkward silence rising between them as they lingered.

She stared at the dirty floorboards, at the toes of his dark boots, and cleared her throat. "Well . . ."

She lifted her gaze from the floor. He had not bothered to don a cravat as most gentlemen wore, and she found herself eye level with the base of his neck.

The shirt beneath his jacket was open at the throat, exposing tan, warm-looking flesh. Even in the corridor's shadow, she thought she saw his pulse hammering against the side of his neck, thought it moved quickly, beating with a rhythm that matched her own galloping heart.

"Thank you for your . . . kindness." She was not sure what word applied to him. No doubt he had been helpful, but his current hard stare did not bring forth thoughts of kindness. He looked . . . angry. Dangerous.

He nodded grimly, his blue gaze as harsh and relentless as it had been when she first collided with him in the village.

"You could have been honest with me," he bit out. "You needn't have told me we would journey here together if it was not your intention."

"You wouldn't accept my answer."

"So lying was easier." He gave a single, hard nod.

Turning, eager to escape him, she fumbled with her key, loathing the way he looked at her . . . as if she had failed him. She squeezed her eyes shut in a hard blink. Impossible. She didn't know him. Didn't *owe* him anything.

His hand clamped down on her shoulder just as she managed to unlock her door. He forced her back around, forced her to confront that damning gaze of his.

"Let me go," she hissed, defiance burning through her chest as he backed her against her door.

His fingers flexed on her shoulder but he did not release her. He stepped closer, those blue eyes intense and burning on her. The hand on her shoulder slid down her arm, circling her wrist. His thumb pressed against her pulse point, holding her, connecting them with that light, burning touch.

Something flickered in his eyes. Something dark and powerful, different from the anger but somehow more dangerous. An answering spark flared to life low in her belly and she ceased to breathe altogether.

After a long moment, his hand slipped from her, freeing her. Yet she still felt bound by the pull of his eyes, branded by his touch.

"Take care of yourself . . . *Duchess*," he drawled in that rich, whiskey voice of his that reminded her of warm nights and the smoky peat scent of fire.

Without another word, he turned away, his

boots thudding along the floorboards, echoing through the narrow corridor.

Pressing a hand to her stomach, she regained her breath. Dragging air into her too-tight lungs, she watched as he disappeared inside his room, wondering at the sudden hollow ache in her chest that had nothing to do with the death of her husband. And everything to do with a man she barely knew. A man she would never see again. And yet she did not feel the relief she should over that fact.

Chapter 8

"**Y**ou have an Englishwoman staying here, Tom?"

Griffin looked up from his tankard at the two men addressing the innkeeper, his pulse spiking at the question. They wore grim expressions on their faces and he instantly surmised they served as the law in these parts. And he had a fairly good idea what Englishwoman they sought.

"I did." The portly innkeeper returned from behind the bar, wiping his thick hands on a soiled apron. "She settled her account and left early this morning."

Griffin knew as much. He had knocked on her door at sunup to make certain she was on her way. Why he bothered, why he cared, he could not say. He owed her nothing. Still, mingled relief and regret filled him when that door never opened.

Relief that she had taken his advice to depart at first light, and a peculiar sense of regret that he would never see her again, never look on those dark, haunted eyes.

"I saw her," he heard himself say before he could consider what he was doing.

The two Scots looked his way. "Did you, now?" They approached his table, looking him over closely.

He took a swig from his tankard, thinking fast. "A fetching bit of skirt."

"You know where she's headed?"

He took his time answering, biting into a hunk of tough bread. The food in these parts left much to be desired. With the famine, he expected no better. Still, his stomach craved something more palatable.

"Real huffy sort. Took offense to my . . ." He pretended to search for the proper word. "Interest."

"And? Do you know where she is?"

Figuring every moment he bought her could only help, he lied. "Said something about going to church."

"Church?" The two Scotsman exchanged disbelieving looks.

He shrugged and tore off another hunk of bread with his teeth, doing his best to appear unaffected. He had seen the church at the far end of town, a ramshackle building with a cross nailed to the gabled roof. Perhaps they would believe a suspected murderess craved the Lord's forgiveness for her crime.

After a moment, one of the Scots grinned. "Thank you, sir." With a nod, they turned on their heels, their tartans whipping on air.

Griffin held his seat, watching the two men hasten from the taproom. Once the door banged shut behind them, he stood. Wasting no time, he gathered his saddlebag and settled his account with the innkeeper. Stepping outside, he crossed the road toward the stables, pulling up the collar of his coat to ward of the slash of wind.

He halted in the stable yard, recognizing the fine coach with the elaborate coat of arms on the door. With a sinking feeling, he rounded the coach and halted.

She stood there, in the process of being assisted within.

"What the hell are you *still* doing here?"

She spun around at the sound of his voice. "Mr. Shaw."

Her driver blinked. Looking Griffin over, he gave a slight nod of acknowledgment. "Is there a problem?"

"You could say that," he ground out, eyes trained on her. "I thought you would have been gone by now."

She motioned to the coach. "It's a team of six. It took John some time to ready them."

Griffin looked over his shoulder, almost expecting to see the two Scotsmen from earlier bearing down on them.

Her soft voice penetrated. "Is there a problem, Mr. Shaw?"

He turned back around. Stepping closer, he closed a hand around her elbow. "The problem, sweetheart, is that they're already looking for you." He motioned to the coach. "Even if you leave now, I have no doubt they can overtake you in this lumbering beast of a contraption."

The color faded from her cheeks. "Oh." After a moment, she gave a small shake of her head and lifted her chin. "I shall merely explain to them—"

"What? Who you are?" He snorted. "After they hear your tale, they will have no doubts you murdered your husband."

"I did *not* murder him." Her dark eyes flashed fire, locking with his in challenge.

"They will believe you did." Hell, he almost believed she had.

She shook her arm free of his hand. "What do you suggest, then? It sounds as though I have little choice. I either confront these men or try my luck on the road."

Neither of which would serve her well. He studied her a moment, knowing there was little time. A decision needed to be reached and soon. He didn't have time to stand around staring at her, looking into those dark eyes and marveling at how much she reminded him of *her*. Absurd. The woman had died years ago. Griffin did not even know her name. He only knew that she had felt soft, helpless, light as wind in his arms, drowning in her own blood from the thrust of a bayonet.

A death he did not stop . . . but should have.

But *this*. This, he could stop.

"Come," he said, the word dropping like a stone in the air, hard and fast. He snatched one of her bags—the smaller valise from where it sat on the ground beside her—waiting to be loaded.

Her eyes rounded. "What are you doing with that?"

He grabbed hold of her hand. She gasped at the touch. When she would have pulled free, he tightened his hold, twining his fingers through hers.

Facing her driver, he grimly directed, "Continue on. Hurry, man. With luck, they will follow you and give us time to get away. Tell them nothing of your mistress."

The coachman nodded dumbly.

"What are you doing?" she demanded as he pulled her behind him, deep into the shadowed confines of the stable, searching for the stable master.

"Saving your neck."

And perhaps righting past wrongs . . . gaining for himself a shred of redemption at last.

The village dozed, still as stone in the morning silence. Gray light broke over the thatched rooftops. A dog barked as they passed the blacksmith's, and Astrid started in the fractured silence, jerking in the seat of her saddle.

She glanced at Griffin Shaw beside her. His gaze scanned over the village with the alertness of a hawk. She held her breath, following his gaze to a single man emerging from a house.

"Is that—"

He cut her off with a sudden lift of his hand and a hard shake of his head.

She bit her lip.

He urged his horse faster. Her mount increased its pace, following his. The feel of the horse, large and undulating between her legs, felt alien, but a sidesaddle was not to be found. They were lucky enough to have obtained a mount for her with such haste.

Griffin glanced back over his shoulder at her, a too-long lock of dark hair falling over his cheek.

She gave a small nod, and inhaled thinly through her nose, telling herself that she was doing the right thing in placing her trust in him. He had saved her life. And for whatever reason, he sought to help her now.

She felt her brow crease at the strangeness of *that*.

No man had ever made it a priority to look out for her. Her father had left her to the care of servants. And Bertram had simply *left* her.

She gave herself a small shake as if she could toss off the dark thoughts. The *why* didn't signify. He would take her to Edinburgh. From there she could take the train the rest of the way home. And that would be the end of it. The end of them.

She would return to Town and see about putting Bertram's affairs to final order. Duty demanded it. No matter how his grandmother and sister felt about her, they deserved to know what happened to him. His heir, a distant cousin whose face she could not recall, deserved the right to claim a title he may or may not wish to possess. No matter that a part of her preferred to delay and remain in this wilderness, preferred hiding from the call of duty, to embrace freedom. To pretend, for once in her life, that Astrid, the Duchess of Derring, did not exist.

They rode in silence, their pace slow as they left the village far behind and delved deeply into heavy mists. The drawing rooms of the *ton* fell even farther behind. Another world. One she felt in no hurry to see again.

They made their way through mountainous landscape, climbing and descending steep inclines, during which she was heartily glad to be riding astride and not sidesaddle.

She suppressed her misgivings over the fact that she was riding into a wilderness with a stranger. *Trust him.* She allowed the whisper to weave through her head, as unrelenting as the wind whistling off the deep crags around them.

They stopped midmorning, leaving the winding road behind and following the sound of rushing water to a nearby brook. The waters raced cold and fast as they guided their horses to drink.

"How are you faring?" he asked, the first words he had spoken since he bustled her from the stables.

She nodded, accepting a corked flask of water from him and taking a sip. "How far are we from Edinburgh?"

He glanced at the horizon, blue eyes narrowing as he studied the sun over the treetops. "According to my map and the stable master I consulted back in Dubhlagen, we'll probably reach there tomorrow."

"Is there another village along the way?"

He shook his head. "We'll bed down outdoors."

"Outside?" She had never slept a night outside.

His lips quirked. "What's the matter, Duchess? Never slept beneath the stars before?"

"No."

He nodded slowly, his gaze dragging over her face with a thoroughness that made her chest suddenly tight. He did that. Looked at her as no one had. As though he saw her, truly saw her and not the cold veneer she presented.

"Well." His eyes held hers for a long moment before she looked away, focusing her attention on the dark waters moving swiftly at their feet. "There's a first time for everything." He chuckled, the sound running through her, slow and warming as tea going down.

"I suppose you sleep outdoors often?"

"Often enough. Texas is a big place."

She looked at him again. "And what do you do in Texas?"

"Corn, beans, potatoes." He lifted his good shoulder in a shrug. "Depends what I think will sell well the following year."

"You're a farmer?" She reassessed him. He didn't fit with her idea of a farmer. She never imagined farmers to be expert marksmen.

"I s'pose you could call me that. I do whatever I can to survive . . . if I'm lucky I make a little money in the process. I ranch. Tend livestock. Cattle. Hogs."

"Hogs?" she echoed, wrinkling her nose.

Laughter shook his voice. "They're easy to care for and bring a nice purse at market. As large as they are, they're unlikely to be carried off by scavengers and Indians."

"Indians?

His well-carved lips twisted. "They're not just myth."

She lifted her gaze from the water and studied the hard cut of his profile, handsome and sharp as carved marble. A man that lived in savage lands. With savages. She had never seen his like. Never imagined such a man existed. Her heart beat harder and she forced her gaze away, pulling cool, bracing air into her lungs. "Of course," she murmured.

She watched beneath her lashes as he moved to check the cinch on his saddle, marveling at the life he led. Her father would never have deigned to speak to such a man—a man who *worked* for a living. He would have considered Griffin Shaw beneath his regard. Weak. Unimportant.

And yet she could not help but see him as anything other than strong. Her gaze flicked over the broad expanse of back. An impressive specimen. A man with strength and honor. Rare characteristics, indeed.

"And you prefer that sort of existence?" she heard herself say.

"What *sort* of existence do you mean?" he asked, clearly not understanding as he moved around to the other side of the horse.

She wet her lips. "The sort where you work for a living. Where you must stand vigilant against Indians?"

He burst forth with a sudden rich chuckle. The skin at her nape tingled in the most bothersome way at the sound.

"For most of the world, there's no choice in the matter. Preference has nothing to do with it." He glanced at her over the top of his horse, a single dark eyebrow quirked. "It's a grueling life, I admit. The frontier's not for everyone. But it's the only life I've known, and I can't say I would want the *sort* you've led." His eyes gleamed down at her without a hint of apology. "I suppose that surprises you? Makes me seem a primitive?"

She opened her mouth to deny the suggestion, but then snapped her lips shut. Yes, she supposed that did make him somewhat primitive. A man who *preferred* sweat and hardship over a life of leisure and comfort. Certainly not a gentleman.

Then his other words penetrated. "You know *nothing* about the sort of life I've led."

"No." He nodded once, a hard shake of his dark head. "I don't." Dropping both hands on his saddle, he leaned forward. "But I imagine being born with a sense of entitlement, knowing only a life of pampered privilege, makes it especially hard when you fall." His words hung in the air, part question, part statement, resonating inside her in a way that made her shift uneasily where she stood.

She gave a small nod. Swallowing, she stared starkly at the rippling water, thinking her biggest challenge had not been the loss of wealth. Not the dearth of pretty dresses or jewels. Not the lack of food whenever she desired . . .

None of that bothered her. Not as much as the loss of her self-respect. Which is precisely what she lost when she acted with the cold calculation her father had taught her.

"Where I come from," he continued, "men are not born to prestige and wealth. A man must earn any success to be had in life." He moved to her horse then, checking the cinch as well.

She watched him for some moments, wondering if her father had ever once left the walls of their home to inspect their property, to oversee the fields or inquire after his tenants. He always entrusted such matters to his steward. Griffin Shaw's notions would have confounded him.

This man was a different breed. She wondered what duty was to him . . . and somehow doubted it had anything to do with propriety and societal expectations—everything she had been brought up to value.

"Ready?" he asked.

Her body protested at the idea of getting back atop her mount so soon. Rather than complain, she tightened her jaw and brushed her hands on her skirts.

"Ready," she answered, her eyes meeting his.

His gaze followed her stiff movements. "If you need some more time—"

"That's unnecessary," she assured, gathering a fistful of her horse's mane and bouncing on the balls of her feet, preparing to mount, determined that she not appear weak and frail, someone he must cater to over the next day. He had done enough already. She'd not have him think her totally helpless. A female in need of rescuing, totally dependent on a man to coddle her.

His voice scraped the air, sending unwelcome tingles along her spine as he helped her swing atop her mount. "As you say, Duchess."

She suppressed a flash of annoyance at his mocking form of address, watching him swing himself up in one fluid motion, his muscles bunching and flexing beneath his clothing. Nothing in his movements hinted at any stiffness or soreness.

Both mounted, she followed him across the brook, frowning as she thought over their conversation. She couldn't recall talking so freely with a man before. Especially a man she had known for such a short duration.

Drawing a thin breath through her nostrils, she let the cold air fill her with a familiar chill, ice in her veins, cold, numbing. Chasing away all feelings, freezing them dead.

Chapter 9

G riffin eyed the horizon, noting the fading twilight with grim acceptance. He had pushed her as far as he could. Although he had hoped to cover more distance, it became apparent that she was not accustomed to hard riding, despite her tight-lipped endurance. He did admire her mettle though. Who knew that a duchess would never complain?

Confident he'd found a suitable spot to break camp, he pulled up his mount and swung down. Without a word, he gripped the lady by the waist. Her dark eyes flared wide as he swung her down, sliding her along the length of him, enjoying the feel of her slim figure against him, the mash of her breasts against his chest surprisingly erotic.

When he released her, her hands grabbed his arms, her legs buckling.

"Easy," he murmured, his hands flying back to her waist.

She watched him with the wariness he was coming to expect. At first it annoyed him that she should still distrust him. If it weren't for him, she never would have made it out of Dubhlagan. She'd be facing Scots' justice . . . perhaps in the form of a noose.

And yet she was entitled to her distrust. From what he knew of her, it would take a great deal to thaw her reserve.

"My legs feel like jam," she muttered, her soft clipped speech stoking some place deep inside him.

Sliding his hands from her waist, he grasped her arm and led her to a grassy spot. "I'll tend to the horses. You just let the blood return to your legs, Duchess."

Her chin went up, as he knew it would. That jutting chin had become her trademark, especially when she was annoyed.

A smile tugged his mouth. He wasn't certain what bothered her more. The reference to her title or the fact that he addressed her with such irreverence. He wasn't privy to the proper manner of address among the British peerage, but he was fairly certain calling her Duchess did not qualify as due respect.

Turning, he unsaddled their mounts. He slapped Waya on the rump to let him wander, knowing he wouldn't stray far and would return at once with a whistle. Hobbling off the little mare, he returned with his saddlebag slung over his shoulder and bedding tucked under his arm.

Squatting beside her, he shook out a tarp and patted for her to sit. She obliged, watching him all the while with that steady, unflinching gaze. Dark, fathomless. Direct and frank, pulling him in.

He handed her his water flask and moved off to hunt down kindling for a fire, grateful for a moment alone, for distance from that mesmerizing gaze.

"It's going to be a cold night," he commented upon his return. He glanced up at her as he arranged the kindling, eyeing her navy gown, the wide skirts and tight bodice with buttons straight up to the throat. Dressed so modestly, it was a wonder she roused his interest. Standing, he brushed off his hands and searched through his leather saddlebag, pulling out a small bundle of oilcloth wrapped in twine.

"Here. "Unfolding the paper, he offered her the jerky.

She took the dried meat from him as if it might

come alive and bite her. Turning it over in her hand, she asked in those proper accents that twisted his insides into knots, "What is it?"

"Jerky." At her blank look, he added, "Dried venison."

"Oh," she murmured, lifting her gaze and watching him tear off a bite with his teeth. After a moment, she followed suit, her small perfect teeth gnawing daintily on the meat. Something curled in his gut at the simple sight. So basic, so elemental, that he immediately imagined that mouth on him, those pearl teeth grazing his flesh, nipping at his mouth, his neck, his chest.

Clearing his throat, he shoved the image away, fighting it back down his suddenly tight throat. The woman had just lost her husband, and here he was imagining tossing her skirts over her head.

"It's just for tonight," he assured her. Tomorrow he would leave her in Edinburgh and he would continue on his way to Balfurin. Although he could not say for certain whether he would receive any hospitality when he reached his destination. He did not even know if the man he sought still lived.

"I'm tired," she murmured on a sigh as she finished her jerky, the first comment she had volunteered in awhile.

"Get some rest," he encouraged, doubting she had slept much last night.

Nodding, she snuggled down onto the tarp, pulling a blanket up to her shoulders. Several moments passed in which neither spoke. He looked away, deciding he needed time to get a grip on his attraction before he looked her way again.

He assumed she slept until he heard her voice, strong and clear. "I don't believe I've thanked you, Mr. Shaw."

His eyes met hers over the spitting fire. He broke a twig and tossed it into the writhing flames, noting the way the flames gilded her hair honey gold. "No, ma'am."

Her dark eyes clung to his for a long moment, glowing in the firelight like polished jet. "Thank you."

He gave a hard nod, unnerved by that dark mesmerizing gaze.

He breathed with relief when her eyes drifted closed, shuttering the dark, compelling pools. Soon she slept, her chest rising and falling in slow, deep breaths beneath the wool blanket. Her stern features softened, and he realized she was younger than he first thought, not as old as himself, perhaps only five and twenty. Too young for someone to be so grave, so sad.

He thought about the husband that had left her, the man that had wanted to marry another woman while still bound to her. An angry burn centered in his gut. He stirred the fire, watching as it chased shadows over her fair skin. She really was beautiful, mysterious and solemn . . . so haunted by propriety, constrained by the dictates of her proper British upbringing.

She shouldn't remind him of a blood-soaked battlefield. Or the woman buried there.

She shouldn't. And yet she did.

She made him remember. Remember everything. All he sought to forget. San Jacinto. The violence of their surprise attack. The blood. The needless killing. They had the enemy whipped, but still they fought, still they had killed, cutting down so many. He remembered that massacre . . . and the woman that had been caught amid it all. Perhaps she had been a laundress, a camp follower. He didn't know. It didn't matter.

He had shouted at her . . . at his fellow soldier charging her with a bayonet. Useless. She dropped, her dark-eyed gaze locking with his through the smoke-shrouded field.

He remembered her. Remembered the plea he had failed to answer in those dark eyes. Liquid dark eyes. Black as sin. So like Astrid's.

And he remembered his father never looked at him the same way after the war. Aware of that day's butchery, Donald Shaw never disguised his shame in him.

With his father's death, Griffin finally felt free to put that behind him. Or at least try. He hoped to learn the truth, to solve his mother's deathbed ramblings and perhaps find his place in the world . . . to obtain a measure of redemption for himself. To discover if he was perhaps more than the man his father had judged him to be. A better man than even he believed himself.

His prickly duchess rolled onto her side with a soft sigh. He studied the fine arch of her brows, several shades darker than her fair hair. Her lashes, dark smudges of coal, fanned her cheeks while she slept. His fingers itched to trace their inky lushness.

He gave himself a hard mental shake, reminding himself that he liked women with blue eyes. Blue eyes full of mirth. *Never dark eyes. Never.*

He liked women with humor, who knew how to laugh and smile. Not somber females with ghosts shadowing their eyes and diffidence in the curve of their mouth. That would make her too much like him.

* * *

She was beneath the bed again. Blood crawled toward her on all sides. *Bertram's blood.* Dark and thick as grease, it slid up her fingers, rolling over her hands and wrists, up her arms. She parted her lips to scream, but then the blood was in her mouth, choking her, drowning her . . . *shaking her.*

Hard hands gripped her, jarring her very teeth.

"Wake up. Duchess, wake up!"

Astrid blinked, a scream lodged deep in her chest as she focused on the face above her. The fire's glow licked at the shadowed features staring down at her, concern etched in the hard lines.

"You're safe now," he murmured, brushing a lock of hair from her forehead. She flinched at the touch, and he hesitated, his hand hovering over her face, his palm wide, his fingers long and blunt-tipped, both elegant and masculine.

"You're safe," he repeated, lowering his hand back down with infinite slowness, as if she were a skittish animal he must reassure. The tips of his fingers brushed her forehead, tenderly, gently.

Her eyes locked with his, drowning in the pale blue of his stare. Tearing her gaze away, she looked around her, noticing for the first time that they shared the tarp and blanket. Some time during the night he had joined her. The air caught in her chest. A space no more than an inch separated their bodies. Her lungs tightened.

"What are you doing?" she demanded, tugging at the blanket that cocooned both of them, drawing it to her neck.

His dark brows drew together over his eyes. "Waking you from a bad dream."

"No." She shook her head and arched her spine to increase the space between the two of them. "What are you doing *here*? With me?"

"I thought that obvious." He blue eyes gleamed down darkly at her. "Sleeping. At least I was until you screamed in my ear."

"You cannot sleep with me," she protested, wincing at the squeak in her voice. Clutching the blanket to her chest, she sat up.

"We only have one tarp. And with the weather as it is, I thought it sensible to take what warmth we could from each other. I don't relish the feel of cold ground beneath me."

Sensible. Her lips compressed. Glaring at him in suspicion, she wondered why he had not mentioned the specifics of their sleeping arrangements before she fell asleep. *Before* he crept beside her like a thief in the night.

As though he read her mind, an angry glint entered his eyes. "You needn't look at me as if I've sullied you. I was sound asleep with no designs on your person until *you* woke *me*."

Astrid continued to glare at him, fingers tightening on the blanket as if he would rip it from her.

"Jesus, lady," he snarled, lying back down on the bedroll. "You really hold a high opinion of yourself, don't you?"

She watched him as he settled onto his side, his back to her, suspicion still centered tightly within her chest.

"I'm going back to sleep, Duchess," he tossed over his shoulder. "Do whatever you like."

She stared at the rigid line of his broad back for several moments, suddenly feeling the fool. Could he not simply be as he presented himself? Honest and considerate. He'd had plenty of opportunities to molest her. Instead he had only aided her.

Clearly, it went beyond her power to trust another soul. But was it any surprise? The most important people in her life—her mother, her father, Bertram—had failed her in some way.

And when her turn had come, she had failed Portia.

Not liking the realization that she trusted so little, that she was so jaded she imagined everyone disingenuous, that she herself was not to be trusted, she settled back down. Positioning herself on her side, she tucked her cheek on her forearm, the heat from his body radiating toward her.

She held herself motionless, listening to rhythmic sounds of the night, the steady fall of his breath, deciding that she had overreacted.

"Astrid," she whispered, a peace offering of sorts.

Moments passed and she assumed he had not heard her until he spoke. "What?"

"Astrid. My name is Astrid." *Not Duchess.* An empty title that meant nothing. Had brought her nothing. That rang with mockery when he said it.

"Good night, Astrid," he murmured at last, the rich rumble of his voice softening her name, making it sound almost pretty when she had always thought it rather harsh. Whenever her father had said her name it sounded like an epithet on his lips.

Sighing, she closed her eyes and allowed

herself to relax, letting her back brush against his . . . and telling herself she took no pleasure in the hard length of him so near her, touching her.

That the warmth of another—a man—was not something she missed. Something she never had before.

Something she now craved.

Chapter 10

An arctic cold arrived around dawn. With a shiver and several groggy blinks, Astrid lifted her head and assessed the mist-shrouded surroundings.

She and Griffin no longer slept with their backs to each other but, in this early morning cold, sought warmth and cocooned together. Her upper body was pressed against his, breasts cushioned on the warm wall of his chest.

Cheeks flaming, she attempted to slide her leg out from between his but found it wedged tightly between rock-hard thighs.

His voice purred in her ear. "If you wanted on top, you only had to ask."

Her gaze collided with his heavy-lidded blue stare. Heat scored her cheeks. Her hair had come loose in the night and she blew at the blond strands falling in her face.

Pressing her hands on either side of him, she pushed herself up, opening her mouth to reprimand him, well accustomed to putting gentlemen in their place.

His hand came up, seizing her by the back of her head and dragging her down to him, smothering her words with the hot press of his mouth.

His lips claimed hers, warm and soft, a tender caress that seemed at odds with such a rough man.

He angled his head, taking more, trailing the warm tip of his tongue along the seam of her lips in a quest for entrance. She gasped and he deepened the kiss, sliding his tongue inside her mouth, gliding it against hers in a sinuous dance like nothing she had ever experienced.

A lick of heat twisted in her stomach, thrilling in its strangeness. Frightening.

She relaxed against him, melting into his hard length, her blood simmering, liquefying her bones.

He tasted good, so good, like the way he smelled. Of wind and woods and man. For an insensible moment, her hands curled into his shirt, pulling him closer, mashing her breasts into his chest.

He growled against her mouth, rolling her beneath him, settling himself between her thighs. Even with her skirts bunched between them, she felt the hard ridge of him, prodding and insistent against her belly. He shifted lower, rubbing against her groin, the very center of her—a place that throbbed with desperate intensity, a burgeoning ache that demanded satisfaction and made her squirm in need.

Her fingers clenched the warm wall of his chest, clawing and twisting the fabric of his shirt. Her hips rose, thrusting against the delicious hardness of him.

His lips lifted from hers on a hiss of air, just long enough for him to grit a single word against her mouth. *"Duchess."*

His lips fell back on hers, ravenous, his tongue delving past her lips . . . still, that feverish utterance struck like an arrow to her heart, reminding her of who she was. Who he was. Only one day widowed and she was rolling around on the ground with a man she barely knew? Without dignity. Without pride. No better than her mother. Easy pickings for some silver-tongued devil's misuse.

She shoved him off her, disentangling herself from the solid strength of his arms. Scrambling back, she put distance between them. Hugging her knees to her chest, she glared at him in the light of dawn.

He rolled onto his side, watching her with a lazy, seductive gaze that fired her blood . . . and indignation.

"Don't think that my gratitude runs this far," she hissed, rubbing the back of her hand over her mouth as if she could wipe clean the burning imprint of his kiss.

He stared at her for a long moment, his eyes turning hard, the gleam of desire fading. "Gratitude?" he echoed.

"Yes. Accepting your assistance does not grant you free use of me."

"I don't recall forcing you to crawl atop me."

"It was unintentional, I assure you—not an invitation!"

"And when we kissed? I heard no protests. Far from it." One of his dark brows winged high. "You certainly did not hesitate to rub yourself against me."

Heat flooded her face. "I did not!"

He laughed cruelly. "The sweetest whore never responded so readily."

"Oh!" She lurched forward, swinging a fist at his face.

He caught her hand and hauled her against him. "Enough," he growled, squeezing the breath from her. "Your virtue is safe with me. I don't make it a habit to force myself on unwilling women." His lips twisted. "One word of advice, though . . . if you are unwilling, you best learn a little restraint. Otherwise, you may find yourself on your back and getting more than you bargained for." His hand splayed wide on her waist, fingers digging through her garments, searing into her flesh. "Understand?"

She nodded fiercely.

Chuckling, he released her. Astrid dropped back on the tarp, glaring at him as he rose to his feet and strode from the clearing.

She trembled with fury. Restraint, indeed. As if she needed lessons on restraint. Her whole life had been about restraint. More than the likes of him would ever know. She was not about to change now.

They broke camp quickly. The sun breaking over the horizon did little to chase off the chill, and she burrowed into her cloak as they advanced through trees and gorse thickening all around them, encroaching on their trail and slowing their progress.

When they finally stopped at a sun-dappled glen late that afternoon, she eagerly slid off her mount, not waiting for his assistance, unwilling to risk him putting his hands on her.

A brook burbled nearby. She followed him, ducking under low hanging branches, heeding his warnings of the rocky ground as he led their mounts ahead of them through the heavy undergrowth.

At the brook, she lowered herself to the ground. Succumbing to mad impulse, she stripped off her boots and stockings. With a covert glance at him, she dipped her aching feet in the frigid water, hissing at the first contact.

He grimaced over the back of his mount at her. "You're braver than I."

She shrugged. "Doubtful. I can't even swim. This is as bold as I get." Frowning, she thought back to her youth, to a day when she was seven. "My mother loved to swim. She tried to teach me. Once."

She shook her head, resisting the memory of her mother's face, tight with frustration that her daughter did not share her spirit of adventure, that despite all her efforts Astrid had turned out as dull and remote as her husband.

"Once?" he inquired.

"I didn't take to the water as she hoped." Rubbing her chin, she shook off the memory. Looking up, she found him watching her with a thoughtful expression on his face, almost pitying.

Shrugging, she added, "I did not inherit my mother's adventurous streak."

"I don't know about that. Not many ladies that would hare off to Scotland to bring their errant husbands to heel."

Shrugging again, she clawed a small pile of pebbles into a mound on the ground beside her with focused concentration. "I wouldn't call it a sense of adventure. Obligation perhaps." She tossed a pebble into the dark waters before her. "I had to stop him from ruining another woman's life."

Tossing another pebble, she watched it plop into the water before shooting him a glance.

He squatted beside her. Plucking a pebble from her little pile, he hurled it, and she watched it splash in the brook with more force than her efforts.

She brought her knees to her chest, propping her chin and taking care to cover her toes beneath the hem of her skirt, mindful that she not reveal even an inch of flesh. She dared not. Not after his wholly unfair remark about her needing to learn a little restraint. *Her*. It was too absurd to believe.

Glancing sideways, she studied his hands as he selected another pebble. They were broad with a sprinkling of hair, the veins running beneath the tanned surface manly and intriguing. She remembered the feel of those callused palms on her. Their texture had been erotic, rough and arousing against her skin.

She squeezed her eyes shut in a tight blink before turning her attention back to the swiftly moving waters, willing herself to stop feeling this way around him. In truth, to stop *feeling* at all. To return to the Astrid she knew, the Astrid in control of her emotions, who never let things like anger and desire rule her. Cold. Like her father. Stronger, she had always believed, than selfish, emotional creatures like her mother who thought only of their own pleasure and happiness.

He began to speak, then stopped suddenly.

His eyes changed, grew hard, scanning the landscape like a hawk.

All at once, he reminded her of the man she first faced on the roadside, the primitive who had shot three men dead without blinking an eye.

"What?" she whispered. "What is it—"

His hand sliced the air, the gesture silencing her. Her heart beat faster, the pulse at her neck a furious pounding beneath her flesh.

She looked around them, seeing nothing except the still of a Scottish wood. She glanced back at him, trying to determine what he saw, what he heard.

Suddenly, he grasped her wrist and dragged her off the ground and into his arms with a swiftness that stole her breath. His hands came up on either side of her head, holding her motionless as he stifled her cry with his lips.

She shoved at his chest, stilling the instant she realized he was not kissing her. Not as a man bent on ravishment would. His lips were firm against hers, warm, moving but not caressing . . . talking, whispering. "They're watching us from across the brook. In a moment I will move toward my rifle. And you will run. Do you understand? Run for the brush behind me. Hide. Don't come out unless I call for you."

They're watching us from across the brook.

His words and their implication slithered through her like a snake winding in grass.

A hiss of breath escaped her mouth, fanning his cool lips. She nodded, her wide eyes staring into the glittering blue of his.

He gave a single curt nod. And then released her.

Stumbling, she ran, the metallic taste of fear

rising thick in her throat, flooding her mouth. She didn't look over her shoulder. Didn't dare. Not even as she heard shouts and splashing water. She did as Griffin commanded, even as her heart clenched at whatever was happening to him.

Panic fed her limbs. Her feet struck the earth in hard thuds, pounding in her ears, matching the heavy thrum of her heart. As she tore through trees and tangled gorse, she soon realized that her racing footsteps were not the only sound. Someone followed her, crashing through the brush, his breath a harsh wheeze, building fast behind her.

She ducked beneath a low hanging branch just as a crack of gunfire split the air. She jerked to a halt, terror striking deep in her heart. *Griffin.*

A hand caught and snagged hold of her cloak, yanking so tightly the strings at her throat cut into her flesh. Gagging, she clawed at the ties. With a spin, she fell into a pair of thick arms.

"Quick little thing," a thick burr gasped against her ear.

Astrid caught only a flash of dark eyes set within a gaunt face before she was tossed through the air. A brawny shoulder dug into her belly. His every step bounced her until she thought she would be ill. Just when she thought she could stand it no more, he stopped and dropped her unceremoniously to the hard ground.

Wincing, she shoved the hair that had fallen loose from her face and looked about, taking in a scene far different from moments ago. Gone was the peaceful afternoon, the quiet song of the burbling brook, the still and silent woods.

A dozen men garbed both in breeches and kilts circled Griffin. The latter sat in their midst, battered and bloodied, a cross expression marring his face.

Astrid surged to her feet and charged into the circle of men. "What have you done to him?" she demanded, bunching her skirts in one hand and squatting to inspect his ravaged face.

Griffin looked at her with his one good eye, the blue circling the other all the more startling against his tanned and bloodied face.

"Looks worse than it is," he assured with a wry twist of his mouth, wincing as the stretch of his lips pulled at a tear splitting his bottom lip. Blood seeped steadily from the cut and she pressed her fingers gently to it, the gesture impulsive, tender, and nurturing in a way that she never knew she could be.

"Animals!" she declared, glaring at Griffin's attackers. "Take our things . . . or whatever it is you want and leave us be!"

The Highlanders glanced at one other, clearly caught off guard.

Griffin motioned to his saddle bag. "You heard her."

Silence fell. Only the howl of the wind through the trees and the gurgle of the brook could be heard.

One of the brigands finally spoke, a dark-eyed man that might have been handsome if not for his twisted nose.

"You shot Lionel."

He waved to a tawny-haired man at the edge of the brook who clutched a bloody thigh, a pained expression tightening his face.

"And what of you?" she demanded, surging to her feet. "Charging us like a pack of wolves! Count yourself fortunate only one of you suffered injury!"

The dark-haired man blinked.

"Astrid," Griffin growled, voice low with warning.

The leader assessed her, his eyes sliding over her in appraisal. "Are all Sassenach women as sharp-tongued as you?" He chuckled and looked to his men. "Perhaps I need to venture south after all."

His men laughed.

Griffin grabbed her hand in an attempt to

bring her beside him, but she held her ground, chin lifting as she stared down the brigand leader.

"This is no jest. Cease your laughing."

"Beggin' your pardon," he continued, sobering. "'Tis dangerous indeed to earn the wrath of so fiery a woman." His dark eyes fixed intently on her. "I might get burned." His rangy frame executed a mocking bow. "Lachlan Gallagher. Pleased to make the acquaintance of one so lovely."

She sniffed, unsettled, but did her best to conceal it.

"What's your name, lass?" He glanced to Griffin. "Ashley, did you say?"

With a grunt, Griffin pulled himself to his feet. Clasping her arm, he pulled her behind him. "I call her wife. You may call her Mrs. Shaw."

"That so?" He clucked his tongue. "Pity."

Astrid peered around Griffin, finding the dark-eyed man's eyes still fixed on her. A small shiver coursed her spine and any thoughts she held of refuting Griffin's claims vanished. She would take what protection she could in pretending to be his wife.

"Well, it happens that you've stumbled upon me and my men availing myself of some fine Mac-Fadden sheep."

"Thieves," Astrid muttered.

"We're not thieves," the dark-eyed man corrected. "Reivers. A fine Scottish custom. And we raid only that which belongs to the MacFadden clan, rot the lot of them."

"Then you have no interest in us," Griffin pointed out. "We're merely passing through."

The man shrugged. "Be that as it may, I find that you have *something* that interests me." His dark gaze fell on Astrid again.

She did not miss his meaning. Nor did Griffin. His fingers tightened around her arm. "She belongs to me.".

The leader tsked. "Yes. A wife. Inconvenient." His hand moved to the blade strapped to his side. "I suppose I can take care of that bit of nuisance."

Her fingers tightened around Griffin's arm.

Gallagher gave her an exaggerated wink. "It should be an easy enough matter to rid you of your husband, lass."

"You will do no such thing," she announced, stepping around Griffin, a frisson of fear skimming her spine.

The Highlanders around her laughed as if she had uttered some extraordinary quip.

"Ah, Sassenach, what a gem you are." The Highlander slid a deadly looking blade from the scabbard at his waist. "Choose your weapon," he advised Griffin.

With a grim set to his lips, Griffin pushed Astrid out of the way. Tugging up his pant leg, he pulled an even deadlier looking blade from his boot.

Astrid stared at him in amazement as he turned to face the other man. Her stomach clenched.

Could he mean to fight in his condition? She could not allow him. With his recent head wound and freshly battered body, he could not stand up to such a contest.

She had to stop him. He had done enough for her already. More than enough. She would not accept his life as sacrifice for her. He would lose, die, and she would still be at the mercy of the Highlander.

Stepping in front of him, she ignored the feel of his hard stare on her back and announced, "I'm not his wife. He lied to protect me. I'll come with you."

"Astrid," Griffin hissed, the sound sharp and furious.

The dark-eyed Scot smiled. "I see." He shot Griffin an almost empathetic look. "Clever of you to lie. But not worth your life. You should thank the lass. You'll live because of her."

The leader turned to his men then. Sheathing his blade, he instructed, "Let's move before Old MacFadden catches wind that we've been at his flock."

Astrid turned and faced Griffin. His look of acrimony flayed her like a whip, leaving her bare and bleeding before him. She held his gaze, suffered his stare, willing him to understand, hoping he would. If not now, then perhaps someday.

"Could you not trust me?" he asked, his voice soft, wounding her more than if he shouted fiery words.

She blinked, her hand drifting to her throat, to the pulse there that suddenly thrummed wildly.

Trust him? This man? A relative stranger?

"Griffin, I . . ." she paused, wetting her lips, looking away from the hot accusation of his gaze.

"Dammit, look at me," he hissed.

"I do you a kindness," she whispered in a rush, facing him again.

Her words made his eyes darken with fury. "You forget," he rasped, wiping the blood from his lip with a fierce swipe of his hand, "there is nothing *kind* about you."

Stung, Astrid stepped away, startled to hear her own words flung back at her. "You are correct, of course," she replied crisply, gathering her composure and wrapping her familiar reserve like a cloak about her.

"Yes." He snorted. "I should have believed you when you told me."

Lifting her chin, she confessed. "I'm not sorry. I won't have you kill yourself over me." She shrugged one shoulder.

The muscles knotted along his jaw. Hot fury burned in his eyes, reaching out to singe her. "We're not finished, you and I."

She shook her head. "Good-bye, Griffin." The words caused a deep ache beneath her breastbone that she could not have anticipated. Even when Bertram had abandoned her she had not felt this way. Like a cord had been forever severed, a part of her ripped open . . . almost as if they had been bound. As Griffin suggested back at the inn. Absurd, but the pain of it was there.

The Scotsmen mounted, the jangle of harnesses and horses' hooves filling the air. She held Griffin's gaze, unable to look away, knowing this would be the last time she saw him—the intriguing man that made her feel as no one had, a woman to be honored, protected. The memory of the heat in his eyes before he kissed her flashed through her mind, a taunting farewell.

Lachlan Gallagher plucked her from the ground and set her before him on his horse. "There you go," he murmured in her ear, "make yourself comfortable."

She shivered as he slid an arm around her waist, pulling her close. Her eyes fixed on Griffin. He watched her with an intent expression on his face, eyes a pale, silvery blue that seemed to echo his earlier words. *We're not finished, you and I.*

"Let's be off, then," the brigand at her back called out, his voice smug, grating as he nudged his mount to the front of the line, removing Griffin from her sight. But not from her mind.

His face stayed with her as they rode away. Even with one eye blackened and swollen, the memory of his rancor gleamed clear as lightning in a dark night.

Her belly twisted, knowing he thought she had failed him. Betrayed his trust. Even though she *knew* she had done the right thing in stopping him from gambling his life for hers.

She inhaled cold, stinging air through her nose and reminded herself it would not be the first time she had failed someone with pure intentions. Her sister-in-law still refused to speak to her.

"Don't be afraid. I'll not rape you." The brigand's breath fluttered her hair as he spoke. "I'm not the sort to force a woman."

"No?" Despite herself, his words allowed some of the tension to ebb from her.

"I'm a patient man. I can wait. You'll grow fond of me."

"I don't think so."

"You'll soon forget him, little one."

Astrid sniffed, deigning not to answer, and knowing that whatever happened, she would never forget Griffin—the first man to risk anything for her. *Everything*. The first man with whom she had dropped her guard. Even if only for a few mad moments.

He was not a man she *could* forget.

Hard hands tightened on her waist. "I'll give you something else to concentrate on."

"Unlikely," she could not help biting out.

He laughed, sliding his hands around her waist, palms flattening over her belly. "You have fire. But it's buried deep. I shall enjoy bringing it out of you."

"Go to hell."

He laughed again. "Oh, yes. You and I shall rub along very well." His hands moved higher, his fingers tracing her ribs through her gown.

She closed her eyes, willing herself not to flinch,

not to think about what—who—she left behind. Not to feel anything at all as his fingers inched higher and his voice rolled over her like a dark tide, blotting out all light, all hope.

Chapter 11

They didn't travel far before they encountered a flock of sheep milling about in a grove, pathetic creatures that looked half starved and wore the same hungry look as the half dozen men standing guard over them, waiting for the return of the rest of their party.

The motley bunch showed no surprise at the sight of her ensconced on the saddle before their leader. They surveyed her with flat eyes and hard mouths that made her wonder if they frequently abducted women along with the livestock they reived.

Soon they were moving again, pushing a hard pace even with the flock herded before them. A harder pace than what Griffin had subjected her to. Squeezing her eyes shut, she told herself she would have an easier time if she learned not to think about Griffin anymore, to forget the look in his eyes when she had left. And most importantly, to forget all that nonsense of being *bound* to one another.

They climbed deeper into the mountains. The bite of wind and cold on her face honed to the sharpness of a knife's edge with each passing moment. The air thickened, making it a struggle to draw its frigid density into her contracted lungs.

The brigand used her name freely when addressing her, as freely as the hand that held her about the waist, his fingers at times crawling over her torso or dropping to caress her thigh in a manner that set her teeth on edge.

And still she could not stop thinking of Griffin, worrying over his injuries, hoping he fared well alone.

That final look on his face replayed itself in her mind. She knew the look. Knew it as well as anyone could. In his mind, she had betrayed him. For whatever reason, he had appointed himself her defender, and she had failed to permit him to protect her. A sigh swelled up from her chest. She had done the practical thing. Perhaps he would come to see that later.

She forced her thoughts ahead, to her own fate. Once she reached their destination, she had to find a way out of this mess. She would appeal to the clan's laird and pray he possessed the sense that Lachlan Gallagher lacked. Surely he would see it was one thing to steal sheep and another to abduct an innocent woman.

Astrid glanced around them. They moved up a particularly steep incline and she could not resist sneaking a peak over her shoulder. The sight only made her stomach squeeze.

"You'll not see your man behind us."

"I did not expect to," she snapped, facing forward, sitting tall so that she did not lean back against him. Only too late did she even realize her reply signified acceptance of Griffin as *her man*.

"Even if he were not injured, these mountains aren't for the faint of heart. Only a Highlander could maintain our pace. Don't be looking for him to rescue you."

"I'm not."

"Good." A moment of silence fell before he added, "Because if he were to come after you, I would have to kill him."

She twisted around to study him, reading the truth in his gaunt features. "You think he will come," she muttered, a touch of surprise in her voice.

His lips twisted and his dark eyes gleamed with a feral light, as if Griffin stood before him

148

now, challenging him in some primordial contest to the death.

"Aye. I saw his face when you left him."

So had she. Every time she closed her eyes, she saw him.

He continued, "It may kill him, but he will not quit."

She turned back around and mulled over her abductor's words. True, Griffin had said they were not finished, but that had been pride and anger talking. Once he cooled off, once she was gone, he would certainly remember whatever it was that brought him to Scotland and return to his purpose. The fate of a woman he barely knew would not plague him, would not cause him to act rashly and risk his own life.

The grueling pace eventually sapped her energy and she could not stop herself from relaxing against the man behind her, from taking support in the length of him. Nor could she seem to stop from drifting off into a state of half-consciousness, somewhere between sleep and wakefulness, eager to escape the rigors of the journey. She did not know how much time passed before a hard hand on her shoulder jostled her fully awake.

"We're here."

She blinked out at the dark, moonless night. As far as she could see, *here* appeared to be . . . nowhere.

Then she saw it. At first it seemed they floated on inky air, sinking down toward winking stars.

They left the wooded hills behind, descending onto flat terrain. Far ahead, hundreds of tiny lights flickered like stars in the night.

"Cragmuir," he announced at her back, the pride in his voice evident as the outline of a castle took shape against the dark veil of night.

"Cragmuir," she repeated, marveling at the stone edifice looming larger than life before her. Like something out of Arthurian legend.

A great drawbridge lowered over a moat that smelled of rot and refuse, the chains creaking in the night wind. Two men stood high on the battlements, cheering down at them.

The men in their party called back, the laughter and triumph in their voices mingling with that of bleating sheep.

"Sheep not being the only prize caught," Lachlan whispered in her ear, the tips of his fingers brushing the undersides of her breasts.

She drew a hissing breath through her teeth and forced his hand down.

He chuckled against her cheek. "You'll grow accustomed to my touch. Come to like it, I vow. I've had no complaints before."

Griffin's furious eyes flashed through her mind again, a burst of fire in a dark night, and she shoved down her misery. She chose this fate, and she would find a way out of it.

They thundered into the yard to the welcome of barking dogs and a burgeoning crowd of Highlanders. Lachlan dismounted and swung her down beside him, a hand circling her wrist like a manacle, forcing her close to his side as he dragged her through the keep and into a cavernous hall that resembled something out of the middle ages.

Several massive tables littered the room in no apparent order. An old man sat at one, enshrined in a great wood-carved chair. His blue eyes watched their approach with keen interest.

"Uncle," Lachlan greeted.

"Nephew," the older man—Gallagher, she presumed—returned, "I see by your grin that your mission went well."

His hand flexed on her wrist. "Very well."

The volume in the hall intensified as the rest of the men spilled inside behind them. Serving girls poured into the room, carrying trays and trenchers, beaming smiles on their faces.

Her stomach clenched at the smell of fresh-baked bread and roasted pheasant.

"And what have you there? A present for me? Something else you stole from MacFadden."

"Sorry, uncle. This prize is mine," Lachlan declared. "A reward for successfully completing my task."

"Oh?" the older man asked, his voice a scratchy growl on the air as he lifted bushy brows. "Since when do you decide your reward? You're not yet lord and master here."

She tugged anew on her wrist, deciding now the best time to plead her case, while the uncle appeared to be hovering between favor and disfavor with his nephew.

"I belong to no one! I was abducted! Taken against my will." She fastened a beseeching gaze on the clan's laird. "Please, sir. Surely you can see such an uncivilized act is a poor reflection on you and your people. I am an innocent traveler in your land. Your nephew viciously beat my traveling companion and—"

"Och, a Sassenach?" The old man shook his head in disapproval, the rest of her words lost on him. His gaze skimmed over Astrid in new estimation, as if his nephew had brought home a serpent. "Why would you want such a creature?"

"She's different—"

"Aye, she is that. Trouble, she is. Not a sweet Scottish lass that can keep her tongue behind her teeth and show her man proper deference, to be sure."

"Uncle," Lachlan chided, his voice knowing, "I don't recall my aunt being a reticent woman—"

The old man's eyes softened at the mention of—presumably—his wife. "Nay, she was not."

"Well, perhaps I want the same thing for myself."

"And you would compare her to your dear aunt?" He flicked a large, gnarled hand Astrid's way.

"Pardon me," Astrid interjected. "So that there is no mistake here, let me clarify that I'm a hostage."

"A hostage, eh?" Gallagher mused. "In that case, what sort of recompense shall I demand for your release?"

"Uncle," Lachlan broke in, his voice a whine.

His uncle waved a hand to silence him, eyes still trained on her. "And," he added, "to whom shall I make these demands? Family? Friends that might miss a fine Sassenach lass such as yourself?"

Astrid considered what he was asking of her. Should she give up the names of her friends? Certainly Jane or Lucy would pay whatever ransom request these Highlanders made. She had resisted prevailing upon them before. But had the time come to put her pride aside and take their help?

"Yes," she admitted. "I have friends. Extremely wealthy, important friends that would care a great deal to have me safely returned."

"Interesting." The laird combed fingers through his scraggly beard.

"Uncle, she is mine," Lachlan insisted.

"Ah, hell, man. Would you cease thinking with that twig between your legs. If you're to take my place someday, then you better start thinking like a laird and put your people before your own needs."

A sudden commotion erupted at the front of the hall, drawing the attention of the laird and his nephew.

Astrid turned to watch as a small crowd of Highlanders advanced on them, nearing the head table. Grumbling and foul curses filled the air, gaining volume as the men reached them.

A sudden hush fell over the ragtag group. They parted, revealing an imposing, tartan-free figure in their midst. Even battered and bruised, he stood heads taller than most of the men, his carriage erect, proud, eyes a deep, glittering blue.

Astrid's heart seized in her chest. A sob rose in her throat that she barely caught from spilling into the suddenly charged air. He had come. Unbelievable. She took one step forward.

Lachlan growled at her side, his hand clamping down on her arm. "What are you doing here?"

Griffin trained his gaze on her, his eyes blistering with hot accusation. Not once did he glance at the man who addressed him. After a long moment, his drawl rose strong and defiant over the hall. "I've come to claim what is mine."

A breath shuddered through her.

"Lachlan," his uncle demanded, "who is this?"

"My name is Griffin Shaw."

Astrid looked nervously to the clan's laird, knowing he held their fate in his hands. The old man's eyes flitted over Griffin in hard-eyed scrutiny. "The lass belongs to you?"

Griffin and Lachlan answered simultaneously.

"Yes."

"No."

Lachlan sneered. "A man who cannot hold on to his woman, does not keep her long in these parts. You lost your right to her."

"I'm here now," Griffin stated, his hand moving toward the knife at his side. "And I'll cut down any man that tries to stop me from leaving with her."

Astrid closed her eyes in one tight blink. What on earth was he doing here? *Bloody fool.* Did he have a death wish? He should never have come. She could not even fathom how he managed to show up only moments after them. In his condition, he should have barely been able to stay mounted.

"You're welcome to try," Lachlan bit out, his own hand moving for the blade strapped to his side.

"Enough," the laird growled, his bushy beard moving about his lips as he spoke. The older man's keen blue eyes assessed Astrid. "Can't see what's worth getting so excited over." His gaze roamed her and Astrid stiffened her spine, meeting his stare with her frostiest expression. "No meat on her at all. And that dark-eyed gaze of hers could chill a man to the core."

Astrid did not to flinch, accustomed to reaping such judgment. Especially from men. It was what she had come to expect . . . what she in fact had cultivated over the years. "She'll fill out nicely with proper feeding," Lachlan assured.

Proper feeding? As if she was some kind of pet?

Emotion burned darkly in her chest and she struggled to control it, shove it back to that place deep inside where feelings hid, where she kept them bottled and suppressed so she could go about the world with stoic resolve.

Lachlan's gaze cut to Griffin as he added, "I know how to nourish my women. In and out of bed. Something the lass here will soon learn for herself."

Griffin bared his teeth in a snarl and lunged forward.

Several men stepped in his path to restrain him.

The old man laughed a rusty sound. Leaning back, his massive wood chair creaked from the pressure of his girth. "Appears he takes exception to that, Lachlan." He cocked a reddish-gray brow at his nephew, his blue eyes intent and serious. "I see only one solution."

Lachlan turned to assess her, his dark gaze moving over her slowly, thoroughly, before swinging to Griffin, spending little time considering his bruised and ravaged face before saying, "You want her? Then take her back, my friend. If you think you can."

Griffin nodded resolutely. "If I win, she's mine. We walk out of here unharmed." He swiped a hand through the air. "No one gets in our way."

"Aye. On my honor."

Griffin's mouth twisted, the crimson tear in

his bottom lip deepening. "I'll have to trust that counts for something."

Lachlan's eye twitched, the only indication that he took offense. He set her from him, handing her off to one of his men hovering nearby. He pulled back his rangy shoulders in a stretch.

Angry breath escaped Astrid in a hiss. She yanked her arm free of her new captor and leveled her coldest stare on him when he looked ready to snatch hold of her again.

"This has gone far enough," she declared at Lachlan's back as he moved toward Griffin. Ignoring her, they moved to the center of the great hall. Everyone cleared out of the way. She shot a frustrated, desperate look at Griffin. "I'm not a bone to be fought over. I'm done with being treated like property!"

The two men continued to ignore her.

The uncle laughed and addressed Griffin. "You've been challenged, Shaw. Are you man enough to accept?"

Astrid fiercely shook her head. Lifting her skirts, she stumbled forward gracelessly, gritting her teeth when a wall of men merged to block her. "No," she cried, trying to shove past. "He cannot! He's injured. Your men beat him only this day! How can this be a fair contest?"

"Enough, Astrid," Griffin growled, his eyes glinting furiously at her. "I will fight."

She stomped a foot. "No, you—"

"Silence!" the old man roared. "Hold your tongue, woman, and learn your place." He wagged a gnarled finger in her face. "This is men's business. They'll fight. Hand to hand. No weapons. And the winner shall claim you. Now sit beside me like a good lass." He motioned to the chair beside him.

She closed her mouth with a snap, heat flooding her face as long-suppressed emotions bubbled to the surface, dangerously near spilling forth. A set of hands forced her into a chair beside the laird.

Helpless, she watched as tables were pushed aside. Griffin and Lachlan shrugged free of their coats. She studied the strong lines of Griffin's face, the bruises only heightening his good looks, and feared she would be sick.

Lachlan stretched his arms over his head, the picture of health and vigor. She pressed a hand to her rolling stomach and tried to believe that Griffin knew what he was doing. He had already proven himself strong, following them through mountains and bitter cold, arriving only moments behind them—an occurrence she had not considered even remotely possible.

The old man beside her rubbed his hands together, clearly relishing the upcoming fight.

"What happens if he loses?" she demanded, a desperate fire burning in her chest as her eyes devoured the sight of Griffin. *God, keep him safe. Let him win.*

"If?" he snorted. "Hate to tell you, lass, but your lad there doesn't look too—"

"What happens?" she spit out.

"Och, well, that depends on Lachlan."

Astrid shook her head, not feeling at all heartened. "Yes, but, in these instances, what's usual?"

He slid her a bemused glance. "Usual? You're a strange lass." He shrugged one beefy shoulder. "His life is forfeit. His fate would be in Lachlan's hands."

Bile rose high in her throat. "That's barbaric!"

If Griffin lost. . .

Shaking her head, she braced herself for the violence to come, telling herself she had done all she could to stop it. Still, the thought was cold comfort as she watched Griffin prepare to wage his life. For her.

Chapter 12

Griffin stripped down to his vest, deliberately unbuttoning his cuffs so that his sleeves would billow and flutter with his movements—a measure he knew would help distract his opponent. He smiled grimly as the Scot stripped to his trousers, grinning and flexing his bare arms for the crowd.

He deliberately avoided looking at Astrid—sitting so silent and pale beside the clan's laird—lest his rage return and cloud his focus. He needn't look her way to remember her lovely face, so calm, so cool, dark eyes infuriatingly detached as she rode off with the Highlander and left him.

Her utter lack of faith in him galled him still. He might be a stranger in these parts, but he knew a damn sight more about survival than some haughty Brit better suited to the pomp of London drawing rooms.

She had made her choice, going with the Highlanders rather than letting him protect her as any man worth his salt would have done. He should have left her to her fate. *Faithless female.*

Shrugging past his stinging pride, he reminded himself of what losing would mean to Astrid. Not even a stubborn female lacking the sense to follow his lead deserved to be left to the mercy of these men.

Determination sealing his heart, he ducked Lachlan's first swing and quickly countered with one of his own, his right fist connecting with his opponent's jaw in a satisfying crack of bone on bone.

Keeping his left arm close to his side, he pulled back to deliver another jab . . . only to be swept off his feet from a swift kick to the knee.

He fell to the ground. Lying on his side, he rolled hard and watched as a boot slammed down inches from his nose. He grabbed at the ankle and twisted it savagely, bringing Lachlan down with a howling curse. Before he could rise, Griffin pounced, flinging himself on the other man's back. Grabbing a hank of his hair, he brought Lachlan's face crashing into the ground. Again and again.

The cries and jeers of the crowd registered dimly, but adrenaline pumped hotly through him.

He didn't look up, didn't seek out *her* face through the red haze clouding his eyes even though he knew she was there, watching, her dark eyes no doubt fathomless and unmoved as ever . . . even as he fought for his life . . . and hers.

The thought only heightened his rage, sent a burn of aggression rushing through him, firing a path through his veins, fierce and swift as the wind howling outside.

A sharp elbow to the ribs propelled him backward. He grunted from the force. The Highlander broke free and spun around. Rage glowed in his eyes and a wet trickle of crimson streamed from his nose into his mouth. "Bastard," he hissed, blood spraying from his teeth.

They squared off again, circling each other like two great jungle cats, wary, tense, waiting for the moment to spring at the other.

Griffin's fingers flexed at his sides. His senses sharpened, twisting, swinging into razor-sharp pinpricks that gathered along his nerve endings. He honed in on his opponent with the alertness of a stalking wolf, the pain in his body disappearing in a heated rush of warrior instinct.

Lachlan moved first, charging Griffin with a roar.

They came together like two angry rams, careening across the room and crashing into a table. Griffin's head slammed into the hard surface. His vision blurred for a moment, spots dancing before his eyes at the grinding scald of agony where he'd been struck by the rock days ago.

Reaching out, he fumbled along the top of the table, knocking over dishes until his fingers closed around a goblet. He brought it crashing over the Highlander's head.

Lachlan released him and staggered sideways, clutching a hand over a bloodied face embedded with glinting glass.

Griffin snatched a pewter platter off the table, sending a leg of lamb flying. With a grunt, he smashed the serving dish against the side of Lachlan's head, throwing him back onto the table.

Griffin raised his leg and positioned his boot dead center in his chest. With a great shove, he launched the other man off the table and across the room.

A hush fell over the hall as Lachlan swayed drunkenly, arms flailing at his sides before dropping with a heavy thud to the floor.

Blood pumped through him, liquid heat in his veins that numbed him to any pain that his body might be feeling. Griffin brushed pieces of shattered crockery from his clothing. His gaze immediately shot to Astrid. She stared at him with wide eyes, coal dark and unreadable in her ashen face.

Chest rising and falling with great drags of breath, he faced the old man, a despot overlooking his domain. At the moment, his expression looked almost comical with shock.

"I would like food and a bed," he announced.

The old man snapped his gaping mouth shut and looked from the unmoving Lachlan to him. Clearing his throat, he replied, "Of course."

Griffin's gaze moved back to Astrid, her lovely face etched in stone. "And my woman," he added, hoping to provoke her, to see some change in her calm demeanor.

She stiffened where she sat and that chin of hers went up.

He quirked a brow at her, daring her to object. With the hum of battle still whistling through him like a hot wind, his patience had reached its end.

The need to possess, to dominate, thrummed through him, as blistering and swift as the blood quickening in his veins. He stared at her, ready to claim her in the truest sense.

He watched her mouth open, saw her lips move, her head begin to shake side to side.

Unbelievably, she intended to speak, to refute him. After he had just fought to save her from becoming some Highlander's plaything. She still could not look at him with gratitude. Could not hold her tongue. The woman possessed the sense of a pea. Instead of biting her tongue and simply feigning submission until they managed to escape their audience, she had to show her shrewish nature and force his hand.

His hands clenched at his sides.

"I'm no man's—"

"Enough!" he roared, satisfied to see her eyes widen at his shout. *Emotion from her. Finally.* It would not be the last, he vowed. Before this night was finished, he would have more than emotion out of her. He would have it all—nothing less than her total surrender.

Griffin's vision blurred in a red haze of fury . . . and something else. Something wild, savage, and hungry.

A hushed silence fell over the hall. He uncurled his fists and took several halting steps toward the table where she sat, watching him with large eyes.

The laird watched him, too, his eyes measuring, assessing, waiting to see if Griffin was the kind of man to let his woman set the rules. He didn't need to glance around the hall to know that everyone else watched him, too.

Seeing no choice in the matter—these Scotsmen would expect him to teach her proper deference, especially after waging a fight for the right to claim her—he strode forward and pulled her from her chair.

"Woman," he ground out, the word a scathing drip from his tongue. "I believe it's time to show you who is master."

A rumble of agreement broke out in the hall and Griffin knew he had said the proper thing in the eyes of these Highlanders. Crucial if they were to walk away from here.

Astrid's dark eyes narrowed and flitted about the hall, a hare snared in the watchful gazes of a hungry pack of dogs. He knew she resented their murmurs of accord. Stiffening, she pulled herself to her full height, reminding him every bit of the haughty duchess despite her bedraggled appearance.

Her gaze moved back to his face. "My name is Astrid," she hissed. "And you're not my master."

His anger flared hotter yet at her words. Damn little fool, she didn't know when to quit.

With a sigh, he bent and tossed her over his shoulder.

He braced himself, expecting her shouts and struggles. Instead she stiffened, rigid as stone over his shoulder.

The hall burst into loud applause and feet stomping.

"Teach her a lesson she won't forget," a serving girl shouted.

"Aye, silence that mouth of hers!"

"Ride her good for me!" one of the men shouted crudely.

"Aye, no sparing the rod for that one!"

Loud laughter followed that ribald suggestion. A quiver of indignation coursed her rigid body, passing through her slight frame and into him.

He reacted to the comments as well . . . felt an answering burn in his blood to show her, in the most basic, primitive way, that she was his, that she belonged to him. At that moment, it had nothing to do with proving his dominance to their audience. He could give a damn about any of them in that moment. He wanted to do it for himself—wanted *her* for himself.

The blood pumped thickly through him at the thought of stripping her naked and spreading her alabaster thighs before him. Of lodging himself deeply inside her and stroking her flesh with his until her cries filled the air. Of watching her dark eyes glaze over with passion, chasing away the hollow, empty look that he had come to loath. That reminded him of another.

"This has gone far enough," she whispered near his ear, that soft voice of hers sending sparks through him. "Put me down at once and cease treating me in this humiliating fashion."

He answered her with a swift slap to the bottom that earned him a gasp. With his hand still on the curve of that rounded bottom, he addressed the clan's laird. "Our room?"

"Aye," the old man chuckled, wiping at the corners of his eyes where tears of mirth pooled. "You've earned it." Nodding, he snapped his fingers at one of the serving girls. "Show them to their chamber."

A flame-haired girl rushed forth and Griffin followed her up a winding set of stairs, the stones slick with condensation and mildew. She sent him several intrigued glances over her shoulder as they progressed down a dimly lit corridor, the lighted sconces along the walls casting eerie shadows before them.

"Here you go, love," she said, iron hinges creaking as she opened a thick wood door to a large chamber, an impressive four-poster bed positioned in the center.

Furs covered the enormous bed and various areas of the stone floor. A fire burned in a hearth large enough for him to stand in, its pervading warmth flowing throughout the chamber, further warming his desire-heated body.

"This will do nicely. Leave us," Griffin commanded, his hand still caressing Astrid's bottom, enjoying the feel of her flesh tightening and contracting beneath his palm.

With a knowing smirk, the maid left, the door thudding shut after her.

He strode farther into the room and dumped his burden unceremoniously on the bed. She vaulted off the mattress as if he had tossed her in a pot of boiling water. Face flushed, eyes glowing dark as lit coals, she squared off in the center of the room, her skirts an angry swirl as she moved.

At first it appeared she would come at him with fists swinging. Then she caught herself. Stopping, she inhaled and straightened, smoothing one hand over her fair hair, gathering her composure in the simple gesture even if it did nothing to tidy the honey strands of hair that haloed her face.

He felt a flicker of annoyance. He would have preferred her mad and fighting. Not this return to the frigid duchess rarely given to emotion. He knew she had it in her. Had seen it only that morning—*tasted* it when she woke so warm and pliant in his arms. As sweet and responsive as any hot-blooded woman could be.

Crossing his arms over his chest, he suffered her chilly gaze, suffered the coldness and aloofness she wore like a shield of armor. He cocked a brow and grinned, mocking her, daring her shell to crack, daring her to let go.

Her eyes narrowed in on his face.

"What's wrong, Duchess?" Something dark and dangerous unfurled inside him. "Never had a man toss you on your back before?"

The stinging crack of her palm against his cheek sent his head snapping back.

"Christ," he ground out, fingering his cheek as he dropped his gaze back down to glare at her.

"How dare you!" Her arms dropped to hang straight at her sides, fists so tight that her knuckles went white where the blood ceased to flow. She took several stiff strides back.

"Me?" He shook his head, marveling at her gall. He took a step forward, followed by another and another, intent on closing the distance between them. "If it weren't for me, you would be on your back servicing some Highland brute right now."

Her nostrils quivered with anger. "I seriously doubt it would have come to that."

"No? You were willing to take that risk, were you?" He grasped her arms and gave her a little shake, the burn in his blood heating to dangerous degrees at her foolish words . . . to say nothing of what the *feel* of her in his hands did to him. "Damn fool, your mistake is not knowing when to hold your tongue." He shook his head. "Have you never considered you might not know all the answers? That someone else might know more about a situation than you?"

For a moment, he thought something flickered in her eyes. An emotion he couldn't name. Then the dark veil returned, hiding everything from him, hiding *her*.

Rather than answer, she tugged her arm free, inching back until she bumped into the bed. Which was fine with him. The bed was precisely where he wanted her. Ever since he had carried her from the hall, he'd been consumed with one purpose.

With a hand on her shoulder, he shoved her down, watching in satisfaction as she toppled back in wide-eyed wonder.

"I take that as no," he growled.

"I don't claim to know everything—"

"No?"

"It's not in my nature to let a man I hardly know

lead me," she said in that starchy voice of hers. As if she were addressing one of her servants and not an equal, not a man burning with a feverish hunger for her.

A man I hardly know. Is that all she considered him? A stranger?

She held his gaze. *So proper. So cold.* Her eyes dark and fathomless as the night sea, pretending nothing existed between them.

His eyes dropped to her bodice, to the rise and fall of her breasts beneath—the slight mounds that would fit his hands perfectly, that he had craved to taste and explore for long enough now. But no more.

He would have passion and heat from her.

And he would have it now. This very night.

He climbed onto the soft mattress, his knees on either side of her hips.

She blinked several times, her tongue darting out to moisten her lips as she tried to pull herself back with her elbows.

"What are you doing?" her voice trembled on the air.

He squeezed his thighs around her, trapping her beneath him and stopping her from scrambling free.

"I'm going to have you, my little Duchess," he

growled, grabbing her by the back of the neck and hauling her up off the bed, flush against him.

Panic widened her eyes. "You'll force me?" she sneered.

"There will be no force involved." He smiled, flexing his fingers along the soft skin of her nape, relishing the crush of her breasts against his chest. "Before we're through, you will have loved and begged for every moment of it."

"Arrogant pig," she hissed. But despite her words, twin flames gleamed at the centers of her eyes and her hips shifted, nudging his hardness, seeking him out even as her words denied him. "We both know that this won't be—"

His lips crushed hers, intent on silencing her, punishing her, destroying her infuriating attempt at indifference.

Until his lips met hers. Until he tasted their softness, felt their fullness. And quite simply, he was lost. His lips gentled, tongue sweeping inside her mouth, consumed with a need that had nothing to do with punishment . . . and everything to do with desire.

Chapter 13

His mouth tasted of man and heat and heather-kissed winds. Hunger surged inside her, dark and dangerous, ravenous as a beast released to prowl the woods. It had been so long since she felt the warmth of another. Perhaps never.

Astrid clenched her hands and shoved them between their bodies, trying to wedge the two of them apart, resisting the overwhelming temptation to flatten her palms against his hard chest and feel him, savor the hard press of muscles surrounding her.

She willed her lips to still, willed her body not to respond to the magic of his mouth on hers, coaxing forth feelings and emotions long denied. New feelings. Terrifying, exciting feelings she had been so careful to stifle. Freed from a dark well, they spiraled through her like warmed wine, dizzying, exhilarating, emboldening her as nothing before. A strange, intoxicating elixir she could not resist.

His hands slid into her hair, scattering the remaining pins. Her scalp tingled beneath his hands. Her fingers trembled between them, yearning to unfold, to caress and explore his pulsing warmth.

With a strangled sob, she let all her resistance slide away and parted her mouth, meeting the slick glide of his tongue with her own.

Opening her hands, she clenched fistfuls of his vest and returned his kiss with wild fervor, pulling him down over her, sinking back into the soft bed.

He growled low in his throat, dragging his mouth over her jaw and down her throat. Astrid opened her eyes and shut them again, afraid that she would wake from this dream.

His fingers moved to the tiny buttons at the front of her gown. His hands fumbled, shaking over the small buttons.

"Damn buttons," he muttered, his voice strangely hoarse.

She set to work on his clothing, shoving the vest off his shoulders and pulling the shirt over his head.

His hands trembled over each button as she leaned up and rained kisses over his jaw, neck, and chest, skimming her palms over his hard chest, scraping her nails through the short crisp hair, stopping to trace the small dusky circles of his nipples.

He moaned. Because he reached the end of her buttons and could now shove her dress to her waist or because of her hands and mouth on his chest she could not be certain. Nor did she care. He made quick work of stripping her free of her dress, the feverish movements of his hands exciting her only more. Her undergarments followed, the cambric a flash of white on the air, doves flying over their heads.

Naked beside him, not a moment of shame or hesitation seized her. It was as if she were someone else entirely, someone unafraid, someone willing to trust, to give herself over to another. To him.

His hand roved her thighs, callused fingers and palms rasping her tender flesh. His blue eyes shone darkly in the firelight as he stared down at her.

"You're beautiful," he murmured, and she believed it, believed she was, believed he meant it. Not too thin, not too pale, not too strange with her liquid-dark eyes and fair hair. Not herself at all.

Propping herself up on her elbows, her hands reached for him. He watched her, eyes burning, his large body unmoving, still as stone as she unfastened his breeches and shoved them down his narrow hips.

Head cocked to the side, she studied that part of him for a long moment, biting her lower lip as an unfamiliar heat swirled through her, pooling low in her stomach. Her belly contracted and she fidgeted restlessly in attempt to ease the throbbing ache between her legs. Her hand reached out and touched him with a single finger, something she had never done before, never wanted to do.

A tremor rushed over him as she wrapped her fingers around the hard length of him, luxuriating in the feel of him, silk on steel in her hand. Encouraged by the sound of his rough approving growl, she stroked him, her fingers gliding over his length, her breath increasing, matching the harsh sound of his.

He swallowed visibly, his throat muscles working.

Excited beyond endurance, every nerve in her body screaming with a desperate urgency, she parted her legs, leaving herself exposed to his searing gaze. Cool air rushed over her, caressing that most vulnerable part of her.

One hand still holding his throbbing member, the other clutching the counterpane, she urged him closer, thumb rolling leisurely over the velvet tip of him, eyes never moving from the taut lines of his face.

A bead of moisture rose up to kiss her thumb and want twisted deep inside her. She rubbed the evidence of his desire over him.

Guided by her hand, his body came closer, beautiful and glistening in the firelight, his hips widening the gap between her thighs.

Squeezing his pulsing length in her hand, she teased him at her opening, nudging him against her, watching hungrily as his eyes dilated with desire. His chest lifted on a ragged breath as she traced the head of him over her folds, rubbing him in her moistness, tormenting herself—tormenting them both.

"God," he gasped, eyes burning blue fire as he bucked against her hand, trying to bury himself inside her.

She smiled coyly and shook her head.

"What are you doing to me?" he groaned.

Making it last. Making it so good and so perfect that it would be enough. Enough for a lifetime.

Unable to stop herself, or the siren that she had become, a siren that she never knew she could be, she bent forward and tasted him, savoring him with a single, deep lick of tongue.

He shuddered, his hand diving into her hair, tangling in the loosened strands, gripping her head as she took the head of him in her mouth.

Her gaze flicked upward, relishing the sight of his head flung back, the tendons in his neck stretched taut, the muscles in his chest strained tight with tension. Urged by some dark, unknown part of herself, she devoured him, loved him with her mouth, fueling her arousal as she wrenched groans and cries from deep within him.

Leaning back, she released him, beyond teasing, beyond delaying the desire that had turned her into a wanton creature.

Falling back on her elbows, she met his gaze. "Take me," she whispered.

He came over her, his arms falling on each side of her, caging her in. His gaze held hers, dark and dangerous, feral as a jungle cat cornering its prey. He prodded her opening with his hard heat.

Legs wide, she lifted her hips to meet his first thrust, ready for it, taking him in as deeply as she could, crying out and arching beneath the invasion that stretched her, filled her to capacity.

Leaning forward, her hands clawed down his back, seizing the tight mounds of his buttocks, urging him on, needing the ferocity of this union, the sense of coming apart inside herself from his each and every thrust.

He dragged his mouth down her throat to her shoulder in a blistering trail.

"Harder," she gasped in his ear and he increased his thrusts.

In answer, he plunged fiercely, burying her deeper into the soft bed.

She moved beneath him, desperate for more, for all, for an end to the torment, an end to the aching emptiness . . . for him to never stop . . . never leave her.

"Astrid," he gasped, biting down on her shoulder.

She arched beneath him, breasts pressed into his sweat-slick chest, his crisp hair against her nipples incredibly erotic. He followed his bite with a kiss to the bruised flesh, his tongue licking and laving, sliding upward, over the column of her throat.

She let go then, surrendered, muscles squeezing and tightening in a blinding flash of pleasure and pain.

Her vision grayed at the edges and she wondered if she had perhaps died, the feelings rippling through her too great, too powerful, too . . . much, reminding her with startling suddenness why she hid from such tumultuous emotions.

Her muscles relaxed, body liquefying into a puddle as he moved a final time inside her, the heat of him pouring into her.

She lay utterly still for a moment, her legs spread wide beneath him, his large body heavy and sticky atop her, his member still twitching inside her.

As the pleasure ebbed, so did the feelings, the emotions she had allowed herself to feel. Like water spilling from a cup, they poured from her, fleeing from the hidden depths of her soul.

Slowly, Astrid returned to herself. She looked down at herself, at his dark head resting against her shoulder. One bare breast peeked out from beneath him, gleaming golden in the glow of the fire.

Her legs, spread widely, indecently, appeared to belong to someone else, some other wanton creature of the night that permitted emotions to tumble from her as easily as her clothes. *Someone like her mother.*

Damnable tears pricked her eyes. It had come to pass. Just as her father said it would. She had become as capricious as her mother. An amoral creature that succumbed to passion and emotion without a shred of sense or dignity. Without a thought to the obligations weighing on her.

No. She would not be that person. Would not become her. One fall from grace did not constitute a total lack of control or loss of responsibility.

Her knees trembled slightly, shaking at the effort to stay upright. The slopes of her thighs glistened with a fine sheen of perspiration, the muscles beneath the flesh quivering. Unable to hold them up, she let her legs slide down, the bottoms of her feet gliding over the furred coverlet.

He stirred against her—in her—and lifted his dark head. Staring at her, his lids heavy over the light blue pools of his eyes, a familiar lick of heat twisted inside her belly.

"You're incredible," he murmured, rising on his elbows over her.

His words caused a deep pang near her heart and she blinked tightly, willing the hurt away.

His fingers combed the hair from her shoulders. His chest lifted with a deep inhalation, the crisp hairs tickling her breasts.

"I knew, you know," he drawled, his voice a rough scrape on the air. "You're a wildcat. Full of heat and passion. Nothing cold or proper about you." His beautiful mouth curved in a smile.

Her chest tightened, his words salt in an open wound.

He shifted, easing the weight of his chest off her and sinking his hips deeper against her. Her eyes widened at the deep thrust of him within her. His member stirred, hardening inside her again, coaxing a response. One her body was only too willing to give . . . even if her mind screamed that she resist.

She shook her head side to side on the fur coverlet and shoved at his chest. It was like pushing at a wall.

"No," she whispered, her voice a desperate plea. She could not go there again, could not lose herself all over, not so soon. It was disgraceful.

"What?" he rasped, lowering his head and pressing an open-mouthed kiss to the thrumming pulse in her neck as he slid his hard length out of her.

"You don't want to?" He pushed back inside her and she gasped at the sensation. "Where's my little hellcat now?" he purred against her throat.

"No," she whispered, but her body betrayed her, her inner muscles tightening, squeezing him like a glove, pulling him deeper inside her.

He moved again, nearly sliding all the way out, his flesh a hot drag of sensation against her own.

Her nails dug into his forearms, her body arching and straining against him as he inched back within her by slow, agonizing degrees.

The friction unbearable, a sob escaped her. Defeated by her own body, her hips rose to take as much of him as she could, mindless from the slow, steady pace he set, wanting it hot and frenzied like moments ago.

Her hands clawed at his chest, nails digging into the supple flesh.

He moved, slipping out of her and rolling onto his back, leaving her empty and aching.

Her head whipped sideways to glare at him in reproach, the core of her throbbing, empty and crying out from the loss.

He cocked an eyebrow. "You said *no.*"

Folding his arms behind his head, he held her gaze, his blue eyes burning like winter fire. "You want it? Take what you want, Astrid."

She dropped her eyes down to his manhood. It sprang boldly from the nest of hair between his legs, beckoning her. With a bitter curse, she rolled over and mounted him, lodging him deeply inside her, hating him in that moment for filling her so perfectly. For making her seize control, making her claim him so that there could be no confusion, no doubt that she wanted this—

wanted *him*. That she was as weak as her mother had been.

Dismissing the unpleasant thought, she sighed with gratification and closed her eyes against the sight of his satisfied smile as she rode him, setting the frenzied pace her body craved, taking herself to that final pinnacle until her body shuddered and stilled atop him.

Chapter 14

For some time, Astrid didn't move. Draped over him in a boneless puddle, her chest rose and fell with rapid breaths. Rolling to her side, she brought her legs together, their length slick and damp with perspiration. She flinched when his large hand fell on her hip in a possessive gesture, fingertips curling and sliding toward the jut of her hipbone.

She felt him inch closer to her back and closed her eyes, squeezing them tight, his touch, his closeness unbearable, stirring the deep *want* for him all over again.

A hard knock sounded on the door, startling her and sending her scrambling beneath the counterpane.

"Easy," he chuckled, rising and sliding his breeches over his nudity.

Peering over the edge of the covers, she watched

as he strode across the chamber and pulled the heavy wood door open.

A maid stood there, bearing a large tray, steam wafting from its contents. Astrid sat a little taller, attempting to identify the source of steam and tantalizing aromas.

The servant took her time eyeing Griffin's chest, her eyes gleaming with wholly feminine appreciation. Dark, possessive feelings tightened Astrid's chest and she glared at the girl.

"Thought you might be wanting some food." Her voice rang coyly as she attempted to step around Griffin.

He blocked her and removed the tray from her hands. "Thank you."

The girl frowned as he removed her burden. Craning her neck, she caught a glimpse of Astrid on the bed and grinned slyly.

Face burning, Astrid sank low on the bed, well imagining how she must look, hair wild around her naked shoulders. No doubt her appearance gave evidence to the carnal nature of their activities. And the maid would waste no time informing everyone that Griffin had taken their advice, crudely worded as it had been. The skin over her face tightened, heating with shame.

The door thudded shut and she released a

pent-up breath, glad to have the girl's prying eyes gone.

"You must be hungry." He lowered the tray before her.

Stomach clenching, she gave a quick nod. Tucking the counterpane tightly beneath her arms, she snatched a chicken leg from one of the plates and tore into it with a snap of her teeth. She moaned briefly in appreciation.

"I guess making love isn't the only time you make that sound," he murmured as he sat beside her.

Her eyes flew open and she covered her mouth with the back of her hand, forcing herself to chew more slowly, silently. She scooted back from the tray as if distancing herself from the fare would keep her from gobbling down the dish full of buttery rolls. Almost as if eating with more restraint would prove that she was not a creature of passion, not a woman given to impulsive behavior. At least not again. Not with him.

"Don't," he rebuked, lowering onto his side and propping himself on an elbow. "I like a woman with an appetite." He selected one of the rolls and waggled it before her mouth. "C'mon," he encouraged. "You know you want it."

She looked from him to the buttery roll.

"Astrid," he said, his voice firm, matter-of-fact. "You have to eat."

Leaning forward, she forced herself to take a dainty bite from the roll.

Shaking his head, he looked back at her as she ate. Flipping a hank of hair over her shoulder, he glided a finger over the smooth slope of her shoulder, marveling, "How can you be so thin and eat like this?"

"I rarely eat like this," she replied. "At least not often. My friends call me a camel."

"A camel storing water," he mused, rolling a date between his fingers, staring at her as though he would like to devour her and not the food.

"Only I store food." She smiled ruefully, recalling the afternoon Lucy had made the comparison. Astrid had been halfway through a platter of ham salad sandwiches at the time. "Accurate description, I suppose."

"You know, that's the first time I've seen you smile."

Astrid's mouth hardened automatically.

"And then it's gone." He sighed. "I suppose I shouldn't have said anything."

She dropped her gaze to the tray and selected a wedge of cheese.

"Why can't you smile?" he murmured, tilting her chin up with a finger. "Is it so very difficult?"

She returned his stare, answering with a solemn honesty that surprised her. "I've had little to smile about in my life."

"So you won't let yourself smile because of what has happened in the past?"

She shook her head, dislodging his finger from beneath her chin. "It's not that simple."

He popped a date into his mouth, watching her intently as he chewed. "Why is it so complicated?"

Because smiling leads to other things. Feelings. Emotions that lead to crazy, reckless sex with a man she had known less than a week. Her stomach heaved, her hastily eaten meal threatening to return on her.

"Astrid? What is it?" Griffin leaned in, his body an encroaching wall of heat that she immediately responded to. Like a fire in winter, his heat drew her, called to her, beckoned.

Blast. Her body wasn't her own anymore. She had to get away from him. Quickly. Before she did anything more foolish, more reckless than she already had. Before she drew too close and went up in flames.

Long fingers traced her jaw. "Astrid," he whispered, his drawl beguiling, a lure to her long frozen heart.

She shook her head fiercely and pulled away with a shiver.

His eyes frosted over, clouds drifting over a pale blue sky. "What?" he bit out. "I can't touch you anymore? What precisely has changed from moments ago?"

She blinked once, long and hard. Inhaling deeply, she opened her eyes to the tempting sight of him and plunged ahead. "I can't do this again."

"*This?*" he demanded.

She motioned between them. "Yes. This. What we did . . . are doing."

His jaw hardened. A muscle jumped wildly in his cheek. "You can't say it?" he ground out.

She fought off the rising burn in her cheeks, struggling to reclaim her usual composure. "You know my meaning."

"Sex. I suppose that's the universal word for it. Although there are more colorful alternatives."

Heat swept over her face, licking her cheeks. "Griffin, please."

"What?" he snapped, eyes sparking blue fire. "I'm a common man, Astrid. What did you expect?"

She swept a hand over her burning face. "It can't happen again. It's wrong."

"*Wrong?*" He shoved off the bed as if her nearness tainted him. "Easy to say now. After the fact."

"You're angry."

"And you're observant," he snapped, adding in a growl, "Why the sudden change? You scratched your itch, satisfied your curiosity so now you'll return to being the haughty bitch? Very well. Just remember I will always know the truth."

His eyes scoured her and she tightened her fingers on the fur counterpane, pulling it higher. She didn't know why. The way his hot gaze slid over, she knew he remembered every inch of her, every line and curve.

"What truth?"

"That you're a fraud, pretending to be the dignified lady, the haughty duchess who's really as hot as any whore for it."

Astrid stared, his words ringing in her head, every bit the truth.

She had been hot for it, on fire—for *him*. Only him.

She bit her lip to keep from confessing this, to stop from giving him any excuse to think that what they had shared went beyond a sordid tryst.

"Make no mistake," he assured her, first tugging on his boots and then pulling his shirt over his head. "I won't lay a finger on you again. I'd touch a rattlesnake before approaching you. Less likely to get bit."

That said, he stalked across the room, wrenching the heavy door open.

"Where are you going?" she cried, leaning forward, fingers digging into the covers.

"I'll take the company of a rough bunch of Scots over you. At least they don't pretend to be something they're not."

She jerked at that remark, then again as he slammed the door, the sound reverberating throughout the chamber, throughout her heart.

She sat still for a long moment, her fingers flexing in the soft fur. Her eyes lowered, taking in the food before her. So much still uneaten. And she didn't crave a bite. Nothing would satisfy the gnawing ache inside her. Not this time.

With a choked cry, she sent the tray crashing to the floor, food flying in so many pieces . . . like the shattering of everything she had once held to be true. About herself. About the unlikelihood of ever losing herself over a man.

* * *

Griffin stormed into the hall, glad to see that much of the crowd had dissipated. The last thing he needed was to face questioning stares. He grimaced, recalling that this crowd wouldn't limit themselves to questioning stares. No doubt they would demand an explanation. Details he had no wish to share.

He approached the massive fireplace, skirting the tall scarlet-cushioned chairs and extending his hands out to the life-giving warmth, watching the hypnotic dance of flames within the giant rock hearth.

"Did your woman throw you out, lad?"

Griffin whirled around, hand instinctively flying to his side where he usually wore his holster.

Laird Gallagher sat in one of the chairs, his brawny arms resting on the wooden arms, reposed and regal as a king surveying his domain.

"I left of my own will," he muttered.

The man chuckled. "Aye, we all say that. And we swear nothing will bring us back to them, but then we always return. Likes bees to the honey pot. Ah, it was the same with my bonny Maggie. She had the fiercest temper." He shook his grizzled head with a snort. "She could make me see red with that smart mouth of hers. I'd swear we were finished. Done." He swiped a large gnarled hand through the air. "I'd move my things into another chamber, start looking among the women, swearing one of them would suffice to take her place."

The man smiled then, a light entering his eyes that struck Griffin as both fond and sad.

"And?" Griffin prompted, certain he wasn't finished.

Gallagher leaned forward in his chair, his voice lowering as if sharing some secret. "All it took was a look, a sway of her hips, and I'd say or do whatever it took to get back into her bed." He fell back, chuckling and threading his fingers through his beard.

Griffin swung around to face the fire again, crossing his arms over his chest. "Not me," he vowed.

"Not you," he mocked. "And why not? You're too strong, too smart, hmm?" He winked. "You're just like the rest of us. A slave to your cock . . . and that little lass upstairs owns it."

It burned on the tip of his tongue to deny this to the coarse old man, to inform him that any woman he'd known less than a week could not possibly matter to him. But the words stuck in his throat.

"Now," Gallagher announced, "why don't you sit here and tell me what brings you to Scotland. By the time you're finished the wee lass may be asleep and you can crawl back into bed without her even knowing."

Griffin grinned despite himself and dropped into a chair beside him, admitting to himself that he liked the crusty old man. He reminded him of his foreman back home.

"Where are you from?"

"Texas."

"Ah, dust and Indians."

"Well, it's not exactly dusty where I live."

"Hmm," the laird murmured. "Shaw is a Scottish name."

"My parents immigrated to Texas—well, New York first. Texas soon after."

"And what were you doing on MacFadden's land?" He sniffed, rubbing his nose with a thick sausage finger. "Don't tell me you know that ol' battle-ax." His eyes narrowed. "No relation, I hope."

"No," he answered. "My mother died several years ago. My father, a few months past. I thought it time to see the country of their birth." To find out if his mother had been telling the truth.

"Hmm," Gallagher murmured in response.

Griffin leaned forward in his chair, resting

his elbows on his knees. "I'm not going to have a problem leaving here, am I?"

The old man studied him for a long moment before replying, his tone deceptively off-hand, "Well, now, I think I might enjoy your company for a bit. I would be vastly interested in hearing about these Indians of yours."

Griffin tensed. "I appreciate the offer, but—"

"And," Gallagher continued, "I would especially like to hear more about these wealthy friends your woman mentioned. The ones that would miss her a great deal if she were to get lost in the Highlands for an extended amount of time."

"Wealthy friends?" he asked grimly, wondering what precisely Astrid had said before his arrival . . . and convinced that whatever she had said had been the *wrong* thing to mention to a clan of Highlanders desperate to feed their people through a famine.

"Aye," Gallagher murmured, "we may want to contact them."

Nodding, Griffin rose to return upstairs, understanding at once he and Astrid wouldn't be permitted to depart any time soon. At least as far as the laird was concerned. He, however, had other plans. And they did not include sitting around this place for an indefinite amount of time regaling the old Scotsman with tales of snakes and Indians.

The laird's voice stopped him. "A word of advice while you're here." Griffin slowed and looked over his shoulder. "Best keep an eye on that woman of yours. She's got a cold manner about her that gives many a man a notion. You needn't worry further about Lachlan, but there are others in the clan. A man likes to imagine he can be the one to light a fire in a woman with such a chilly way about her."

Unbidden, the image of Astrid wild and frenzied beneath him flashed through his mind.

"Yes, I understand your meaning," he returned, thinking that was the first thing he had noticed about her. That damnable aloofness, those obsidian eyes that the light never quite reached. Damn fool that he was, he had wanted to see the light flare in those eyes—had wanted to put it there.

"I'd keep her close."

"I'll keep that in mind."

He waved a broad hand in the air. "You have only my hospitality during your stay here."

"Thank you." Griffin turned and strode from the great hall. Marching up the stone steps, he hoped to find Astrid asleep when he entered the chamber. Cowardly, he supposed, but he had no wish to see her now with the light banked in her gaze.

The heavy wood door didn't make a sound as he eased it open. He paused in the threshold, assessing the still form lying on the huge four-post bed.

He approached slowly, circling the bed, dipping his head to get a better look at her. Asleep, she looked every bit an angel, countenance relaxed, her lashes smudges of coal on her milky cheeks. The firelight cast entrancing shadows over her creamy shoulders, smooth and elegant as polished marble above the fur counterpane.

His gut tightened and he knew he had never beheld a woman like her. Fire and ice. Elegance and dignity. Even bedraggled and travel weary, she pulled at something deep inside him. He could not imagine her in his world. Life on the frontier would change her. Break her. Like it did so many women. Robbing them of their youth and putting them in the ground too soon. With a curse, he shook his head. Why was he even thinking such thoughts? It wasn't as if he would be taking her home with him. Nor would she consider going with him. Even if he asked. And he would not.

He reached out to touch her face, then stopped. Dropping his hand, he removed his clothes, pausing when he noticed the tray on the table, the dishes shattered, the food, still mostly uneaten, in chaos amid the shards.

He glanced back at her, wondering if she had dropped the tray or thrown it. Dropped, he decided. The frigid duchess would not have succumbed to temper and shattered the dishes. And why should she have lost her temper anyway? She had announced that they would never make love again—had called what happened between them *wrong*. A mistake.

He slid in bed beside her, careful not to make a sound, heedful that he should not come in contact with one luscious inch of her.

A quick glance beneath the fur revealed she had donned her nightgown. He quickly lowered the fur, staring instead at the flowing mass of hair fanned out over the pillow, golden silk, a huge improvement from the tightly drawn bun that made her features look pinched.

He let his fingers stroke the loose strands against the pillow, confident that such a light touch would not wake her. He smiled ruefully. What happened to his penchant for dark-haired beauties?

His mind drifted to Adelaide, the girl he had always counted on marrying. At least one day. His own parents had expected as much. And he had never discouraged them from the notion. Nor had he encouraged it. Adelaide's father, a neighbor, held the same expectations. A union between them would benefit both families, eventually merging their properties. And Adelaide was a nice girl. If uninspiring.

But now, lying in the dark, he could only dimly recall her face as he stared at the woman asleep next to him.

In truth, it all seemed so faint in his mind. Hazy. Adelaide. Texas. The life he left behind. The longer away, the less certain he was of where he belonged.

This journey was intended to give him answers, to fill the void his mother's deathbed confession had left in him. To forget the way his father had looked at him, so full of disappointment and shame in his only son.

Only the closer he came to discovering those answers, to finding the truth eluding him . . . the more adrift he felt.

Sighing, he closed his eyes against the sight of Astrid, flinging his arm above his head, hand tugging idly on his hair.

Still, he could only see one face in his mind—the face of the woman next to him. The pinpoints of light glinting brightly in the dark of her eyes when she surrendered and let the fire take her.

Chapter 15

Astrid stretched upon waking, her muscles pliant and relaxed as warmed milk. Smiling softly, she drew her arms high above her head and released a tiny mewl-like moan.

"Sleep well?"

Eyes flying open, she pulled her arms down, memories of the night before—and who she had spent it with—flooding over her. The warmth evaporated from her body as she recalled how the night had ended. The harsh words. The venom of his gaze.

Her eyes sought Griffin, finding him sitting beside her, thankfully dressed.

He fixed his eyes coldly on her, the passionate lover gone, his eyes chips of blue frost, looking at her as if they had shared nothing. Nothing special. Nothing intimate. As if their bodies had not so thoroughly loved each other only hours before.

At your own request, a small voice in the back of her head reminded. *I did this.*

She tore her gaze away from him. Morning light washed the room, altering it, giving it little resemblance to the shadowed, dreamlike chamber of the night before. Appropriate, she supposed. That night was over. *A thing of the past.* Already more dream than reality. It could never happen again.

"Yes," she answered, tucking her hair behind her ears. "And you?"

She readjusted the counterpane around her and darted a glance to her valise across the room, longing to dress herself and repair her hair—to reclaim *some* normalcy, to reclaim herself.

He stared at her, a strange little smile curving his lips. "Like a log."

"Lovely," she murmured.

His smile deepened, turned mocking. "So we're to this now? Social niceties? How civilized."

Flushing, she ignored the comment and asked, "Could you give me a moment please? So that I might dress?"

His mocking gaze made her feel the fool for even asking. "A little late for modesty now, don't you think?" he asked in the same hard voice he had used before he stormed out of the room last night. A voice she loathed now as much as then.

She missed the way he had spoken to her before—all heat and velvet . . . melting her insides.

Foolish, she knew. She had asked for this. Foolish, she supposed, to now want to shield her body from his eyes. But how was she to put what happened behind them if she did not at least try to reclaim some distance?

He cocked an eyebrow and crossed his arms over his broad chest, not moving toward the door to grant her the privacy she requested.

Annoyed, she flung back the counterpane and stood. Chin high, she moved to her valise, walking proudly, boldly.

Holding his gaze, she worked the ties free at the front of her nightgown and shrugged the prim cotton off her shoulders and down her arms, letting it drop to her feet in a whisper . . . letting him look his fill.

Naked before him, she resisted the urge to cover herself with both hands.

His eyes gleamed, the dark centers seeming to grow, darken, bleeding out the light in his blue gaze as he surveyed her, eyes moving up and down her body slowly.

Dark satisfaction spiraled inside her. She was glad to see that his plan to humiliate her had ended in his own punishment.

Intent on torture, she dressed herself slowly, enticing him, letting him watch as she proceeded to cover herself bit by slow bit, taking her time sliding her stockings up her legs and tying the garters at her thighs.

Her satisfaction grew, burning through her at the sight of the ruddy color staining his cheeks.

Only by the time she finished buttoning her last button, her perverse pleasure backfired and she felt as hot and flustered as he appeared.

Rounding the bed, she smoothed her hands down her green and blue striped skirts, averting her eyes and striving to regain her composure. The gown had once been the height of fashion. Now the green and blue were so faded one could scarcely tell where the stripes began and ended. Pride had prompted her to add white lace to the cuffs at her elbows in an attempt to keep up with fashion.

She faced him, proud and erect, dressed but still burning with the knowledge that he had stared at her as she attired herself, his angry, hungry eyes following her every movement.

"Will we breakfast before departing?" she asked, moving to her valise, presenting him with her back. "Or are you eager for us to be on our way?

"We're not leaving," he announced. "At least not today."

She straightened and swung back to face him. "Pardon me?"

"They're not letting us go. A circumstance owed much to you."

"Me?"

His eyes still roamed over her as if she stood nude before him. "Yes. You."

"Why won't they let us go?"

"Apparently," he bit out as he lowered to the bed and tugged on his boots, "you mentioned some wealthy friends to the laird."

"Yes." She shrugged. "What does that matter now? I was desperate. I would have said anything for him to let me go."

"Well, it seems the ol' laird is highly interested in these friends of yours . . . and their willingness to fill his coffers for your safe return."

"No," she gasped, realization sinking in.

"Yes. Being an enterprising sort, Gallagher intends to ransom us. Or rather you. I suppose I could take my leave if I so wish."

If I so wish.

"And will you?" she asked, fighting to keep her voice level, to sound unaffected at the prospect. She could not blame him if he left her. She had insisted they were nothing to each other. He owed her nothing.

He stared at her a long moment before saying, "No. I won't leave you here. I'll see you safely to Edinburgh. As I promised."

Unable to hide her relief, a shuddery breath rippled through her. Sinking onto the bed beside him, she propped her chin into her hands. "What are we going to do?"

"Never fear," he assured her in derisive tones. "They'll treat us as honored guests." Rising from the bed, he extended his arm. "Come. Let's eat. I'm famished."

"Are we not going to discuss this more? You don't plan on accepting this situation. I can't stay here."

He lifted one broad shoulder. "I'll take care of the matter."

She gnashed her teeth. Didn't he know her well enough yet to know she would not sit on her laurels and leave it to the *strong* man to handle everything? With reason. She learned long ago to rely on herself. And old habits died hard.

With all the cold hauteur she could summon, she rose to her feet and accepted his arm. "Unnecessary. I shall simply explain that I was bluffing . . . afraid for my safety and merely attempting to procure my release."

"Yes, you do that," he suggested, his voice

mocking as ever as he led her from the chamber. "So far, you've been very successful at managing things on your own."

"If you have a better strategy, by all means share," she snapped. "What do *you* suggest we do?"

"*We?* Nothing. Me? I plan to scout the castle today and plot the best escape route."

"Escape?" she echoed as they moved down the corridor. "What are you planning to do? Climb down the castle walls with your bare hands?"

"If need be." He cut her a glance, the hard set to his jaw telling her that he could . . . and would.

She assessed the unforgiving lines of his profile, the bruises still visible, and reminded herself not to underestimate him. He'd already proven that nothing could best him. Likely he had never failed anything in his entire life. Or anyone.

"And what of me? Do you expect me to scale walls, too? Or will you leave me here?" she asked, regretting the question the moment she posed it. He'd already said he would take her to Edinburgh. Must she provoke him into retracting his promise?

He stopped on the stairs and turned, backing her against the cold stone wall. Her pulse thumping madly at her throat, she held her breath as he caged her in, his arms coming up on either side of her head.

In the dimness of the stairwell, his eyes glowed with a predatory light. "You think I would abandon you here?"

Astrid swallowed down the thickness in her throat. "I'm quite aware that you're vexed with me—"

"Vexed?" he repeated. "Oh, no, Duchess. I'm not vexed. You gave me the ride of my life. Why would I be vexed with you?"

She flinched, stung.

Feeling little more than a tart—no doubt his intention—her hand rose to strike him.

He caught her hand in his. "Careful," he warned, fingers squeezing her fist.

"Or what? You'll leave me here? Perhaps you should." The words dropped from her lips recklessly, hot and furious. "I'm beginning to wonder if I might not fare better with some Highland brute."

"Shall we find out?" he drawled.

His gaze dropped, eyeing the rapid rise and fall of her breasts against her bodice. His voice lowered, as did his head, his lips brushing the side of her neck. "Would you prefer that, Astrid? Would that help you forget me?"

Unable to stop herself, she angled her head, giving him better access to her throat, her breath escaping in a fast tremble of air. His tongue laved her quickening pulse.

Forget him? Impossible. She brought her hand up, threading her fingers through his hair.

"You think another man can do the things to you I do? Make you feel the way I can?"

Her mouth moved silently. *No.*

Dropping his arms, he stepped away, simply left her leaning forward like a plant seeking light, her treacherous body aching, her neck tingling from the feel of his mouth, the rasp of his tongue.

Turning, he strode down the stairs, leaving her to follow. Fisting her hands at her sides, she drew a steadying breath and trailed after him.

To her surprise, she found him waiting at the base of the stairs, expression cool, remote. The hard-faced stranger again. She took his arm and accompanied him into the hall. All eyes turned on them.

Gallagher motioned for them to occupy the two seats beside him at the table. As if they were indeed guests of honor. Lachlan sat a few chairs down, his face as battered as Griffin's—perhaps more. His already mangled nose looked as if it had been broken yet again.

A serving girl set steaming bowls of porridge

laced with honey before them. Astrid tucked into her bowl, consuming the tasty fare. Her mouth watered at the platter of buttered bread dropped on the table. She started to reach for one, then stopped, feeling Griffin's stare. Self-conscious, she dropped her hand back in her lap.

"Regular little martyr, aren't you?" he leaned close to whisper in her ear.

Fighting down the swarm of heat that licked her cheeks, she set her chin at a firm angle and took a small bite of her porridge.

Swallowing, she turned her attention to the laird sitting on the other side of Griffin.

"My lord," she began, leaning forward, not certain the appropriate form of address for the laird of a clan, but thinking it wouldn't hurt to address him with the utmost respect.

He turned light blue eyes on her. "I fear my words yesterday evening have been misconstrued."

"Misconstrued, eh?" he mumbled, lifting a spoonful of porridge to his mouth and leaving much of it on the beard surrounding his lips.

"Yes." She nodded, pressing on determinedly. "I had only hoped to convince you to release me. You see, I have no wealthy friends willing to pay for my release."

He stared at her with narrowed eyes. "You freely admit you lied then?"

"Yes," she declared, then frowned at the look Griffin shot her—one of pity and mild disgust. As if she were the village idiot. He shook his head.

The laird wrinkled his nose. "You're not to be trusted, then. That much is clear to me."

"No," she quickly denied.

"Aye," he nodded, leaning forward and plucking a slice of bread off the platter before them. Wadding the thick slice into a ball, he took a considerable bite. Giving her a conspiratorial wink, he asked around a mouthful, "Come now. A starchy Sassenach like you doesn't have a few friends with blunt to spare?"

Her spine stiffened at his description of her, however true . . . however much she had cultivated that very image of herself. "No. None that can be relied upon for assistance."

"No relations?"

For a moment she thought of her in-laws. Thinking of them, she replied honestly, "I don't inspire that sort of devotion, I'm afraid."

Chewing, he measured her with keen blue eyes before answering, "Nay. I don't believe it." With a firm nod, he added, "You will supply me with the names of these friends. And you will remain here until they pay the price of your freedom."

She drew her shoulders back. "I cannot supply you with names I do not have."

"Very well." He shrugged and took another bite of bread. Flakes and crumbs flew into his beard as he spoke, "Then you'll be with us a long time."

Frustration burned a bilious trail up her chest. She swung her furious gaze to Griffin.

He gave her a smug, knowing look before turning his attention to Gallagher. In all mildness, he asked, "Since we'll be here awhile, how might we occupy ourselves? Is there a library perhaps?"

"Of course. We're not unlettered barbarians here," the old man replied, wiping a rough wool sleeve against his mouth. "Just know the guards have orders to stop you or your woman from passing the outer gates. Otherwise, make yourselves at home."

Griffin nodded his assent, his look all innocence.

Until he glanced back at Astrid. And she knew there was nothing innocent in his request, saw it in the glint of his pale blue eyes. He meant to investigate the castle and plan a method of escape. Suddenly such a measure did not seem extreme in the least. It seemed utterly sensible. Their only choice.

Chapter 16

A hard hand on her shoulder shook Astrid awake.

"Make haste. Dress yourself and gather your things."

Rubbing her eyes, she sat up, her eyes adjusting to the dim chamber. Embers from the fireplace provided minimal light. Griffin moved about the room quickly, a dark shadow collecting his saddlebag and swinging it over his shoulder.

Astrid dressed herself in her striped poplin gown. Out of necessity, she had learned to dress herself without the assistance of a maid several years ago, but even long practice did not stop her fingers from stumbling over the buttons.

Looking up, she stated rather obviously, her voice still scratchy with sleep, "We're leaving."

"Yes."

She shook her head. Laird Gallagher ran a lively

household. That much she had observed in their brief stay. Even at this late hour, someone would be found lingering in the hall. They could not simply stroll unnoticed into the bailey.

"How can we?"

He stopped before her, his stare cool, unmoved. "I'm aware that you don't trust me." His lips twisted wryly at this. "But if you wish to leave here, you will follow my instructions without question. Do you understand?"

The *without question* part rankled. She was not the sort to follow blindly. She had been forced to look to herself for too many years to blindly follow anyone.

He must have read her hesitation. He stepped so close their noses almost touched. "If not, then we might as well remain here." He gestured toward the door. "If you badger me with questions out there, if you so much as hesitate, we *will* be caught." His eyes glinted darkly. "With you, it's a certainty. And I assure you that once we're caught, an opportunity to escape shall not come again."

Astrid gave a tight nod, disregarding her stinging pride. "Fine. I'll do as you say."

"Good."

Griffin moved to the chamber's lone window and pried the stained mullioned glass open, its ancient hinges creaking in protest. Sticking his head out into the cold night, he looked below. Taking his bag, he dropped it.

Looking back at her, he motioned her near. "Is your valise ready?"

Despite her curiosity and the questions that burned on her tongue, she handed over her valise, wincing as he dropped it out the window, grateful for the well-worn leather that likely would not crack.

Griffin moved toward the bed then, and she took advantage of the moment, peeking her head out into the frigid night air.

A pale smudge of face looked up at her from below, their bags waiting at his feet.

Turning, she watched Griffin secure a rope around one of the thick bedposts. Positioning his foot against the bed, he yanked hard to make certain it held fast.

Dread sinking into her belly, she shook her head. "You cannot mean—" She stopped cold when he tossed her a dark look, his warning clear. Recalling her promise of moments ago, she bit the inside of her cheek.

Striding past her, he flung the rest of the rope out the window. Presenting her with his back, he squatted. "Hop on."

Astrid blinked. Tucking a stubborn strand of hair behind her ear, she hesitated for so long that he looked over his shoulder. One look into his steady blue gaze and she knew he was deadly serious. He meant for them to climb out that window.

Trust him, a voice whispered across her mind.

Drawing air thinly through her nose, she moved behind him, looping her arms around his neck. He rose with her in one smooth motion, the burden of her weight seemingly insignificant.

Grasping the rope in both hands, he swung a leg over the window and lowered them out. Astrid squeezed her eyes shut, her arms tightening about his neck as the night's cold air washed over her.

"You might not want to choke me," Griffin wheezed.

Her eyes flung wide open and she looked down. And quickly realized she should have kept her eyes closed.

With his feet braced upon the wall, they hung above the earth. The ramparts loomed tall beside them, emphasizing how high they dangled from the ground. Her chest squeezed, lungs constricting until she could not draw breath.

"Astrid!"

The sharp sound of her name penetrated

her panicked thoughts. She loosened her arms around his neck—even if it terrified her to relax her hold—both relieved and alarmed when he began to move, as deft and limber as any jungle creature. Hands moving one after the other, he lowered them down the wall.

She permitted herself to breathe once they touched down. Sliding off his back, she shook her skirts and plucked her valise from beside the waiting man, eyeing him inquiringly. Failing to recognize him from their exploration of the castle today, she wondered when and where Griffin had made his acquaintance.

The man's hand shot out, his palm a pale flash in the dark. He snapped his fingers impatiently.

Griffin reached in his jacket, pulled something out from inside and handed it over.

She leaned forward, trying to see what passed between the two men.

The other man glanced at whatever it was and shoved it into his pocket with a satisfied grunt. "Come," he rasped from beneath his hood, the thread of anxiety in his voice unmistakable, heightening Astrid's own tension. "Your mounts wait beyond the trees."

Burrowing deeper in her cloak, she glanced around them at the encroaching shadows.

The Scotsman led them quickly through the bailey. "Last I checked, the guard on duty was tupping Hilda. But he's well in his cups, so I don't count on that lasting long."

The yard was silent this late hour, the few torches flickering in sconces along the far stone walls lending eerie shadows to the night.

Tension knotted her shoulders as she followed Griffin, fixing her gaze on the broad expanse of his back. They slowed at the gatehouse. Their guide motioned for them to wait as he went ahead.

She shifted from foot to foot as they waited, the heavy fall of each second convincing her that the man had been intercepted and only moments remained until they were caught.

"Easy," Griffin whispered near her ear, his warm breath rustling loose tendrils of hair. She shivered. And not entirely from her current state of anxiety.

She nodded jerkily and leaned against the chilled stone wall outside the gatehouse.

"Who's there?" a deep voice rumbled over the night.

Astrid jolted off the wall, squinting at the dark shape materializing from the shadows.

One of Gallagher's men approached, eyes wary

as he surveyed them. "What are you two doing down here—"

Griffin cut off the rest of his words with a swift, merciless blow to the face. The man fell in a graceless heap. Astrid jumped clear at the last moment, saving herself from being dragged down with him.

Griffin reached out and grabbed him by the shirt, assessing his half-closed eyes for a moment to make certain that he had in fact been rendered unconscious. She sighed, grateful when the man's eyes fell completely shut, saving him from a second blow.

The other Scot returned then, gaping between the unconscious man and Griffin. "What the hell did you do to him?"

Shaking loose his fist, Griffin growled, "Seeing that he doesn't alert the entire castle of our escape. What else was I to do?"

Scowling at his felled compatriot, he bit out, "Very well. I'll put a bottle in his hand and drag him into the hall after I finish with you two. Come on with you, then, before someone else comes along."

Some of the tension ebbed from her shoulders as he led them forward. Apparently the guard on duty was still occupied with Hilda. Hopefully, they would have no more incidents.

They passed through the gatehouse and beneath the half-raised grate. Astrid stood to the side and watched as Griffin and their guide lowered the drawbridge, grateful for the well-oiled chains and levers. Not a creak or clang broke the silence.

The bridge set down and Griffin swung his bag over his shoulder. Taking her valise from her hand, he tucked it beneath his arm. His eyes met hers briefly, conveying urgency. "Ready? You must be swift. We cannot be spotted."

She nodded, a tremor of excitement skating down her spine as he closed his hand around hers. *Crazy.* She should feel nothing but fear. Not excitement. Not . . . freedom. Not pleasure in touch.

Cold wind whistled through the air, chapping her cheeks. She watched him as he lifted his gaze to the sky.

"One moment," he whispered, strong fingers flexing around hers.

She followed his gaze, watching the fast-moving clouds skim the night sky, drifting like smoke over the nearly full moon. Suddenly the clouds thickened, obscuring the bright orb and washing the land in darkness.

"Now," he commanded, his voice fierce.

Adrenaline shot through her. Together, they

dashed forward, racing across the wood planks of the bridge and into the wind's sharp teeth, her hand still clamped in Griffin's as they fled across the open grassland surrounding the castle.

Her breath puffed ahead of her in frothy gusts. She struggled to keep up, pumping her legs as hard as she could. The cold wind rushed her, smelling of snow, clawing at her hair and whipping her cloak back from her shoulders as they plunged ahead. The ties of her cloak chafed her throat. Her heart hammered in her breast, whether from exertion or fear or delight she could not say.

The dark line of trees loomed ahead, and they dove within. Griffin released her hand and dropped their bags at his feet. Gasping, she leaned against a trunk for support.

"Wait here," he instructed, disappearing deeper into the trees.

Silence hung thick around her, punctuated only with the howl of wind and heavy pants of her breath. Clouds moved overhead again, parting. The glow of the moon washed the earth again, limning the craggy snow-capped mountains in the horizon. Hugging herself, she waited for Griffin, studying the chill-encircled castle, a thing of beauty in the night.

A smile curved her lips. In that moment, if she

never returned to Town, she could not summon a scrap of regret.

A horse neighed softly and she looked over her shoulder as Griffin emerged leading their horses. In the soft spray of moonlight, his features looked carved of stone, every angle and line cut from a sculptor's blade, his bruises mere shadows.

"Didn't think we were going to walk out of here, did you?" Anger still hummed in his voice, evident in the curl of his lip as he added, "I said I'd get us out of here."

She didn't reply, merely moved to her mount, accepting his assistance as he boosted her up.

Looking over her shoulder as they rode away, she snuck one last glance at the dark outline of the castle, more mythical than real in the shimmering moonlight—the place where she had surrendered to desire, where she had released her long-suppressed emotions . . . her heart. Where, as a prisoner, she had tasted freedom for the first time in her life.

She stared behind them until the castle was swallowed up by the thick growth of trees.

And then she turned. Facing forward, her back to what was now the past.

Chapter 17

"**W**hy are we stopping?" she asked, looking down at Griffin as he dismounted, the first words she had spoken to him since their escape from Cragmuir.

She slid from her mount unassisted, clinging to the saddle until the feeling returned to her feet. The fear of pursuit still nagged at her. "Don't stop on my account. I would not be the reason we're caught."

"You need to rest." This he uttered without once looking her way, his blue eyes intent on the task of unsaddling his mount, dark brows drawn tightly as though in concentration.

"I'm fine," she protested. "We've traveled only a few hours."

"We rest," he declared, firm lips barely moving around the inflexible words. "A little sleep will do us both some good."

Sighing, she gave a brief nod and glanced up, squinting at the thick canopy of branches high above them, an impenetrable ceiling of foliage, so dense they obscured the sky from her gaze and made it impossible to tell how close they were to daybreak. She wondered if they had even been missed back at Cragmuir yet.

"They'll expect us to ride south. In the area they first encountered us," he offered after some moments. He lifted one shoulder. "So we'll head west and then circle around. It will take a bit longer to get you to Edinburgh, but it's the wisest course."

She stared at him for a long moment, something she could do at her leisure since he continued to avoid looking at her.

Suddenly he looked up, snaring her with his chilly blue gaze. "I'll get you there. As I promised. The good news is that the authorities in Dubhlagan won't likely look for you in Edinburgh so many days after your husband's death. They've likely quit any search they put forth."

She released a shuddery breath. "Good," she managed to say, wondering at the sudden burn in her eyes. With unsteady hands, she hastily turned and began to uncinch her saddle.

The prospect of reaching Edinburgh, of taking

the train home, filled her with a decided lack of cheer. *Home.* The word echoed dully in her heart. Soon this would all be over. And she'd be *home.* Out of each other's lives for good.

He was soon at her side, brushing her hands aside as if they were insignificant gnats. She stood back, wrapping her arms around herself and feeling useless as she watched him tend to her mount.

Turning, she moved to a large ash tree. Leaning against its broad trunk, she slid to the ground, indifferent to the rough scrape of bark through her cloak—the stinging burn welcome for the feeling it brought, penetrating the numbness that tingled up her backside to her lower back from long hours in the saddle.

Her gaze followed Griffin moving about the clearing. Propping her chin on her knees, she swallowed against the tightness in her throat. She had not thought his coldness capable of wounding her. Not her—she, who lived in a state of self-imposed emotional exile. From the start, she had wished for distance from this man, had fought to maintain it, to shy from the fire that drew her, threatening to thaw her.

Now she found the cold unbearable.

He dropped their saddles near her and tossed her the bedroll. "Here."

Without another word, he disappeared, leading the horses from the clearing, no doubt to a nearby pond or brook. He always made a point of camping near a water source.

She made quick work of unrolling the bedding, her hands smoothing out the edges of the tarp, trembling in the most vexing way.

They would no doubt sleep side by side again. It was only practical. Especially in this cold. The smell of snow hung on the air. It would likely grow colder as the night unfolded.

Her heart raced at the prospect of them so close, bodies side by side throughout the night, sharing their heat . . . sharing each other. And yet how could she sleep beside him and not remember, not relive their time together, not turn to him like a moth seeking flame, hungry for him, for more of what her body could not forget?

Finished with arranging the bedding, she propped a saddle against the tree and leaned her back against it, wondering how she might bridge the gap that she herself had forged . . . and why she even wished to. Because quite simply, she must not.

But shouldn't they be civil toward each other? Considering they were stuck together, at least for the time being, it was the proper thing to do.

Proper. She let the word roll through her head, telling herself that was her sole motivation. Not because she craved something more. Not because she craved *him.*

Sighing, she scrubbed her hands over her face. If she were honest with herself, she would admit that she missed him. As he had been before. Caring. Interested. His eyes hungry on her. And she had pushed him away, a flame too hot to bear touching.

He returned then. Tethering the horses to a nearby bush, he disappeared back into the trees without a word, returning minutes later with an armful of kindling.

She watched as he started a fire, the offer to help on the tip of her tongue, but she held back, clinging to her silence, afraid of speaking. Afraid of rejection from the cold man he had become, the man she had pushed him into becoming.

She studied him in silence, her gaze lingering on his muscular thighs, stretched taut against his trousers as he crouched before the fire. Rising, he went about making camp, continuing to make her feel invisible, a mere shadow. Tormented. He rifled through his satchel and took out the twine-secured package of jerky.

At last, he joined her on the bedroll she had

spread out, handing her a hunk of the dried meat.

She cleared her throat. "You never said what you're doing in Scotland." Her hands played about the rough edges of her meat.

"Nothing of importance," he answered, his voice low and gravelly.

She watched him in the firelight, disbelieving. Moistening her lips, she persisted. "Why are you here?"

She began to suspect he would ignore her question until he said, "My mother died a few years ago." Bending his leg, he propped an arm on his knee, rolling his piece of dried venison between his fingers. "I'm headed to a place called Balfurin. The lands of Laird Hugh MacFadden."

She angled her head to the side. "Gallagher's enemy?"

He nodded.

She studied his chiseled profile. The fire cast dancing shadows on his face. *Entrancing*.

He didn't look at her as he continued, simply stared into the fire, almost as if he spoke to the nest of crackling fire and not her at all. "My mother was half out of her mind at the end . . . but she said certain things." He paused, tearing off another piece of jerky with his teeth. He chewed for some moments and swallowed before adding, "At first, I told myself nothing she said could be taken seriously. The pain she was in . . ." A muscle knotted along the bruised flesh of his jaw as his voice faded.

She resisted the urge to touch him, to feather her fingers over his bristly cheek in a soothing gesture.

"Let's just say she couldn't have known what she was saying. And after she died, I convinced myself to put her words behind me."

"But you couldn't."

"My father wouldn't answer any of my questions." His lips twisted and he plucked a twig from the ground, toying with it between his fingers. "Not surprising. We weren't close. Not since the war." Something flickered in his eyes at that confession. "He died recently."

So he was all alone. Like her.

He waved his hand. "So here I am."

"And why is that?" She angled her head, studying him. "What are you looking for? What did your mother tell you?"

He looked at her then, and the intensity in his blue gaze made her breath trip. "She claimed I wasn't her son. Hers or her husband's—the man I had called father all of my life."

Her heart squeezed at this declaration, knowing the anguish it must have brought him at the time, a son watching his mother die. She knew full well the effect a parent's words or actions could have, the way they could haunt you for years—a lifetime even.

"And you think you'll find answers at this Balfurin?"

"Hugh MacFadden, the clan's laird . . . he'll know. He'll have my answers," he replied grimly.

"What did your mother exactly say to you . . . at the end?"

"A fever struck the ship crossing over. My mother took me from a couple who died a day apart of each other. My real parents were Scottish like them, traveling to America for a fresh start . . . like them." He smiled harshly.

She envisioned his adoptive parents, a young couple, indigent crofters like so many in Scotland even now, gambling everything on an uncertain future . . . and a child that wasn't of their blood.

"But then everyone who comes to America is after a fresh start." He glanced at her. "Running from something. Running toward something."

He fell silent, his gaze returning to the mesmerizing dance of flames. And she knew he was talking about himself now. Knew that he was running away from something . . . running to something. Even if he didn't know what.

Just as she was. She'd come to Scotland looking for a second chance. *A chance at . . .*

Staring at his face, realization struck her full force. Her lungs squeezed, chasing the breath from her body. A chance at *this*. *Him*. Freedom. Love.

She swallowed down her last bit of jerky, not tasting it as it settled heavily in her knotting stomach. Why should she want to return to her old life? When she had sampled freedom with him? As crazy as it sounded, this journey had been the most liberating experience of her life. Because of him.

She was more like her adventuresome mother than she ever realized.

"So you're here to find your family," she said, regaining her breath, eager to resume talking, to behave as though she had not just discovered a new, unwanted facet to herself.

His gaze cut to hers, hard and fierce in the muted light. "I *had* a family." He flung the twig toward the fire with a vicious swing. "I don't know why the hell I'm here."

She dropped her chin back on her bent knees.

"I thought I knew what I was doing here. Why I came to Scotland. Now . . ." her voice faded and she shrugged lightly, the careless gesture so at odds with the turmoil she felt.

He snorted. "I thought your motivation perfectly clear."

"Yes. To stop Bertram," she uttered, frowning as she faced a truth she had tried to ignore. "I've never held any influence over my husband. Why did I think I could convince him to do the right thing?" A deep sigh rattled from her chest. "In the few moments I had with him before . . . before he was killed, nothing I said swayed him to cease his charade. He actually offered to pay me if I would simply disappear and pretend I had never seen him."

"Bastard," Griffin growled.

She shook her head. "I don't know what I thought I could accomplish in coming here."

"At least you did something. You tried. I imagine it's more than some ladies would do. It took courage."

She winced. "Courageous, I'm not."

"Nor kind. Or so you've said." His look turned speculative. "I've never met a woman so resistant to hearing herself praised."

She fixed her gaze on the flames. "I don't deserve praise." She drew a ragged breath and confessed, "There's much you don't know about me. I'm not a very nice person." She announced this without self-pity.

"Well, I'll confess you've been a pain in my ass on more than one occasion since we met."

Her gaze flew to his, astounded that he would speak so plainly. But that was Griffin, she realized. Plain-speaking. No mincing words.

"And," he continued, "you can freeze a man with a look." He leaned forward, capturing her gaze. "But I wouldn't say you were an evil person."

She smiled half-heartedly.

"But you think so," he pronounced. "Why?"

She closed her eyes in a slow blink and shook her head. And then she said the words she had not spoken to another soul. Not even to Jane and Lucy . . . too afraid to see the disappointment in their eyes.

"When Bertram first left, things were . . . bad," she explained, at a loss for a better word. "He took anything of value with him. I didn't know what to do. His grandmother lived with us and she was ailing." She grimaced. "We could not even afford a physician. Can you imagine? A Dowager Duchess swallowing down Cook's remedies . . . I don't even know if they helped or not." She paused, wetting her lips. "And then there was Bertram's sister."

She gulped down a breath. "She agreed to marry a wealthy merchant. I thought our problems were solved."

Griffin nodded.

She bit the inside of her cheek, coming to the hard part, the part where she sold her soul for the promise of security and comfort. The part where Griffin would look at her differently.

"Portia backed out."

"With her own grandmother ill?" He frowned. "Rather selfish of her."

"That's what I told myself . . . how I justified what I did next."

"Which was?"

She spoke quickly, as if spitting the words out made her actions less dastardly. "I drugged her and helped smuggle her into the merchant's carriage so he could take her to Scotland and force her to marry him." She shook her head. "I thought she merely suffered a loss of nerve. That she would come around."

"Rather desperate," he commented, his voice mild, lacking the judgment she expected to hear.

She looked at him sharply, expecting to see censure there and finding none. "I did a terrible thing."

"Perhaps," he allowed. "But someone needed to be sensible and save the family. It wasn't as if you could marry the man yourself." He broke another twig. "It must have baffled you that your sister-in-law did not share your sense of responsibility."

Blinking, she gave a single jerky nod, wondering how he understood her motivations so well. "Indeed. I would have married him myself if I could have."

"So what happened?"

"Portia escaped him." *Thank heavens.* "Apparently she had engaged the affections of the very wealthy Earl of Moreton. Only I was unaware of their *tendre* for one another."

He cocked a dark brow. "Might she not have told you and eased your mind? It might have prevented you from resorting to drugging her."

Astrid rubbed her forehead. "I don't know. Portia and I were never close. She was always a dreamer while I was . . ."

"Practical. Sensible," he supplied.

She nodded.

"Your sister-in-law and this earl? Did they wed?"

"Yes." She smiled wistfully. "By all accounts, they're quite happy. A love match, if you can believe it. So rare among the *ton*."

"And here you are." He flicked his gaze over her worn dress. "Still in dire straights?" It was more statement than question. At her silence, he made a disgusted sound.

"I don't expect anything from them," she hurriedly explained. "Not after what I did."

"Her brother abandoned you. I don't think it unfair to expect a little assistance considering she is in a position to lend it. Enough at least to put some meat on your ribs."

"I could never ask—"

"She and her husband should offer."

She shook her head stubbornly.

"So this is your great sin?" he demanded. For some reason he sounded angry, his voice like a lashing whip. "Why you insist you're not a *nice* person?"

"It's enough, isn't it? If Portia had not escaped, she would now be married to the wrong man when she loved another. Then you would not be so quick to shrug off my actions."

His brow furrowed. "And how is it she escaped?"

She waved a hand. "I'm not sure of all the particulars . . . I sent the earl after her and—"

"Wait." Griffin held up a broad palm, shaking his head. "You sent her earl after her? You're saying you helped *save* her?"

"Yes, but I'm the one who placed her at risk in the first place."

"Look, I can see you're determined to wear the hair shirt for the rest of your life, but think on this: you made a mistake, one not so unforgivable in my estimation, but then you repaired it. That's all anyone can hope to do."

She stared at him, amazed he did not find her actions so unpardonable . . . and tempted to believe they weren't.

"No." She shook her head. "I could have never made the mistake in the first place."

Whether one was sorry or regretful or tried to make amends, failed to signify. Mistakes, her father had taught her, were forever that. A weakness in character not to be overlooked. Which explained why, when her mother sent word that she was stranded and without funds in Paris, he had refused to send for her. He didn't want her back. Not after her betrayal. *A person receives only one chance in life, Astrid, and your mother had hers. She can rot in a French gutter for all I care—a fitting whore's death.*

One chance.

Astrid may not have abandoned her husband and child for the thrill of a lover's touch, but she, too, had dispensed her share of betrayal. She already had her chance. She'd gone too far with Portia. Her actions couldn't be undone.

What had she been thinking to come to Scotland? To try and stop Bertram? Like her mother, dead of an unforgiving French winter, redemption was not hers to have.

"Yes, well, life doesn't work out that way, does it? We're not perfect creatures," he bit out.

She stared hard at his furious expression, confused at why he should be so angry.

"We all make mistakes," he continued. "For some of us, the mistakes are far worse than the one for which you punish yourself."

"Oh. And what terrible mistakes have you made?" she demanded.

He looked at her intently, the pale blue of his eyes darkening. "I've killed. In the war."

"Soldiers fight. They kill," she returned. "I wouldn't call that a mistake. It was your duty."

"Do soldiers kill women?" The question fell hard, heavy. "Is that part of their duty?

Unease tripped down her spine. Her fingers flexed around her knees. "What do you mean?"

He continued to stare at her, his gaze steady, unflinching . . . searching. "You remind me of her," he whispered.

She frowned. "Who?"

240

"Not your face. Not your hair. But the first time I saw you . . . I saw her." He rubbed a finger beneath his eye. "I can't explain it. It's the eyes. Dark as coal."

Her chest tightened, the breath freezing in her lungs. He no longer seemed to see her as he talked. No longer seemed to be with her at all. His gaze drifted over her head.

"Her eyes were so dark. You could see your reflection in them." His eyes snapped back to her then. "The same as yours. Haunted. Sad."

"Who?" She asked again, needing to hear, even as she feared his answer.

He shrugged. "I don't know who she was. A laundress. A prostitute. There were a few women there. Amid the blood and gore."

"And you killed her?"

"I didn't save her," he countered, eyes flashing.

"Another soldier killed her, then," she surmised. "You can hardly blame yourself for that."

His eyes locked on hers. "Can't I? I was there. A party to it all. We won the day. There was no need to keep on killing . . . to kill her. A woman . . ." His voice faded to a whisper, but she felt that whisper deep in her own soul. Knew the echo of it, ceaseless, merciless, flaying your heart to ribbons, rendering you useless, worthless for yourself or anyone else.

"My father never looked at me the same way after that."

"Was he there, too?"

"No, but he heard the stories." He laughed then, the sound hoarse. "And I told him about her. I shouldn't have, but I was drunk."

"I'm sorry, Griffin."

"You see," he murmured, his face strangely unmoved as he looked at her, as though he fought to keep emotion at bay. A practice she well knew. "Your sin's not so great."

She opened her mouth to tell him neither was his. That he couldn't blame himself for the actions of other soldiers, that war was ugly for all involved . . . but something in his eyes stopped her, trapped the words in her throat. Nothing she said could alter his thoughts on the matter. Just as nothing he said could change her.

She slid down against the saddle. Folding her arms over her chest, she turned her face to the side, away from him, and closed her eyes.

Chapter 18

Her eyes flung wide open on the wind of a gasp. She drew another gulp of air deeply into her lungs, starved, desperate for breath as she blinked against the cold night. Moonlight filtered through the treetops. Wind whistled through the rustling leaves.

"Astrid?"

Griffin's shadow rose beside her. Instantly, she knew him. His touch, his heat, his smell. She *knew*. She *remembered*. And she craved more. Again.

His hard arms surrounded her. Wide-palmed hands flexed over her flesh, long-fingered and strong, expertly running along her body, drawing soothing circles on her back and making her breath come quicker.

The nightmare was familiar. Rocks. One after another they came, pressing down on her, pushing the air from her chest. Faces loomed above her, each one adding a rock to the ever-growing mound atop her. Her father. Portia. Bertram.

"Only a bad dream." Griffin's deep drawl slid through her, chasing the chill, purging the terror of moments ago, liquefying her bones, imbuing her with a languid warmth, almost as though she had imbibed one too many glasses of sherry.

"I've dreamed my share," he confided, his voice rumbling from his chest and vibrating against her body.

"Yes." Her fingers tightened their grip on his shirt, pulling him closer. "I imagine you have."

His breath ruffled her hair.

Her gaze lifted to his. Blue ice glittered down at her, hooded beneath a fringe of ink-dark lashes. Her breath snagged in her throat. He brushed a tendril of hair off her cheek, the rasp of a callused thumb dragging across her skin.

"You said the first time you saw me . . . you saw her."

He tensed against her.

The notion of him seeing death—seeing all he believed himself to have failed at in his life—when he looked at her filled her with a gnawing ache. She did not want to inspire ghosts or ill memories.

She wanted to inspire him.

Her fingers flexed against him. "Do you still?"

He spoke, his words rough and deep, feathering against her cheek. "I see you."

His words sent a small thrill up her spine, igniting a tiny flame of feminine power within her. She nuzzled the cold tip of her nose into the warm skin of his neck with a small sigh, inhaling his manly scent.

"Cold," he hissed on a strangled chuckle.

Warm me, she thought, pressing herself against the length of him with a shiver that had nothing to do with the cold.

He shifted, hands falling firmly on her arms, distancing her from him.

The fire had burned low, the burnt wood mere embers. Shadows sheltered them, the only light that of the moon and the gleam in his blue eyes.

"Don't," he breathed, the single word final, inflexible, for all she barely heard it.

She held his gaze, understanding what he was telling her with that single word . . . but too aroused from the feel of him, the smell, the look to care that she was going against the very rules she had set forth.

She snuggled against him, dipping her face into the crook of his neck, parting her mouth so that her breath fanned the swiftly thudding pulse at his throat.

"Astrid," he warned, his voice a dry whisper, his throat vibrating beneath her lips. "I'm only a man."

She slid her hands between them, flattening her palms over his shoulders. "That's all I want you to be."

With a stinging curse he rolled her onto her back, the full weight of him coming over her, a wall of humming heat pressing her into the tarp as his lips crushed hers.

His hands dropped between them, hiking up her skirts and sliding her drawers down in a rough, anxious move.

Her breath hitched, his eagerness heightening her own desire.

"Are you cold?"

With him? Never. She shook her head fiercely in response.

He paused, taking care to cocoon them beneath the blanket. She felt sheltered, safe, cherished. He braced one arm beside her head. His other hand delved between them to free himself from his trousers. Without a word, she parted her thighs, allowing him to settle between her legs. She tilted her hips, eager and ready for him.

The long heat of him slid inside her in one slick

motion. Her breath escaped in a hiss. Her neck arched, coming off the ground.

He held himself still, the fullness of him lodged deeply inside her, pulsing in rhythm with her heart.

She dropped her head back down, rolling her neck side to side, mindless and moaning as he began to move, his rocking thrusts slow and deep, stoking her, building the fire, tormenting her, drawing out her pleasure until she thought she would die if it did not come swifter, harder.

She dug her nails into his taut buttocks, bringing him harder against her, trying to increase his tempo, but he continued his torment, easing out of her in slow drags of heated flesh.

"Griffin," she wept, lifting her head.

"Say it," he growled.

"What?" she gasped, senseless, mad with need.

"That you want it. You want me. That you always will." His tongue swept the curve of her ear in a hot brush.

She moaned again. It was the height of manipulation for him to inveigle such a promise from her when she was lost with need. When she had to have him or die from wanting.

And yet she couldn't say such a thing.

Because the day would arrive when she couldn't have him . . . when she had to give him up. And pretending that she didn't want him, pretending they weren't the same, two sides of the same coin, might be the only way to survive such a loss.

Then it dawned on her that he wasn't the only one capable of manipulation.

She tilted her hips, taking him deeper, hugging him tighter inside her. Instead of answering, she raked her nails through his too long dark hair, gently scouring his scalp. Pulling his head down, she claimed his mouth in a deep, tongue-tangling kiss.

He groaned into her mouth, angling his head, deepening the kiss in turn. A wave of moisture rushed between her legs and she exploded in a burst of blinding heat, crying out against his mouth.

Singed by fire, the cold Scottish wood around them became a very distant, very insignificant thing, dimming altogether as wave after wave of sensation shuddered through her, sizzling through her nerves as Griffin continued his sinuous thrusts, his breath a harsh rasp in her ear until he stilled, pouring his heat into her.

The deep panting of their breaths mingled,

frothy white clouds on the air, their chests rising and falling against each other in rhythmic unison. Almost as though they were one being. She chased off the fanciful thought.

And yet the awe, the euphoria lingered. Now she understood the blushes and whispers behind lace fans. Before, she had never imagined what was so scintillating about the subject of sex.

At best, her experiences had always been . . . unmemorable. At worst, painful and undignified, leaving her mortified long after Bertram left her bed.

But now she knew. Now she understood what made sane people behave without good sense. Perhaps she even understood what drove her mother to run away with Mr. Welles.

Astrid feathered her fingers against his chest, wondering at the warmth suffusing her . . . and waiting for it to wane, to depart as it must and make room for the cold.

He rolled his weight off her and tucked her close to his side. Long moments passed and she thought he slept until his rich voice murmured in her ear. "No more bad dreams now," he ordered, pausing to release a contented sigh.

The command made her smile. As if he could simply rid her of nightmares with his simple avowal. Strangely enough, she was beginning to suspect this man could do anything.

"No?" she breathed.

"No," he affirmed. "You have me."

The smile slipped from her face. She had him. But she could not keep him.

Astrid swung her cloak about her shoulders and inhaled biting cold air. A soft smile curved her lips as she gathered their bedding from the ground.

The irony was not lost on her. Lady Astrid, Duchess of Derring, daughter of the late Marquess of Fremont, preferred the hard earth over a down-filled mattress and sheets of Giza cotton. And even more shocking, she preferred sleeping on the hard earth with an unrefined brute of a man. Her lips twisted with wicked pleasure. Not that they slept a great deal.

Her gaze moved along the tall ash trees surrounding their camp. A slate blue sky peeked though the treetops, making it difficult to determine the time of day. She could only guess it to be midmorning.

"Ready?" he asked, coming up beside her.

She nodded, suddenly shy. Heat burned her cheeks. Illogical, she knew.

Accepting his hand, she allowed him to lead her to her mount, the feel of his hand warm and strong.

"We should reach Edinburgh tonight, maybe tomorrow."

She nodded, his words cooling some of the heat in her cheeks. Reaching Edinburgh meant an end to this. To them. He would deposit her and continue on to Balfurin.

He helped her mount before moving away. Her eyes followed him as he strode off, devouring the movements of his strong body as he swung himself atop his stallion. He nudged his horse with his boot heels. She followed suit, falling in beside him.

They moved only a few paces before Griffin pulled on his reins, halting their progress. A sound like distant thunder filled the air. The earth began to shake beneath them.

Griffin circled his stallion, scanning the surrounding woods.

"What is it?" Astrid asked, glanced wildly around them, dread forming a knot in the pit of her belly. Alarm hammered in her chest.

"Riders," he answered a moment before dozens of Highlanders broke from the trees, raining upon them like an invading army.

Griffin positioned himself before her, but she had no difficulty assessing the assemblage of men, instantly recognizing that they were not Gallagher's men.

An older man rode to the front, eyeing Griffin up and down with an oddly intent stare. He was a handsome man, still well formed, his exact age indeterminate. The frigid wind lifted the hair off his shoulders, the long dark locks streaked liberally with gray. "Who are you?"

"Griffin Shaw. We're on our way to Edinburgh."

The old man didn't blink. His blue gaze glittered across the distance, fixing on Griffin in a way that made Astrid's hands flex over her reins uneasily. "And what would your business in Scotland be, lad?"

"That's of no concern to you."

A heavy pause fell.

The older man growled, "My name is Hugh MacFadden, and I'll be knowing your name and business."

"MacFadden," Griffin murmured. "Of Balfurin."

Astrid's gaze flew to Griffin. Anticipation coursed through her. Here he was, then—the clan's laird himself, the very man Griffin sought.

"Perhaps we might speak alone," Griffin suggested, revealing none of the excitement she felt.

Something dark and desperate glittered in the older man's eyes as he stared at Griffin, an urgency that seemed unwarranted in the situation. "I'll have your purpose here. Now."

Astrid nudged her horse forward, and glanced at Griffin's profile, starting in surprise to find the same look there. The same intense blue eyes rife with questions—a hungry need for answers. She looked back and forth between the two men, acknowledging that words were being spoken, passing between them without a sound.

"Who are your people?" the laird demanded.

"My father is dead. Died of a fever crossing the Atlantic. I was told his surname. MacFadden."

MacFadden flinched as if dealt a physical blow.

A subdued hush fell over his men and Astrid suddenly knew that everyone else in the shaded glen knew more than she did about what was transpiring.

"Your father. What was his Christian name?"

Silence fell again. Griffin's gaze skittered over the dozen men flanking Hugh MacFadden. That telltale muscle in his jaw knotted, the only outward sign of the tension swimming through him . . . swirling around all of them like an invisible mist.

"Conall MacFadden," he answered at last.

MacFadden's chest lifted on a deep breath, color bleeding from his face. He looked to his left and right with a slow turn of his head, his pent-up breath releasing in a wintry puff of air. Without a word, he lifted his hand and motioned toward Griffin.

With that single gesture, his men dismounted and mobbed Griffin, hauling him off his horse with quick hands and grim, resolute faces.

Griffin struggled against the horde of men.

"What are you doing?" Astrid shouted.

No one paid her heed as Griffin was flung to the ground and stripped of his jacket, vest, and shirt.

Astrid lurched forward with a strangled cry, hand outstretched as if she could reach him.

Griffin struggled, snarling like a beast, dark hair tossing fiercely about his head as he knocked several Highlanders to the ground with his fists.

Even in her horror, awe filled her as he fought off his attackers, the thick cords of muscles and sinews rippling beneath bronzed skin.

She winced as they overpowered him, forcing him down, his bare chest slamming flat with the icy earth.

One of the clansmen shoved Griffin's face into coarse soil. Another placed his boot to his neck, pinning him still while others held down his arms.

Astrid slid down from her mount and charged forward, only to be yanked back by a burly Scot. An arm locked around her shoulders, and she watched, helpless, as Hugh MacFadden nudged his horse forward to peer down at Griffin's broad back on display before him.

"There." One of the Highlanders pointed to the small crescent-shaped birthmark high on his muscled shoulder. "Just as Molly said it would be."

"Molly," Astrid snapped, her brow knitting. "The woman from the inn?"

A few of the men glanced at her before returning their attention to their leader, anticipation writ upon their faces.

MacFadden's gleaming gaze fixed on Griffin's back, his eyes strangely moist as his breath fell harshly, fracturing the air with harsh wintry gusts.

"Let him up!" Astrid cried, jerking against the unrelenting grip on her arms. "It's freezing!

MacFadden lifted his gaze and gave a hard nod to his men.

Griffin was released. He vaulted to his feet, arm lashing out in a blur. His fist cracked the jaw of the man whose boot had pinned him by the neck. The fellow fell to the ground with a thud, hand cupping his injured jaw.

Several clansmen lunged forward, no doubt ready to retaliate for the attack, however earned, but the laird's voice froze them all.

"Leave him."

With his bare chest heaving as if he had run a great distance, Griffin eyed the older man, venom a cold, dull luster in his blue eyes. Grunting, Griffin pointed an unyielding finger at the man with his arm locked around Astrid. "Unhand her."

The man complied. Freed, she lifted her skirts and stumbled to Griffin's side, pausing to snatch his clothes off the ground and hand them to him.

He took them and redressed, a dozen Highlanders watching his every move as if he were some oddity at carnival. "You're my grandson," the laird announced.

"I know," Griffin returned, his tone matter-of-fact as he pulled his jacket over his unbuttoned vest.

"You know?" Wild bewilderment rushed through Astrid as she looked back and forth between the two men.

"Your mother. What was her name?" MacFadden pressed.

"Iona."

The laird nodded, a dour set to his mouth. "I

thought as much. You've my mark. All the Mac-Fadden men bear it." He motioned to Griffin's person. "But you've her eyes. They bewitched your father." His lip curled in a sneer. "And every other man in these parts."

"Fascinating." Griffin shrugged back into his jacket, his tone droll. Taking Astrid's arm, he guided her back to her mount and lifted her into her saddle.

"It proves you're my—"

"I don't give a damn what it *proves*." Swinging up onto his mount, Griffin glowered across the distance at his grandfather, their resemblance unmistakable. She could see it now.

Staring at MacFadden, she could well imagine how Griffin would look in forty years. Still handsome. Still imposing. Virile enough to twist her heart or any other woman's. Only in forty years he would have a wife. Of course, Astrid wouldn't be with him then. Some other woman would have that privilege. She would be long gone. A memory at best.

"Had you asked," Griffin ground out, "I would have shown you the damn birthmark. At any rate, thank you. Your methods confirmed that I made a long journey for nothing. I have no family here. None I wish to claim."

I made a long journey for nothing. His words resounded in her ears. In her heart. Wrongly. His feelings right now had nothing to do with her and everything to do with his grandfather. So he regretted coming to Scotland. She should not make it about her. About them.

"Where do you think you're going?" his grandfather blustered.

"Home. Texas. Where I should have stayed."

More words to gouge her soul. To swipe a bloody trail through a heart that she had permitted to feel. For the first time in her life.

Absurd, she knew. She had known they would part ways. In Edinburgh, he would be free to go wherever he wished. Be it America or Balfurin.

Griffin nudged his mount around. Astrid followed. They took only a few paces before a wall of Scotsmen gathered before them, blocking their path.

Laird MacFadden's voice carried across the glen. "I waited years for my son to return home."

"Your son is dead," Griffin called over his shoulder.

"Aye, but you're not. You're here. A part of *him*. A part of me. You're not walking away. At least not until I give you leave to do so."

Griffin swung his mount around, angry eyes clashing with his grandfather's.

Astrid blew out a heavy breath. At this rate, she might never make it home . . . but the thought did not alarm her. Not as it should have. *Blast.*

She bit her bottom lip. While the prospect of more time with Griffin tantalized her, common sense bade she put an end to it—to them—now. As she had tried to do at Cragmuir.

She snuck another look at Griffin.

Jaw knotting with tension, he stared straight ahead, eyes drilling into his grandfather. His blue eyes glinted with grim intensity—a determination to go his own way, to leave Scotland. To leave *her.*

A deep ache beneath her breastbone left her strangely breathless. She needed to free herself from him as quickly as he sought to be free of his grandfather.

Before he came to mean too much to her. Before. . .

Dismay filled her in that moment. Because she knew the truth then. It was too late. Her stomach heaved.

It didn't matter how soon she freed herself from him, it was too late.

She had fallen in love with Griffin Shaw.

Chapter 19

Fury radiated through Griffin as he stared at the man he had crossed an ocean to find. His grandfather rode ahead of him, his back broad and straight in his saddle. Disheartening as far as reunions went. Not that he had expected a warm homecoming full of happy tears and embraces. He had just not expected to be thrown to the ground with all the courtesy given an enemy captive.

He glanced at Astrid. She rode beside him, her face paler than usual as they were led through dense foliage. Her liquid dark eyes stared straight ahead.

If anything good could be said of the situation, it was that he did not have to give her up just yet. He grimaced, knowing she would not share the sentiment. No doubt she bemoaned yet another delay. More time with him. A rough frontiersman without connections. Without grace or social standing.

Still, he owed it to Astrid to get her out of this mess. From the stiffness in which she sat her mount and the way she carefully steered her gaze clear of him, she likely agreed.

As promised, he would see her to Edinburgh. He had promised her that much. Even if it meant saying good-bye.

He had a life waiting for him. A life that didn't include her. He could not imagine her in Texas. The heat alone would likely give her a seizure . . .

No, she was destined for elegant drawing rooms, for taking tea from delicate bone china.

As a widow she was free to remarry. To find some lord that would keep her outfitted as a lady of her station ought to be. A man that would see she never suffered from neglect or hunger. A man that would take his pleasure of her, ease himself into her snug heat as Griffin had. . .

Sucking in a breath, he veered his thoughts sharply away from that prospect, fists clenching around his reins. Suddenly this entire journey seemed a colossal mistake. Even more than when, moments ago, he first stared into his grandfather's eyes.

If he had simply forgotten his mother's words and stayed home, none of this would be happening.

What had he wanted? A fresh start? A reunion with family members that did not look at him as his father had, through a tainted veil of war, disappointment rife in their expressions.

He would never have met Astrid. And while an uncomfortable tightness seized his heart at that thought, he knew he wouldn't have missed what he never knew. He could have lived his life blithely unaware of a woman who existed a continent away, a woman who was a captivating mixture of ice and fire.

Gradually, his attention was pulled away from thoughts of Astrid. To the slow, steady pounding swelling on the air, shaking the earth. Wondering what calamity was about to befall them now, he brought his horse closer to Astrid, meeting her wide-eyed gaze.

He tensed, one hand diving for her reins as more riders burst through the trees.

His grandfather's men met the onslaught of riders with warrior cries, drawing pistols and swords.

He caught a glimpse of Lachlan's face, bruised and battered in the melee, as well as the Laird

Gallagher himself, large and daunting atop his horse.

"MacFadden," Gallagher shouted. His gaze halted on Griffin and Astrid, face reddening at the sight of them. "Thieving bastard!" He pointed a gnarled finger in their direction. "They're mine."

"Like hell," MacFadden thundered. "You've stolen all you're going to steal from me. You'll not take the last of my blood now."

"*I've* stolen?" Gallagher jerked his monstrous mount closer to the other laird, his bushy brows pulling together like furry caterpillars. "That's the pot calling the kettle black!"

"Your precious Iona deprived me of my son with her witch's spell. I'll not be having you steal Conall's child from me, too." MacFadden's eyes bulged at this declaration, his knuckles whitening about the dagger he clutched in his wiry fist.

Griffin suppressed a groan and closed his eyes in a pained blink, understanding at once. These two braying mules were *both* his grandfathers. He dragged a hand over his face, suddenly weary. Now he knew what his parents had been fleeing—two crotchety old men that bickered worse than women.

"Conall's child?" Gallagher whispered, looking around as if he expected to see a toddler tumble from the trees. "You mean my Iona and Conall . . ."

"Aye! They had a child." MacFadden waved in Griffin's direction, swinging down from his mount. "And I'll not have you making off with him like you do with my sheep."

For once Gallagher ignored MacFadden, staring only at Griffin. "Iona?" he choked.

"She died," Griffin answered, understanding what was being asked, "long ago. On a ship to America."

The burly Scot's skin turned ghostly white around his beard. He dragged a massive hand over his face, clearly overcome.

Despite himself, Griffin felt the stirrings of sympathy. At least one of his grandfathers took a moment to grieve the death of his child.

"What happened to her?"

"A fever took the ship. Many died. My parents included. Another couple took me in and raised me."

"My son gave you to strangers rather than send you back to me?" MacFadden demanded. "I don't believe—"

"Aye, I believe it. You made life so impossible for them, they had to run away together. They're dead because of you." Gallagher swung down to stand nose to nose with his foe.

Griffin winced at that stinging accusation, sharp as an arrow hitting its mark.

MacFadden's face reddened, a vein throbbing dangerously in the center of his forehead. "Likely he and Iona didn't want to risk you getting your hands on their child."

"Stop it," Griffin ground out, wanting nothing more than to knock the two old fools' heads together. "The Shaws took me because my parents asked them. They claimed you would rip me in half with your squabbling." At the time, he had not understood what his mother meant when she relayed that particular bit of information, but now he did.

His grandfathers looked very old in that moment. Old and tired. A quiet fell over the gathering of men, the occasional horse's snort or jangle of harness the only sound.

"I won't stay here to be fought over," he continued. "My parents ran away for a reason, I see that now. If you have any desire to know me, to have a place in my life, you'll end this thing between you two. Now."

His grandfathers looked from him to each other, their expressions tight and pinched, as if they tasted something sour. They assessed one another for several moments, clearly attempting to gauge the other's willingness. God forbid one of them bend before the other.

At last, they nodded, mumbled something incoherent beneath their breath, and moved back to their mounts. Heads bowed, shoulders hunkered, they resembled whipped dogs as they remounted their horses.

"Good," Griffin declared. "If we're in accord, then we shall *all* go to Balfurin."

"Balfurin! I can't go there," Gallagher growled.

"If you truly mean to bury the ax, then you should have no issue." Griffin angled his head, feeling like a mother mediating between two bickering children.

Gallagher's lips clamped shut.

Griffin arched a brow at MacFadden. "And I expect you to be obliging."

"Aye," he grunted, giving a single, quick nod. As if everyone understood they had reached some level of harmony, they began to move out, Gallagher and MacFadden's men riding side by side. Griffin wondered the last time such an event had taken place. If ever.

"And who is this skinny lass with you?" MacFadden asked after several minutes had passed.

He looked around Griffin to Astrid. "Someone I should know? A daughter-in-law?"

"No," Astrid quickly supplied.

"You're not married, then?" Gallagher asked with a shake of his head. "But you said—"

"No, we're not." She held Griffin's gaze, clearly daring him to object.

Deciding her virtue faced no threat from either one of his grandfathers, he agreed, "No, we are not."

"I see," MacFadden murmured, his gaze turning decidedly lascivious as it roamed over Astrid. And Griffin could imagine what it was he saw. Too late, he realized that by telling the truth he had permitted his grandfather to form a decidedly vulgar opinion of her.

Color swept over Astrid's cheeks, anger lighting the centers of her dark eyes. He suppressed a wave of protectiveness, reminding himself that she had opted for the truth and brought this on herself. Yet again.

"We've plenty of hardy lasses you can wed at Balfurin."

"And Cragmuir," Gallagher quickly chimed.

"Perhaps a young widow," MacFadden suggested with a withering look for the other laird, indicating what he thought of Griffin wedding a girl from Cragmuir. "One that has proven herself a good breeder."

Gallagher nodded. "Aye, we'll be needing sons from you."

Astrid made a disgusted sound between her teeth. "Yes," she mocked, "best find a *proven* breeder."

Griffin shot her a warning look. "Don't encourage them."

Mumbling under her breath, her gaze dropped, appearing to find the earth below of vast interest.

"Aye." MacFadden tossed her an approving look. "Listen to the wench. She has the right of it. Face it. There are women you wed, and women you bed." He chuckled at his quip, his look turning faintly leering. It was clear into which category he thought Astrid fell.

Griffin slid her a dark glare. They should have continued their pretense. Instead his little duchess would have to bide her time at Balfurin with everyone thinking her little better than a whore.

"Griffin." His name fell from her lips in a harsh plea. Those dark eyes pulled him in, compelling as ever.

"Perhaps you could impose on"—her gaze darted to his grandfathers—"one of these gentlemen to see me escorted to Edinburgh?"

Anger sizzled through him. She would ask him to let her go now? To release her? As simple as that?

"No." His answer fell heavily between them.

She pulled back slightly in her saddle. "No?" she echoed, her voice as tremulous as a feather on the wind.

"No," he repeated, shooting a hard glance to the openly curious men riding alongside them, disliking that they should witness the exchange. He lowered his voice. "I made a promise I intend to keep."

She held his gaze, her dark brows drawn tightly over her dark eyes in a puzzled expression.

He looked away, training his gaze ahead of them. "Do not ask me again." He nudged his heels and sent Waya ahead, wondering at the real reason he would not release her, for he had no reason to keep her with him anymore.

Chapter 20

Balfurin sat in the midst of a great lake, a single narrow stretch of road extending from the mainland to its front gates. The water surrounding the stronghold gleamed like glass. Craggy mountains stood sentinel around the lake. Sunlight fought to free itself from a sky of swollen gray clouds, almost the same shade as the castle's gray stone. It was an awesome sight, and one he might have enjoyed if his thoughts were not so tangled up in the woman beside him.

Arriving in the yard, he lifted Astrid off her horse, none too pleased at the bold glances Mac-Fadden's men sent her way. He closed a hand around her arm possessively and shot the men dark looks as he followed his grandfathers inside the castle.

They passed through a great hall until they entered a drawing room of well-polished wood.

Thankfully, the men and their insolent stares were left behind.

His grandfathers made themselves comfortable, one on a sofa, the other in a wing-backed chair.

"Becky, drinks," MacFadden commanded, sending a young, eager-faced maid flurrying into motion. Glass clinked as she poured drinks from a sideboard and arranged them on a tray.

Griffin sank down onto a settee, pulling the silent Astrid down beside him, her body radiating tension next to him.

The maid carried the tray around the room, offering each of them a glass of what appeared to be whiskey. When she reached Astrid, she asked politely, "Can I fetch you some tea, ma'am?"

"Yes, thank—"

"Becky, do something with the lass, would you?" MacFadden interrupted, looking at Astrid with something akin to annoyance, almost as though she had *snuck* into the room with them uninvited.

Color spotted Astrid's cheeks.

Becky looked from Astrid to MacFadden, clearly confused. "*Do* something?" she asked faintly.

MacFadden flicked a hand in Astrid's direction, shrugging his broad shoulders. "Aye. *Put* her some place. Anywhere. I wish to speak with my grandson."

"That's enough," Griffin snapped, rising in one quick motion, pulling Astrid up with him.

"Griffin," Astrid broke in, "don't—"

He cut her off, addressing the maid, "Would you show me to my room, please?"

"Griffin," MacFadden's voice rumbled out, brusque with disapproval, "we have much to discuss—"

"We can talk later," he bit out, knowing he was close to losing control entirely. "Right now I'll be shown to my room."

Tossing an uncertain look at the laird, Becky began to lead them from the drawing room.

Griffin stopped abruptly and turned, the anger in him bubbling up from the surface. "Just a word of advice. You and I will get on much better if you take care in addressing my . . . companion with respect."

MacFadden blinked, looking from him to Astrid and back to him again. "I see," he murmured, nodding.

With a curt nod, Griffin turned and followed the maid out of the room, one hand still closed firmly around Astrid's arm. Only with each step, his anger grew. And it was not solely directed at Hugh MacFadden.

Once again, she had put herself out there, exposed herself. Perhaps not to danger this time, but to scorn and derision.

Becky opened the door to a well-appointed bedchamber. "Your room," she murmured, looking uncertainly between them. "I'm sorry the fire has not yet been lit." She moved in the direction of the hearth, but Griffin's voice halted her.

"Thank you, Becky, but I can see to it."

"Very well." She nodded and exited the room.

He thrust Astrid into the chamber before him and closed the door firmly after the maid.

She rubbed her arm where he had gripped her and moved to the center of the large chamber, watching him like an animal cornered, wary and ready to flee.

His temper burned even brighter at the sight. He dragged a hand through his hair, cursing himself for handling her so roughly, for making her look at him with such trepidation, even if she did manage to infuriate him beyond reason.

But now he only saw red as he stared at her. She cocked her chin in that gratingly familiar angle. The defiant action galled him.

"Have you learned nothing?" he demanded. "Could you not have simply bit your tongue and continued to pretend that we're married?"

273

Her eyes flared, then narrowed to slits. "Don't treat me like a dim child. My honor is not at risk here, among your family. I see no reason to carry on the pretense of being married now."

"No?" he growled. "I do," he replied, uncaring that his reply sounded more like a petulant boy denied a toy than a man in full control of himself and his emotions.

"I would think you would want no lies between you and your family. You've only just met. Your relationship with them shall grow stronger whereas our association shall end altogether in a short time. They should have complete honesty from you. Who cares how they treat me?"

"I care," he hissed, seizing her by the arms.

Her eyes grew wide, lips parting on a whimper. She stared at him a long moment, her lips trembling as if she wanted to say something. He waited, wondering what traipsed through that head of hers.

Her tongue darted out to moisten her lips and he had to force his thumb not to brush the tempting pink lip, to lean down and draw it into his mouth, to taste her.

"Are they so wrong? Have I not done with you precisely what they judge me to have done?"

He shook his head, refusing to accept her logic. "I'll not stand by while you're treated like a whore."

She flinched, but continued in a maddeningly even voice. "Then you should have provided me with that escort and sent me on my way."

"Not that again." He gave her a small shake. "I gave my word to see you safely to Edinburgh."

"When?"

"When I've concluded my business here."

"Rather vague," she muttered. "I'll not be held hostage to your whims."

"You'll be on your way soon," he heard himself promise, wondering if that was a vow he could keep. The feel of her in his hands even now fired his blood. He was not yet tired of her . . . and he somehow suspected he wouldn't tire of her anytime soon.

She stared at him a long moment, her dark eyes inscrutable. "Then you must see how your family's opinion fails to signify. A year from now we shall be but a dim memory to each other. What are we anyway save two people forced together by circumstance?" Each clipped word struck him like a jagged little stone. Her eyes gleamed like polished onyx, reflecting nothing—no light, no sentiment.

Galled at her words, at her emotionless stare, his hands fisted at his sides. *How could she be so cold, so without feeling?*

"*Circumstance*," he growled, the word rolling off his tongue like an epithet. "There is more than circumstance between us, Astrid."

Circumstance had little to do with the fact that they had become lovers. Or that the world faded, disappeared entirely, when he held her in his arms.

Dim memories? Did she honestly believe such nonsense?

He'd been with enough women to know that what was between them was real. *Rare.* He would never forget a moment of their time together. Startled and angered at thoughts that dangerously bordered on sentimentality, he cursed beneath his breath.

"Please, Griffin," she murmured, all coolness and ice. "Don't try to make this more than it can be." She motioned around them. "We've reached civilization now. We cannot continue as we were. You know that."

He glared at her, wanting to deny her words, to tell her he didn't know anything of the sort.

She continued. "I'm sure you intend to stay for a while and acquaint yourself with your family.

Can you arrange for an escort to take me as far as Edinburgh?"

He stared at her for an astonished moment, the dignified angle of her chin, the firm set of her lips, and knew she was serious. She meant to go, to leave him. *And why not? She spoke the truth.*

He could send her on her way under the care of escorts, confident in her safety. That had been his motive for helping her in the first place. Nothing demanded he keep her with him now. Still, his mind searched, seeking a reason. To *not* accept that the time had come for them to part ways. To let her burrow back into her privileged shell and return to her life among the echelons of High Society. No doubt she would remarry a proper aristocrat like herself who would bank the fires Griffin knew existed within her, hungry to be lit.

"No," he heard himself declaring in an intractable voice. "I would not entrust you to someone else's care. I said I would see you as far as Edinburgh and I will. I'm a man of my word. You were seen leaving Bertram's room. You're still a likely suspect in his death. For all we know, they're still scouring the countryside for you." A sound reason, completely justifiable, to keep her with him a bit longer.

277

Her smooth brow wrinkled. "A man of your word." Her lip curling back over her teeth. Angry splotches broke out over her smooth complexion. "How singular."

"I'm aware that such a man is unfamiliar to you," he shot back, calling himself a bastard when she recoiled.

And just like that, he knew.

As much as she drove him mad with her inconsistencies, fire in his arms one moment, the ice-cold duchess the next—he *wanted* her. More than he had wanted any other woman. Even if keeping her a while longer meant everyone at Balfurin would continue to see her as his mistress. He would challenge anyone, his newfound family included, who treated her shabbily again. Because he could not give her up. Not yet. *Perhaps never.*

"I'm certain you're being overzealous in your concern. I don't think it necessary—"

"Nonetheless, this is the way it shall be. You will depart when I do. I, and no other, will see you safely onto that train." He dropped onto the large tester bed, bouncing on it a bit as though pleased at its spring. "Until then you shall remain with me, under my protection."

And in my bed.

She watched him warily as he stripped off his jacket and vest. "And how long before you decide to depart? You've only just met your grandfathers."

"I don't know." He shrugged, removing his boots.

"Am I to be your prisoner, then?" Further color spotted her fair cheeks, breasts rising enticingly against her gown. "I have a life waiting in London."

"And it shall continue to wait." He leaned back on his elbows, eyeing the length of her, wondering when precisely he had come to find waifish blondes with demon dark eyes so appealing. He had never favored women of her coloring before. Hell, he had never favored women of her prickly temperament.

Her lips compressed into a hard line, those eyes sparkling like chips of coal. With a disgusted snort, she began to pace, her hands folded tightly before her as she moved. Stopping abruptly, she expelled a great breath and faced him again.

"I'll not remain here as a *toy* to *serve* your needs during your stay, if that's what you have in mind. No doubt there is some willing girl about for that. One with proven breeding potential." She added this last bit with a decidedly cruel twist to her lovely mouth.

He rose in one fluid motion, catching her around the waist and pulling her down to the bed with him, determined to thaw her, to recover the sweet, responsive creature he had enjoyed before his grandfathers discovered them and brought them to Balfurin.

"Don't behave as though you want nothing to do with me. We both know the truth."

She struggled in his arms. "The truth?" she sneered. "And what would that be?"

He coiled his arm tighter about her waist and brought his other hand down on her breast, cupping the firm mound. Her nipple sprang to attention against his palm, pebble-hard. The heat of her flesh burned through the fabric of her gown, singeing him, firing his blood, turning him rock hard in an instant.

She stilled, her breast rising and falling fast against his touch, her heartbeat a speeding drum alongside his palm.

"That you want me—this—every bit as much as I do." He rubbed his palm over her breast in a fierce motion, imagining the blushing crest of her nipple in his mind, pretty and velvety as rose petals.

"I know what you want," he growled, moving to knead the other breast. Small mewls of desire escaped her mouth, each tiny sound twisting him tight as a bow string ready to snap.

Her eyes gleamed darkly, lids falling low as she thrust herself up into his hand.

"I know," he repeated, his voice thick and unrecognizable to his ears as his thumb traced her nipple in feverish circles, drawing widely over the tip before closing in, squeezing and rolling the nub between two fingers, "what your body craves."

He forced his hand to fall away, pleased at the sound of her disappointed moan, evidence of the desire she would pretend not to feel for him.

Her head fell back on the bed, breasts rising on sharp breaths, lids still heavy over her eyes.

"I know *you*, Duchess." He grasped her hips and pulled her roughly against him, letting her feel the proof of his desire. "Don't hide from me anymore. Not after everything that's passed between us. You'll leave when I'm ready to let you go," he announced.

A thoughtless, absurd edict, he knew. And yet he was selfish enough not to care. Wanted her too much to care. Wanted her enough to damn both of them.

Defiance sparked in the dark depths of her eyes

and he knew he'd touched a nerve. She wedged a hand between them, trying to shove them apart. "Arrogant pig," she hissed.

He reached for the hem of her dress, determined to ease the straining ache against his trousers, to sink into her heat, to prove to her that they were far from finished, that they would share a bed. And their bodies. For however long they were together.

She was a fool to think otherwise, to think they could return to being polite strangers . . . that he would allow that to happen.

He had grown too accustomed to the warmth of her body.

A knock sounded at the door.

She ceased struggling.

Stifling a groan, he released her skirts and climbed down from the bed.

The maid that had shown them to their chamber stood in the doorway. "I've been sent to fetch you to dinner." Standing on her tiptoes, she tried to peer over his shoulder, no doubt hoping to catch a glimpse of Astrid in a state of dishabille, worn and sated from a thorough loving.

Exactly what he had hoped for as well.

Looking over his shoulder, he motioned out the corridor. "Dinner is served, Duchess."

Sliding down from the bed, she straightened her clothing.

Later, he vowed. Later he would prove to her that barriers did not exist between them. At least none that he couldn't tear down.

Chapter 21

D inner was a celebratory affair. Astrid, originally seated three down from Griffin, now sat to Griffin's immediate right. He had seen to the change of seating, despite the disapproving frowns of both his grandfathers.

Griffin kept her close to his side, talking over her when addressing MacFadden and Gallagher. Occasionally his hand would slide beneath the table to cover her thigh. In those moments, her breath would snag and she would strive for a neutral expression, praying he did not realize his effect on her.

"The loss of one crop should not devastate an entire population," Griffin volunteered when the conversation turned to the current famine. "A thriving economy needs variety in its crops . . . and at least one high-value commodity for exportation, especially in the event of bad harvests."

This spiraled them into a deeper conversation about crops and possible solutions to battle the famine. Astrid shifted uneasily in her seat, uncomfortable and feeling invisible throughout their conversation. An observer. An outsider.

At one point, Griffin drank from the mug in front of him and complimented Laird MacFadden, "Now, that's a fine whiskey."

"Distilled right here," MacFadden announced proudly.

"Aye," Gallagher grudgingly admitted, no doubt loathing to give a compliment of any kind to his old adversary. "MacFadden has the finest whiskey in these parts. Always counted myself lucky when a barrel or two fell into my lap."

"You mean when you *stole* a barrel."

"You produced this here?" Griffin asked, intercepting what appeared to be the start of an argument.

"Aye. MacFadden whiskey. We've made it since the fourteenth century."

"Fine Scotch whiskey is a commodity. You should market it," Griffin suggested.

His grandfather frowned. "Sell our whiskey?"

Griffin nodded. "This is what I was talking about. A product like this would meet high demand in English markets. Hell, worldwide."

"I don't know," he mused, delving through his long, gray-streaked hair to scratch his scalp. "Don't know if we have enough grain for such a large operation—"

"But combined we would," Gallagher announced.

The two old men eyed one another warily, clearly taken aback to see each other as something other than enemies. As potential partners.

Astrid glanced at Griffin, marveling that he had wrought such a change in these men. And in so short a time. She wondered if he realized that they had changed for him. All for the love of him. A sentiment she could too well imagine.

MacFadden turned to look at his grandson now. "Would you be interested in heading up such a venture? Take our two clans into the future? I could only stomach such a partnership if you were to lead the enterprise."

Gallagher leaned forward, earnestly nodding. "We need you. Your people need you."

Your people? Astrid could not suppress a small smile from curving her lips. They certainly knew how to heap on the guilt and obligation.

Griffin lifted his mug and savored another sip, contemplating, she guessed, a future in Scotland versus one in Texas.

He turned his head and his gaze caught and held hers. Something flickered in his blue eyes.

A long moment passed before he echoed her earlier words, saying, "I've a life waiting for me at home."

Her smile slipped and she looked down at her plate of half-eaten food.

Indeed. They both had lives waiting for them. She in England. He across the ocean.

"Think about it. You're needed here," MacFadden insisted, casting Astrid an accusatory glare, as if she had something to do with Griffin's refusal to stay.

She stared back, keeping her expression cool and unmoved.

A sudden disturbance drew their attention to the front of the dining hall. A tall middle-aged man in a swirling cloak entered, a thick scarf of MacFadden blue and green tartan wrapped around his neck and shoulders. A woman followed him, cloaked from head to toe in a rich dark blue cloak. She hung back several steps, her movements slow and hesitant.

"Cousin," the man called, striding forward, eyes widening as they shifted from MacFadden to Gallagher. "I had barely stepped from the carriage when I was beset with all manner of outlandish tales. Although none so astonishing as the sight of you breaking bread with this devil."

"Thomas," MacFadden rose in greeting, chuckling wryly as he came around to embrace the visitor, the older man's large frame swallowing that of his cousin. "It's not something I expected to happen in this lifetime, to be certain."

"Well, what brought about this miracle?" Thomas asked, slipping off gloves of fine kid leather and snapping his fingers for a servant to bring forth a chair. He untied his cloak and tossed it at a serving girl. Dropping into the chair, his gaze roved first over Griffin, then Astrid, his sharp eyes lingering on her face in a way that made her want to fidget in her chair. She clasped her hands tightly in her lap and forced her spine straight.

No one moved to fetch a seat for the young woman or offered to take her cloak. She remained standing, an unobtrusive shadow lurking beyond Thomas. Only Astrid seemed to notice her, and she decided that the girl likely made a habit of being invisible.

Indignation burned darkly through her as she strained for a glimpse of the face hidden within her cloak. Ink-dark tresses escaped the hood to coil over her breasts like the curl of a demon's fingers.

"Griffin, this is my cousin, Thomas Osborn."

Griffin nodded in greeting at the man sitting across the table from them. Osborn returned his nod with an uncertain one of his own.

"Wondrous news, cousin." MacFadden grinned and leaned forward, heedless of the fall of his hair in his stew. He clapped Griffin on the back heartily. "Conall's son has returned to us."

Osborn stared, speechless for several moments, looking back and forth between Griffin and his cousin. "H-how can that be? Conall did not have a son."

"Like I always suspected. Conall ran away with Iona Gallagher." His gaze flitted to Griffin. "They had a son together."

"I see," Osborn drawled slowly. "And how can we be sure this man is their son?" His eyes flickered over Griffin as if he were some mangy cur come to beg for scraps.

"Aside that he looks just like Conall?" An edge entered MacFadden's voice, defying his cousin—anyone—to challenge him on the matter of Griffin's paternity. "And that he bears the same birthmark on his shoulder that his father did? And me?"

"A coincidence, surely."

"And why," Griffin inserted, his voice dangerously smooth, "are you so certain that I cannot be Conall MacFadden's son? What is it you stand to lose?"

Color spotted Osborn's narrow cheeks. "I merely think someone should question the arrival of a stranger and examine his motives before accepting him so readily into the fold."

"I seek nothing here," Griffin stated with remarkable evenness. "I only came to learn a bit about the parents that died before I could know them."

"'Course, lad," Gallagher's voice boomed out as he glared at Osborn. "We only hope to convince you to stay and take your rightful place here. You're a part of us."

A part of us. Astrid wondered what that would be like. To be part of a family. To belong. To be wanted.

Osborn shoved to his feet, the chair clattering to the stone floor. "This is madness! Let me see this birthmark."

Griffin's eyes glittered in warning, no doubt recalling the indignity of being forced to the ground and stripped of his clothes against his will. "I will *not* remove one stitch of clothing."

"Thomas, calm yourself. You're acting the fool. I've already seen it."

Osborn turned beseeching eyes on MacFadden. "Cousin, you cannot mean to offer everything to this . . . stranger!" His face twisted with anger as the woman behind him quietly set his chair upright again.

"Calm yourself, Thomas," MacFadden advised. "As I have no intention of expiring soon, I don't see your lot having altered much. I'm only eight years your senior, after all. Now cease delving into my affairs. Tend to your own. Shouldn't you be preparing for the grand nuptials? What are you doing here anyway?"

"The wedding's off." Osborn's declaration sent goose bumps over Astrid's arms. "Which is why I've come. As head of the family, you need to be apprised of any matter that may bring shame on us."

MacFadden's eyebrows dipped together. "Speak plainly, man."

"It appears Petra's betrothed has been murdered."

Griffin tensed beside Astrid. She resisted the sudden urge to reach for his hand beneath the table.

Osborne dragged a hand sprinkled with dark hairs over his face and suddenly she knew. She remembered. The skin of her face suddenly felt tight and itchy. A knot of dread settled in her stomach, a heavy pull that made it difficult to draw air.

"You," she managed to get out. Her trembling hands fisted in her skirts. "It was you."

"Astrid," Griffin hissed in warning.

Shaking her head, she rose slowly to her feet, gaze fixed on the man before them, awareness sweeping through her in a flash of heat. The memory of Bertram's face as she had last seen him filled her mind.

Griffin seized her wrist and tried to pull her back down, but she twisted free.

Osborn stared at her as if she had sprouted a second head.

"You killed him," Astrid ground out. "You came to his room, argued with him and shoved him into the mantel."

"Is she mad? What's the lass talking about?" MacFadden looked at Griffin.

Osborn's eyes narrowed on her. "You were the woman seen fleeing Powell's room." A cruel smile curved his lips. "My, my. What a small world."

She nodded jerkily, not bothering to remind him that Bertram wasn't Powell.

"You're his wife," the cloaked woman spoke softly from behind Osborn, the first sound she had made since entering the hall. All eyes swung to her. She dropped her hood to reveal a moderately pretty face. At first, Astrid thought a shadow darkened the lower half of her cheek, extending along her jaw and trailing down her throat. And then she realized the shadow was reddish in color—not a shadow at all, but a birthmark.

Her eyes, a soft doe brown, settled on Astrid with surprising intensity.

"Yes," Astrid admitted. "I was his wife."

"What the hell is going on?" MacFadden exploded.

"Powell wasn't who he claimed to be," Osborn explained. "He was a married man. A fugitive, in fact."

MacFadden's eyes bulged and he motioned to the cloaked woman. "You would marry your daughter off to such a man?"

"I did not know he was married," Osborn gritted through clenched teeth. "Like everyone else, I simply thought it a blessing any man of quality wanted to marry Petra."

Astrid flinched, stung at his words even if they had not been directed at her.

A quick glance at Petra revealed nothing save her bowed head. If her father's callous words affected her, she gave no sign.

"He claimed to be a man of property. Vast coal mines in Cornwall. A knighted gentleman," Osborn defended hotly.

"And no one thought to verify this information before he married into the family?" Griffin questioned.

Osborn cut him a swift glare. "Not even here a day and you presume to stick your nose into our family affairs."

"He is one of us," MacFadden declared with a pound of his fist on the thick table, rattling the crockery.

Osborn shook his head in disgust.

"I think everyone is failing to miss the point here," Astrid inserted, waving in Thomas's direction. "He killed Bertram."

Everyone stared at her with dull, unmoved expressions, almost as if she had not uttered anything of significance.

"And," she added, "he let everyone think I did it."

Osborn shrugged. "I don't owe you anything. It was simply easier than explaining the situation. I did not mean to kill the wretch, after all. He fell and struck his head—"

"Because you were beating him," Astrid hotly reminded.

"Aye," he agreed, with no sign of remorse.

"You took his ring," she added, suddenly recalling the missing signet ring. "I'll thank you to return it to me."

"Fine."

Astrid watched as Bertram's murderer slid a ring from his finger and tossed it to her. She fumbled to catch it. Sucking in a deep breath, she looked to each of the men, waiting for their outrage, their sense of justice to surface. Whatever Bertram had done, he had not deserved to die. "Well?" she prodded.

"So the knave is dead, then." MacFadden shrugged. "Good riddance. A just end."

Gallagher nodded in agreement. "Highland justice. A man doesn't desecrate another man's daughter."

"He only attempted to," Astrid pointed out. "His perfidy was brought to light. Petra was spared."

At this, Osborn lurched from his chair to grab his daughter by the arm, yanking her forward. Petra stared at her with wide, soulful eyes. The eyes of a wounded animal. Astrid's stomach twisted, a deep sense of foreboding crawling through her with the insidiousness of creeping fog.

"Is that so?" Osborn growled.

As though Griffin sensed what was coming—or perhaps he simply sensed her apprehension—his hand closed over hers, strong fingers lacing with hers in a way that made her heart squeeze. It took everything in her to resist squeezing those fingers back, taking the comfort he lent.

Petra's cloak was yanked open to reveal the slight bulge of stomach.

"Considering your husband took his husbandly rights early and filled my daughter's womb with his bastard, I had every right to end his cursed life."

"No," Astrid croaked, a red haze tingeing her vision. Knees weak, she fell back into her chair, staring pityingly at the woman who had clearly fallen victim to Bertram's charm.

"Och," MacFadden grumbled with a shake of his head. "How could you permit such a thing, Thomas?"

"They were weeks from marriage," Osborn cried. "I did not think they required constant supervision." He released Petra as if her touch repulsed him. "Now what shall I do? I've a ruined daughter on my hands."

"Clearly she needs a husband," MacFadden stated.

"Who will have her? Stained with the devil's

mark"—Osborn motioned to Petra's face with his hand—"a bastard swelling in her belly."

"Stop!" Astrid cried, unable to hear another slur cast upon the poor girl. "Stop speaking of her in such a way!" She rose to her feet on trembling legs and rounded the table in a swish of skirts. "Come, Petra. Let's walk."

Seizing the young woman's arm, she led her quickly from the dining hall.

The men resumed talking, clearly unbothered by Astrid's outburst, their voices a deep rumble behind them. Indeed, their hasty departure went unnoted.

By all save one.

One pair of eyes followed her.

She felt his stare drilling into her back with familiar intensity—would recognize it anywhere. Unable to resist, she snuck a glance over her shoulder to find Griffin watching her, his gleaming eyes unreadable.

Her heart beat faster, wondering what he thought of her now—wife to the man that had ruined his kinswoman.

Another realization settled heavily in her chest.

Now free of any suspicion in Bertram's death, Griffin was released, free of his vow to protect her. He need no longer feel obligated to personally escort her to Edinburgh. He could not argue the need for her to remain even one day longer at Balfurin—with him.

Nothing barred her from leaving.

So why did her heart squeeze painfully in her chest at the thought?

Chapter 22

Arms looped together, the two women stepped outdoors into the thin wintry mist. Astrid shivered from the sudden blast of cold. Petra slowed beside her.

"Should we go back for your cloak?"

"No." Astrid shook her head, the notion of possibly facing any of the men again holding little appeal. "Let us walk. I'll warm quickly enough."

"The view is lovely from the ramparts," Petra offered, lowering her hood back over her head to ward off the cutting wind.

They took the slick stone steps leading to the high walkway carefully. At the top, Astrid stared out over the scene. The sun had dipped low between the mountains, streaking the dark waters of Balfurin's lake several shades of gold.

"It's beautiful," Astrid murmured, the wind biting her face.

"It is," Petra agreed. "I come here often when I visit. Always have."

Astrid glanced sideways at the cloaked figure beside her, imagining her as a young girl, escaping the family that treated her as though she were invisible. She could well identify. Conversations with her father had been few, and those mostly centered on her responsibilities to him as a daughter. She grimaced, supposing she should be glad the conversations numbered in the few.

The wind played with Petra's hood, and Astrid leaned forward for a glimpse of her face.

"The devil's mark." Petra's soft voice stroked the air.

"I beg your pardon?"

"The mark on my face?" Petra pushed back her hood and held her face high, revealing the port-stained birthmark. "It's always a point of interest."

"I wasn't staring at that," Astrid hastily assured. "I just could not see your face."

"I'm accustomed to people staring at me. At my mark."

Astrid nodded, after a moment murmuring, "I'm sorry."

"Don't be. It's not your fault. Contrary to what

everyone thinks, I'm not marked by Satan." A humorless smile hugged her lips. "Only now"—she held her arms wide, parting her cloak to reveal her swelling belly—"everyone will believe they were right."

Astrid sighed and rubbed the back of her neck, hating Bertram all over again. "I'm sorry this happened to you."

"Why are *you* sorry?" Petra asked with surprising evenness. "None of this is your fault."

Astrid winced, reluctantly reminding, "He was my husband and—"

"And what? If you had been a better wife he might not have done the things he did?" She shook her head ruefully. "I don't think so."

Astrid fell silent, mulling over her words, and after some moments deciding Petra was correct. For once, she did not need to blame herself. Her husband's actions had been beyond her control. Bertram was Bertram before she ever married him, entrenched in vice and corruption that went beyond the customary pursuits of gentlemen: conducting illicit relationships with the demimonde that he could ill afford, gaming away a fortune, forging banknotes. It was only a matter of time before he tangled himself in a peccadillo from which recovery was impossible. Evidently public trial and the threat of hanging had not been risk enough.

Shaking her head, her gaze slid back to Petra. "You mustn't blame yourself. Or feel ashamed. Bertram could be charming. Persuasive. It is what made him such a consummate swindler." A bitter smile curved her mouth. "I remember the first few times we met—"

"It wasn't like that," Petra cut in, her voice sharp as a whip, all her earlier softness gone.

Astrid frowned. "I don't understand."

"I never thought he was particularly charming. At least he never was to me. He focused most of his attentions on Father and the subject of my dowry. I never wanted to marry him and told my father as much."

She blinked and swiped a loose strand of hair back from her cheek. "You did?"

"We met Bertram while in Aberdeen." She heaved a sigh. "Soon, he became part of the furniture. Once, in the hotel lobby, Father and Bertram were talking to a group of gentlemen, ignoring me." Her lips twisted grimly at this comment. "A lady approached me and asked if your husband was the Duke of Derring. I said no, but she seemed so certain. I could not forget about the encounter, and I began to wonder what if she wasn't mistaken?

When Father invited him home with us, I decided to find out for myself if he was who he claimed to be. I made inquiries that led me to you."

"You wrote the letter!" Astrid exclaimed, her respect deepening for the young woman who had the courage and strength to protect herself when she questioned her father's judgment. Had Astrid done such a thing, had she not been trained so well in duty and stoicism, following her father's edicts without question, she may have avoided marriage to Bertram altogether.

"Aye." Petra nodded. "I feared you would not arrive in time." She exhaled, her warm breath puffing out in a frothy cloud on the cold air. "So I went ahead and told Bertram I did not want to marry him. That my father could not make me. That I loved someone else." She looked down at her hands suddenly, as if seeing something there beyond flesh and bones.

Shock rippled through Astrid. "You love someone else?" She shook her head and stammered, "Th-Then how could you allow Bertram to seduce . . ."

"He raped me." The words fell bluntly, sharp as broken glass scoring her heart.

"What?" The question slipped through numb lips.

Petra turned and resumed moving along the walkway, her steps quick, as if she wished to escape her words.

Astrid fell in step beside her, watching, waiting for her to elaborate, wishing she, too, could escape Petra's terrible words.

"One evening after dinner, my father retired early and left us alone. Bertram suggested we walk the gardens." Petra lifted one shoulder in a weak shrug. "There's a lovely pergola at the center of it where my mother used to read to me as a child. Sometimes we sketched together there. She was a very good artist, my mother."

Perplexed at the conversation's digression, Astrid gently prodded, "What are you saying? Bertram forced himself on you in your family's garden?"

A faraway look entered Petra's eyes, and Astrid knew she was there again, in that pergola. With Bertram. "I spent some of my happiest days there. Before Mama died and I was left alone with Father."

Staring into her pale face, Astrid suddenly felt sick. She pressed a hand to her stomach, attempting to curtail the nausea. Sucking in a deep drag of icy air, she watched Petra, praying that it was a mistake, that she had misunderstood, that Bertram had not done such a thing.

Petra blinked as if returning to herself. The

distant haze lifted from her eyes. "Afterward, Bertram said that should end any reservations I harbored on the matter of marrying him."

Astrid's thoughts reeled, her head spun, flooded with memories of Bertram entering her room in the still of night, his quick pants against her ear and quicker movements over her . . .

The indignity of those trysts paled beside what Petra must have endured.

"Your father knew that Bertram . . ." she paused, the words choking in her throat, mingling with the bile coating her tongue.

Petra nodded. "I told him. He only insisted we wed sooner."

Astrid stared hard at the shadowed face of the woman Bertram had abused. Her stomach churned, imagining what Petra must have felt . . . what she still felt.

"And this man. The one you love—"

"Andrew," she quickly supplied, her chin lifting and a lightness entering her voice. "He still wants to marry me." And then the lightness faded as she added, "He's our coachman. Father would never permit it, of course."

Astrid nodded in understanding. No, Thomas Osborn would never allow his daughter, ruined or not, to marry so beneath her.

Astrid shivered, rubbing her arms, knowing it would be a long time, if ever, before guilt did not run through her like a frozen wind. Bertram had been her husband, after all. That linked them whether she wished it or not.

"Shall we go back inside?" Petra asked.

Astrid sighed. "Must we?"

A faint smile curved Petra's lips. Taking Astrid's arm, she turned them around. "Since they're likely discussing my fate, I'm interested to hear their plans."

"Of course," Astrid murmured, smiling over Petra's droll tone.

When they returned to the hall, the men were still deep in discussion. Osborn now occupied Astrid's chair, a plate before him, utensils untouched as he used his fingers to pick at stringy meat swimming in thick gravy. Licking his fingers, he looked up as they entered the dining hall, his eyes skipping over Petra to crudely assess Astrid, his gaze crawling over her breasts and hips.

Griffin watched her intently, his pale blue eyes shrewd, leaving her little doubt that he could see the truth. Perhaps not *what* troubled her, but that she was troubled, greatly so.

He began to rise to his feet, but Astrid waved him back down. Turning, she opened her mouth to bid good evening to Petra when MacFadden's voice stopped her.

"Ah, there you are, Petra. Excellent timing. We've settled your future."

Both intrigued and alarmed at how they could have reached a decision in so short a time, Astrid closed her mouth and waited.

Osborn leveled hard eyes on his daughter, plucking a bread roll from the platter before him and waving it at her. "You will marry. With all haste."

"Aye," MacFadden exclaimed. "Can't have you shaming yourself or this family."

Astrid glanced at Petra, her nails digging into her palms as the young woman's lips thinned in martyr-like resolve. Unable to hold her tongue a moment longer, she announced, "I think something needs to be understood—"

Petra grasped her arm, her face pale. "Please, no—"

Astrid held up a hand, determined to say what Petra would not. "Petra did not willingly bring about her . . . condition."

"Condition?" Gallagher echoed.

"What do you mean?" Griffin asked, dark brows drawing together.

"Bertram raped her."

A momentary hush fell over the hall before Petra's father spoke. "A moot point. It does not alter the fact that a bastard grows in her belly. She *needs* a husband."

MacFadden shook his head gravely, sending an almost regretful look at Petra. "Aye. He's right."

"It should at least alter your perception enough to concede that Petra deserves some say in choosing a husband."

Osborn flung a hunk of bread into his bowl, producing a splatter of gravy on the table. "Who is this female to give her opinions as if they are welcome?"

"Someone with more scruples than you, a man that would do nothing over his daughter's rape save demand she marry her violator," Astrid cried.

Ugly red mottled Osborn's face. "Hold your tongue, wench, lest I remove it from behind your teeth."

Griffin surged to his feet and settled one hand on the back of Osborn's chair. "Have a care," he warned, leaning over him.

Osborn glared up at him, taking a long moment to reply. "Is that the way of it then? You've appointed yourself her champion?"

Griffin did not respond, merely moved around

the table to stand beside Astrid, crossing his arms over his broad chest, letting that serve as answer.

Astrid suppressed a small thrill at his display of protectiveness.

With a grunt, Osborn returned his attention to MacFadden, ignoring both Astrid and Griffin, doing his best to behave as though he had not been cowed. "The crux of the matter is that no man in his rightful mind will have Petra if he has to stomach raising another man's whelp."

MacFadden sighed and nodded in agreement. "Aye, we will have to look to our own, then. A loyal kinsman . . ." The old man's eyes swung to Griffin, narrowing.

Astrid's stomach clenched, suspicion slipping into a heart grown suddenly cold.

Osborn followed his cousin's gaze. "What? Him?"

"Aye," MacFadden drawled, a slow smile spreading across handsome, craggy features. "Him."

Him, indeed. Who better than the long-lost son and heir to marry Petra? What better way for Griffin to claim his position, to prove his loyalty?

A sound solution all around. For Petra. For Griffin. Both would have what they lacked, what they needed, wanted even—though perhaps they did not know it.

Petra would marry a good, decent man, even if not of her own choosing, even if not the love of her heart.

And Griffin would marry a good, decent woman, and have gained his family's acceptance and esteem in the process. The very thing he craved, whether he admitted it or not. The very thing lost to him in Texas.

Astrid swallowed and blinked against the unwelcome burn at the backs of her eyes. Cursing her sudden urge to weep, she reminded herself that her preferences bore no significance. Griffin was not hers. No matter how her heart may have pretended otherwise.

It was time to let go. To move on.

She did not deserve Griffin. Not as Petra did. The most decent thing she could ever do would be to encourage a union between Griffin and Petra. Perhaps this was it. Her chance to redeem herself.

Why should such a gesture hurt so much, then?

Chapter 23

Griffin stared in amazement as spirited conversation erupted around him—conversation concerning him, his life, and most astounding, with whom he would live it.

Were they serious? Did they think he would permit others to decide his fate? That he ascribed to some medieval notion of arranged marriages? A man forged his own path in life. A man chose the woman with whom he wanted to share that life.

His grandfathers and cousin talked, droning on without pause, without consideration that he—or Petra, for that matter—might wish to choose their own fates. Both his grandfathers, bitter rivals only earlier, now nodded in perfect accord.

"'Tis right," MacFadden announced.

"Aye, and she is a proven breeder," Gallagher reminded.

"My Petra has the hips of a breeder," Osborn quickly agreed, nodding eagerly.

Griffin shot a quick glance to Petra. Her head was lowered, eyes downcast, making it impossible to read her thoughts, to see if she felt as outraged as he over the discussion. He attempted to speak over the voices. "I'd like to say something—"

Osborn spread his hands wide in front of him in a generous gesture. "I must admit that I can now see the family resemblance to Conall."

Griffin snorted, crossing his arms.

Osborn continued, "It relieves me greatly to know that my only child will marry the future Laird MacFadden."

Griffin felt his lip curl with disgust. "Convenient," he muttered beneath his breath. *Now* Osborn solidly believed in his paternity.

Astrid cleared her throat portentously. "It makes a good deal of sense," she announced in that clipped way of hers.

Something dark and dangerous brewed deep in his chest.

Sense?

"A most practical solution," she went on.

Practical solution? This was his life. And Petra's. Not some damned equation. And yet even Astrid discussed him marrying Petra as if it were a business merger to be negotiated with cool calculation. *Damned English. And Scots, for that matter.*

Anger seethed through him like a prowling beast. He raked his gaze over the woman who had occupied far too much of his thoughts lately. So much so that he had begun to harbor doubts over returning home. That the woman to inspire such feelings should now inform him so matter-of-factly that he should marry another—that doing so was a most practical solution—went down in a bitter wash of betrayal.

Apparently his fascination for her was one-sided.

Apparently Astrid suffered no softer sentiments for him.

Not if she failed to blink at the prospect of him marrying another, but in fact encouraged it.

MacFadden's voice penetrated slowly, worming its way through the anger clouding his head.

" . . . we'll need the reverend."

They had begun making arrangements, and all without a word from him. Or Petra. And they thought he would go along? He could have laughed at the absurdity of it all—if the maddening female beside him did not choose that moment to say, "It seems most sensible if the reverend were brought here. In her condition, Petra should not travel. Nor in such weather."

The men nodded, murmuring their assent. Astrid, though unusually pale, nodded, too.

Their words vanished in a searing flash of rage. He'd had enough. With a curse, he snatched hold of Astrid's wrist. Indifferent to the shocked stares, he dragged her from the hall.

"Griffin," she hissed as she hurried to keep up. "What's wrong with you?"

What's wrong with him? *What's wrong with* her? *With all of them?*

He ground his teeth, saying nothing until he reached the privacy of their room. Spinning her before him, he uncoiled his fingers from her wrist and slammed the door shut, the thick wood reverberating loudly, echoing in the stone-walled chamber, sealing them in, prisoners in a tomb.

She hurried to the center of the room, watching him with wide, wary eyes. Her fingers curled around one of the thick bedposts. Her chin went up in that infuriatingly indignant lift he knew so well.

"Why did you drag me out of there? What must Petra think?" she demanded, her fingertips turning white and bloodless where they dug into the wood.

He advanced on her, stalking her as a predator would. "I don't give a damn what anyone thinks. Never have. Where I come from men live their lives according to their own rules. They certainly don't allow someone else to pick their spouse."

"How terribly convenient," she spat, her thin nostrils quivering, "to live your life so recklessly, free of responsibility."

"I didn't say that." He took a steadying breath, fighting for calm, and the overwhelming urge to shake her until her teeth rattled. "Look, I realize you're a product of an archaic society—"

"Archaic?" Her entire body quivered with indignation. She pressed a palm to her chest. "*I* belong to an *archaic* society?"

Unable to stop himself, his gaze dropped to the curve of her breasts trembling beneath her hand. His palms prickled, remembering the shape and feel of those breasts, the soft undersides so sensitive to his touch. His mouth dried as hunger swept over him.

Shoving the distracting thoughts from his head, he smiled grimly. "If you would pull your head from the sand, you would see that the world's changing."

"Indeed?" she sneered. "Is it changing here, then?" She waved a hand wildly behind her to the thick oak door. "Your own cousin sits below with another man's blood on his hands. But all is forgiven based on an *archaic* system of beliefs."

"That aside, the world *is* changing, Astrid," he maintained, refusing to let her distract him from what he wanted to say, what *needed* to be said. "It's actually a place where you might find happiness, freedom . . . if you would only take it." His eyes drilled into her, and suddenly he knew he was talking about more than her arrogant presumptions regarding whom he should wed. He was talking about *them*. About what might happen between them if they would only let it. If *she* would let it. . .

"No," she muttered, shaking her head and averting her gaze.

He made a sound of disgust. "Very well. Be stubborn. Only know that I'm in Scotland because *I* want to be, and I'll leave when *I* want to." He pointed to the door. "They don't decide my fate. Nor do you."

He inhaled, ignoring the odd tightness in his chest at the prospect of leaving and returning to Texas. He felt a connection, an attachment to this land and people. It felt like *home*. Even more, there was Astrid now.

Ever since the first moment he had seen her, an angel on a muddy roadside, he felt bound to her. His father's disappointed gaze was fading, becoming a dim memory, paling altogether when he stared into her face.

"When I do marry," he continued, "it will be because I decide to, because I can't imagine living my life without a particular woman . . ." He angled his head, studying her. "You're a fool if you don't already know that much about me. And you're an even greater fool if you don't want the same thing for yourself."

"I'll never marry again," she quickly retorted, her nostrils quivering. "Once was misery enough. I'll not give away my freedom again."

"But you'll readily give mine away."

Color spotted her cheeks and her dark lashes fluttered over her eyes. She gave a tight nod, an almost imperceptible movement of acknowledgment. "I've never been able to dismiss duty so lightly. It mystifies me that you can. This is your family, Griffin. Your home. Petra—" She squeezed her eyes in a severe blink, as if the mere mention of the girl's name pained her. Opening her eyes, she stared at him intently, dark eyes glowing like

317

polished onyx. "How can you not offer her the protection of your name?"

"The pity I feel for her does not mean that I should sacrifice my future—and hers. We deserve our own choices."

She looked at him bleakly. "You think her father will give her a choice? I've known men like him all my life. If not you, he will choose someone else."

"So it might as well be me?" he snapped, his anger bubbling to the surface at her determination that he should wed Petra. "You're doing it again."

"What?"

"Deciding someone else's fate based on your own sense of right and wrong. Isn't that your great sin? The very thing you did to your sister-in-law?"

She pulled back, the color draining from her face. Clearly his words struck a nerve. "I am not—"

"Yes," he affirmed, taking a step closer. "You are."

Reproach flashed in the dark depths of her eyes before the cold, familiar mask fell into place, blotting out all emotion.

A tightness pervaded her chest, prickly and hot. Itchy. She lifted a hand to her throat, rubbing the skin there, as if she could rub out the awful truth of his words. *She was doing it again.*

Griffin's hot gaze pinned her, probing, stripping away flesh and bone to all she hid, all she was. She swallowed, fighting the terrible thickness rising in her throat. A thickness that threatened to choke her as he stepped closer.

She shook her head as if she could shake off his words, his relentless stare. And yet she could not escape that gaze, those eyes that *knew*, the words that could not be refuted. Denial burned on her tongue. *You're wrong. You don't know me.* But the words would not come.

Somehow, in a short time, he was able to see to the core of her, to expose all her frailties, to take her past and fling it in her face with the accuracy of an arrow finding its target. But then that should not surprise her. They were the same, after all. Two souls punishing themselves for the sins of their past.

"Always dutiful," he accused. "Always so damned proper. Do you never just surrender to your desires? Do what you want and say to hell with the world?"

The image of them naked, bodies locked, rocking against one another, wild and frenzied, more animal than human, flashed across her mind. A familiar hunger flared to life inside her, burning through her blood and weakening her knees. She curled her fingers around her throat to stop from reaching out. From pulling him toward her. To remind him that she had in fact followed her desires. More than once.

Blue fire lit the centers of his eyes, and she knew that he knew her thoughts, read them as clearly as a book splayed before him.

She closed her eyes, willing for strength, for the resolve to end this thing between them, to let him go. Because it was over. She could go. Leave. He wouldn't stop her now. There was no reason he should.

Petra deserved him.

And Griffin? What did he deserve?

She opened her eyes, the answer washing over her, bitter and true.

Not me.

He made a move toward her. She stepped back as if fire lapped at her feet.

He cocked his head, a dangerous glint entering his eyes. "Astrid," he whispered. His voice slid through her liked a warm wash of sherry.

She shook her head, her fingers tightening at her neck. Hurting. *Good.* Pain was good right now. It woke her up. Made her remember . . .

She could not have him touch her. One brush of his hand and she would crumble, succumb to her own selfish needs. Same or not, they could not have one another.

He closed the distance separating them, his expression hardening with resolve. Long fingers closed around her arms, singeing her through the fabric of her gown.

"You can push me away all you like," he paused. "You can even encourage me to marry someone else, but you can't run away from *this*." His fingers softened, sliding up her arm.

"It's not right," she insisted, her voice low and desperate. "It's not—"

He silenced her with his mouth.

She moaned. In defeat. In pleasure. She wound her arms around his neck, lost at the feel of his fingers, deft and swift on the buttons at the back of her dress. She moaned . . . even as she loathed herself for being weak, for seizing what she had no right to take.

In moments, her gown pooled at her ankles. He plucked her off her feet and wrapped her legs around his waist. She broke her lips from his to drag kisses down his throat and neck.

An invisible band squeezed around her chest. She felt elated, exhilarated to just touch him, to love him uninhibitedly—if only in the physical sense. If only one more time.

His hands flexed on her bottom, strong fingers digging into her yielding flesh as he carried her toward the bed.

"Griffin," she gasped against his neck.

Desperate with need, she clawed at his jacket, shoving it down past his shoulders, eager to feel his supple flesh in her hands.

He lowered her down onto the bed, coming over her in a heavy wall of muscle, settling between her thighs with a familiarity that both thrilled and alarmed her.

Putting aside the latter emotion, she ran her hands over the solid breadth of his chest with feverish hunger, letting herself surrender to the madness of wanting him, temporary as it was . . . as it could only ever be.

"Astrid," he whispered, sliding a hand against her face, his callused palm rasping her cheek, his eyes glowing blue fire. With a slight shake of his head, his mouth worked, preparing to say something. Something serious from the intent, soulful way he stared at her. Something her heart told her she couldn't allow him to say.

Moistening his lips, he said her name again, "Astrid—"

She brought her fingers to his mouth, pressing them against the silken texture of his lips, stifling his words. Words that could change everything between them. She did not know for certain, knew only the stark way he stared at her now, full of emotion—a passion that threatened to consume her in a slow burn.

Whatever he would say, she would not risk hearing it, would not risk feeding hope to her heart.

She held that gaze, enduring the hot crawl of his eyes over her. Dropping her hand from his mouth, she quickly kissed him, giving him no time to speak, tasting, drinking the essence of him—strength, virility. *A man she loved.* Who had called to her heart from the first moment she saw him, strong and proud in the swirling mists, ready to defend her—a perfect stranger.

Choking back a sob, she deepened their kiss, pouring all the emotion she suppressed, all the love she dared not confess.

He growled against her lips.

Desire rushed her as his hands dove for the hem of her petticoats, anxiously yanking the well-worn cambric to her hips. His fingers found the slit in her drawers, touching her briefly, playing in her wetness.

She nearly wept when his hand left her. Whimpering, she arched off the bed, reaching for him, groping to bring him back to her . . . only to fall back at the sudden, probing heat of him entering her, filling her, stretching her with the incredible length of him.

"Yes," she sighed as he held himself lodged deeply inside her, agonizingly still, his member pulsing with life as his hands tangled in her skirts gathered at her hips.

She devoured the sight of him over her, taut as a bow string, muscles bunching beneath the fabric of his shirt.

"Astrid," he cried, fingers digging into her hips, anchoring her to him.

With his head tossed back, throat muscles working, she drank him in, just as her body did, sealing the image of him in her mind, knowing she would never see anything that moved her as he did again.

Griffin watched Astrid sleep in the early hours of dawn, tempted to shake her awake . . . to make love to her all over again.

His fingers hovered over the dark lines of her brows, tempted to trace them. His hand stilled, deciding to let her sleep. For now. His argument for keeping her with him had fled with the arrival of Thomas Osborn. He could no longer claim fear for her safety. Osborn had owned up to killing her husband, however inadvertently. Astrid was in no danger on that account. She could travel without fear of being apprehended.

Leaning back on the pillow, he sighed, still watching her beside him. If he didn't want her to leave, then he was going to have to tell her the truth. That he wanted her to stay. For himself.

Stomach rumbling, he stood and collected his clothes from the floor. Quietly, he slipped from the room, thinking to return with breakfast. The idea of breakfast in bed with Astrid held decided appeal. He didn't particularly relish seeing his newfound family just yet. At least not while they still harbored delusions of him marrying Petra.

He took quick strides down the shadowed corridor, pausing when he heard a soft sound coming from one of the alcoves set in the stone walls of the corridor.

Glancing to the right, he noticed the shadowy figure of a woman huddled on a bench. Early-morning light washed through the stained mullioned panel of glass in the wall, limning her features in a myriad of colors.

"Petra?"

Her head snapped up. Swiping at her eyes, she rose hastily to her feet, sniffling suspiciously. Her eyes cast about, looking over his shoulders, searching before settling back on him. He did not miss the relieved expression that flickered over her face.

"Mr. Shaw," she greeted.

"Expecting someone else?" he inquired.

"No," she replied in a breathy rush. "Why would you think so?"

Without answering, he waved to the cushioned bench. "Are you well?"

Swiping at her nose again, she sank back down and answered in a small voice, "Quite."

He studied her. "It's all right if you're not, you know."

"Is it?" she asked, a surprising edge entering her voice, "How good of you to think so. However, my father would disagree. He expects me to wash away the shame I've brought to the family. To be a stalwart soldier and do as commanded. And to do so I must marry you."

He winced, thinking that not all soldiers should follow the call of duty so zealously. He certainly wished he had not followed its call to a certain grassy plain.

With a shake of his head, he asked, "But what do *you* want?"

Dipping her head to the side, she admitted, "I want to marry."

He nodded.

"But not you." She shook her head in apology. "Sorry."

He smiled wryly. "Don't be."

She bit her lip and released it. "I want to marry Andrew."

"Who is Andrew?"

"My father's coachman."

"Ah. And would Andrew be who you first thought me to be when I joined you in this corridor?"

She averted her gaze, and he caught a hint of blush staining her cheeks in the glow of dawn. A moment passed before she lifted her chin. "He loves me. He loved me before Bertram . . . " Her voice faded. She fisted the fabric of her gown, and he well imagined the dark roads her mind traveled. "He loves me still," she finished.

"Then why not marry him?"

She snorted. "Father would not permit it."

Griffin shook his head. He felt like he was talking to Astrid all over again. "Ever thought of going against Daddy?"

She pulled back, clearly startled. "And live where? How? Times are difficult. Assuming

327

Andrew finds another position, he can scarcely support himself, much less a family."

"So what? You'll marry me, then? Even while you love someone else? Someone willing and eager to marry you? Will that make you happy?" Anger swelled inside him. An anger that could not be rested entirely at her feet. Astrid would do the same thing——had, in fact. She had wed the man her father chose . . . living *unhappily* ever after to the moment of his death.

"Happy?" she murmured. "When has happiness ever been an issue."

"Hell," he muttered, looking away, dragging a hand through his hair and watching the play of light on the stained glass. "You sound like Astrid." Both women too stubborn to escape the prison they were born into. Even when the door was unlocked before them, they remained within.

Reaching a decision, he looked back at Petra and bit out, "Consider yourself engaged."

She responded slowly, "Are you asking--"

"I'm telling you," he ground out.

She stared at him a long moment, her eyes bleak as they scanned his face. "Very well," she agreed.

He nodded. Disgusted. Convinced. Another woman lost to duty's path. Rot them both. She and Astrid. Damned martyrs. Turning, he strode back to his chamber without another word, his hunger forgotten, determination burning through him.

"Griffin! Wait!"

He paused, looking over his shoulder.

Petra rose and took a halting step from the alcove, her skirts rustling. "What are you going to do?"

"Fetch the reverend, of course. Inform my grandfathers I'll be back posthaste, would you?" His lips twisted in a smile. "Meanwhile, prepare yourself for your wedding."

Chapter 24

Astrid woke with a deep stretch. Soft light poured into the room from the single mullioned window. She sat up, holding the linens tightly to her nakedness as she glanced about the large chamber, so different in the light of day, free of flickering shadows. Free of Griffin.

Falling back on the bed, she stared at the canopy above her, fingers drawing small, worrisome circles over her stomach, wondering where he had gone.

Did he regret last night, knowing, as she, that nothing could come of it?

And yet they had surrendered to desire, committing madness with one another again. Selfish, she knew. She had not changed her mind regarding his marrying Petra. She still believed that it would be the right thing, the proper thing. For Petra and Griffin both.

Still gazing at the canopy, she willed herself to rise, her molten limbs to move, to dress and prepare herself to say good-bye to Griffin.

She rubbed chilled fingertips over her brow, wondering how she could return to her old life as though nothing had happened. As if Griffin had not happened. As if she had not changed, experiencing life for the first time. How would she even fit into that world anymore?

Suddenly she felt relief to have woken alone. Better that Griffin was not here as she reached these sobering conclusions. Better that she was granted much needed time to compose herself without his absorbing presence. The last thing she needed was to become confused again. To *feel* again. To let desire cloud her head.

A swift knock sounded on the door. She clutched the counterpane tighter about herself and surged up in bed, her gaze darting for her clothing. The door swung open before she had a chance to call out.

The maid from last night stood in the threshold with a pitcher in her hands. "Ah, you're awake. Thought you might like some fresh water for washing." Her gaze scanned Astrid, knowing and smug. "Slept well, did you?"

Heat swarmed Astrid's face. Wrapping the

covers around herself, she slid from the bed and dropped her bare feet to the floor. Her toes dug into the soft rug. "Yes, thank you."

"I imagine you did." Her expression turned lascivious. "With a bedmate like yours, I would have, too."

Ignoring the comment, Astrid bent and snatched her clothes off the floor.

"I must say," the girl began.

Astrid shot her a wary glance as she shook out her impossibly wrinkled gown with one hand.

"The way he was looking at you, I was a wee bit surprised that he left so early this morning. Especially on such an errand."

The hairs on her nape prickled and her stomach began to churn uneasily. "Left?" She could not keep the single word from escaping.

"Aye. Departed over an hour ago."

As much as it pricked her pride to interrogate a maid on Griffin's whereabouts and plans, nothing could stop her from asking, "Where did he go?"

"To fetch the reverend in the next village." She shook her head and laughed ruefully as she set the pitcher on a side table. "You should see the two lairds."

"Why is that?"

"They're downstairs even now discussing wedding plans like a couple of old women."

Astrid's stomach plunged to her feet in a vicious dive. She dropped back on the bed, her legs suddenly too weak to support herself.

"Never thought to see those two old dogs breaking bread together . . . even if they still snipe at one another in the process." She sighed contentedly. "Can't tell you how happy everyone is. No one ever relished the idea of that Thomas as lord and master of Balfurin. Griffin's homecoming is a blessing, to be certain. And now his marriage to Petra . . . well, everything is coming together."

Astrid nodded dumbly. *Of course*. He had decided to marry Petra. Precisely as she had urged him. For duty's sake. For his family, his people . . . for Petra who had suffered more than any woman should.

For whatever reason, his conscience and good sense must have reared its head at last.

Perhaps that is what he wanted to tell her last night. Before she stopped him, crushing her lips to his. Perhaps last night had been good-bye for him, too. A final farewell before he went about his duty.

"I see," she murmured, the words escaping her tight throat. "Good for Griffin. And Petra." She nodded once in a satisfied manner, contrary to the ache that flared to life beneath her breastbone, calling her a liar and ten kinds of fool. A scathing voice rose up inside her, whispering and taunting her . . .

Did you think this would be so simple? That you could walk away and not feel pain? You don't want him to marry Petra. You don't want him to marry anyone but you.

She shoved down the insistent voice in her head, pushing it to the dark well inside where she had stored feelings she deemed too volatile, too selfish, too much like those that had guided her mother and led her to ruin.

Standing, she gathered her composure, cloaking herself in a sheet of ice strong enough to kill off pathetic sentiments.

Uncaring of her audience, she dropped the counterpane and set about dressing herself with stiff movements. Denying Petra a marriage to Griffin would be pure selfishness. Griffin and Petra were *right*. Astrid and Griffin . . . well, they were something else. Something that could never be——naught but a dream, elusive and fleeting, never intended to last. Fitting that he should have left before she woke. Would that his memory vanish from her heart as easily.

Her husband had raped Petra. That alone stood as reason to bite her tongue and set aside the love she felt for Griffin . . . and whatever he may or may not feel for her. Surrendering the man she loved was the least she could do.

Dressed and composed, Astrid walked down the corridor with brisk steps, intent on speaking with Laird MacFadden about arranging an escort to Edinburgh. With luck, she would be gone before Griffin returned.

A part of her died, withered inside at reaching this decision. No good-byes. No seeing him one final time. No pressing her lips to his in a lingering taste. They would never again have a night in each other's arms.

It had taken her all day to gather her nerve and decide to approach MacFadden. A day spent contemplating Griffin's abrupt departure, and his stinging neglect to inform her of his intention to wed Petra.

It was one matter to have encouraged his nuptials to Petra, but another to watch him marry another with her own eyes. Her heart could not stand witness to such heartbreak. Nor her dignity. She would be gone before such an event took place.

Quickening her pace, she turned the corridor,

noticing a couple ahead. One of them, a female, struck a familiar chord.

"Petra?" she called.

The cloaked woman looked over her shoulder, the action inherently anxious, apprehensive. Seeing Astrid, Petra stopped and shot a vague, inscrutable look at her companion, a young man that held her arm in a plainly possessive hold.

Astrid quickly closed the distance, assessing the man beside Petra suspiciously, her gaze lingering on his hand gripping Petra's arm.

"Is everything all right?"

"Yes. Fine," Petra replied, her voice a bit strident as she looked to the man beside her.

Astrid followed her gaze, arching a brow. "Won't you introduce me?"

"Oh. This is . . . Andrew."

"Andrew," Astrid murmured, somehow not surprised. Her gaze ran over the coachman. Although not particularly handsome, he was strapping, his arms thickly muscled. One of his broad hands clutched the handle of a valise.

Her gaze snapped back up to Petra's face, awareness hitting her. "Good heavens! You're not—"

"Please, Astrid!" Petra rushed forward, seizing her arm in a surprisingly fierce grip. The birthmark on her face seemed to darken with the depth of her emotion. "Don't try to stop me. I can't remain here. I thought I could, but I can't." She looked to Andrew then. Releasing Astrid, she moved back to his side.

Astrid tried to wrap her thoughts around the fact that Petra was actually running away. "But Griffin—"

"Is a good man," she broke in, "but not for me. I appreciate his offer of marriage, but I don't want to marry him."

"Are you sure you know what you're doing?"

"All my life I've done as I was bid and it has brought me nothing but pain." She looked to the man at her side. He smiled tenderly and pressed the back of Petra's hand to his mouth. "Andrew has kin in Glasgow. He thinks he can find work at one of the factories there. Perhaps we can save enough for passage to America." Dark eyes shining, she added in a broken whisper, "I'll follow my instincts for a change and take a chance on love."

Astrid studied the couple in the dim corridor, feeling a stab of envy. Not because they loved each other. It was a simple matter to love someone. She loved Griffin. No great feat, that. Loving was the easy part. It took no strength or courage. The strength came in how one showed that love, what they chose to do with it, whether it survived life's storms.

She had thought herself strong and brave to love Griffin and walk away from him, to encourage his marriage to Petra. She had thought herself so different from her mother, someone who surrendered to her love of another man and deserted her child.

Astrid swallowed, fighting down the sour taste filling her mouth as realization washed over her.

Petra possessed true strength. Astrid did not.

Petra loved and was willing to take a chance on that love, to follow it wherever it led. Astrid felt small standing before her.

Behind her, footsteps thudded over the corridor. Fast approaching. Petra's face tightened with panic. She pressed closer to Andrew, looking left and right, clearly uncertain whether to flee down the rest of the corridor or take shelter in one of the nearby rooms.

Without stopping to think, Astrid motioned the couple down the corridor, "Go! Hurry. I'll distract them."

Petra slanted her head and looked at her strangely.

"Go," Astrid repeated, waving them on.

With a grateful smile, Petra and her lover fled.

Astrid hastened in the opposite direction, ready to stall the new arrival. Rounding the corridor, she stopped abruptly at the man heading her way, suddenly gratified with her split-second decision.

"My, you're up early," Osborn announced with a leer. "Did Shaw fail to properly tire you out last night?" He stopped before her. "You know, I would be more than happy to accommodate if you find yourself hungry for more—"

"How kind of you," Astrid broke in with false charm. "I can think of no one whose company I would rather have than a remorseless killer such as yourself."

The smug grin disappeared from his face in a flash. "I would think you would thank me for ridding you of that worthless cur. It has certainly left you free to squeeze your thighs around the first buck to cross your path."

She sucked in a sharp breath and resisted the impulse to turn on her heels and leave him and all his crude insults where he stood. No matter how revolting his words, she stayed put, her fingers twitching at her side, itching to make contact with his face. She took comfort in the fact that with every moment that passed, she helped Petra thwart him and all his ruthless ambitions for her.

"You, sir, are a pig."

His gaze crawled over her, glinting with mirthful spite. "And you, *Duchess*, are little more than a whore . . . no matter your fancy airs."

She flinched.

"And you mustn't be very good," he continued with an arrogant cock of his dark head. "First one husband. Now Griffin. You can't keep a man to save your life, can you?" He flashed her a cruel smile. "Whatever you have beneath your skirts mustn't be very appealing or Shaw would not have roused himself so early to leave your bed and fetch the reverend to wed him to my daughter."

Stepping nearer, he ran the backs of his fingers against her cheek and down the column of her neck. She turned her face sideways, closing her eyes against the feel of him.

"That must have pricked your pride," he continued, his voice a slow, insidious murmur that skimmed over her skin as nimbly as his hand. "Perhaps the right man could teach you how to properly please a man." He stood so close now that she could smell the onions from last night's dinner on his breath. Her stomach churned. Opening her eyes, she glared at him.

"What say you?" he murmured. "Would you like that? To learn what a real man is like?"

This time she could not stop herself. She flung his hand off her neck and stepped around him. With one hand rubbing her skin as if she could rub out the stain of him on her flesh, she backed away.

"Never put a hand on me again," she hissed.

"No?" Straightening, he brushed away the invisible wrinkles in his coat. "Pity. Then it appears you're quite finished here. Why not salvage your pride and leave? Today, in fact. Don't be here when Griffin returns." The last suggestion was uttered somewhat ominously. "His whore needn't be standing on while he weds my daughter." Shaking his head, he clicked his tongue. "That wouldn't do at all. Not at all."

Without gracing him with a reply, she turned and hurried back to her chamber.

Salvage your pride and leave.

The fact that his suggestion mirrored her intentions did not make it any easier to hear.

Pacing the length of her chamber, she rubbed her neck, the feel of his hand an irksome imprint there.

She was not fool enough to think Osborn cared about her or the status of her pride. She knew his intent. He wanted her out of the way. Would not risk Griffin changing his mind with the shadow of her presence. Apparently only she knew the unlikelihood of that happening, knew that honor would prohibit Griffin from going back on the promise he had made to Petra.

But Petra would not be here, a small voice reminded. *Surely you could stay . . .*

And what? Be pathetic, desperate, lacking in all dignity? Sniffing about Griffin in the hopes of a future together?

She still had the matter of her own life to resume. She needed to notify Bertram's family of his death, meet with the solicitors, inform the next in line that he had inherited the vast, insolvent estates of the Duke of Derring. No. Better that she leave now. Before Griffin returned.

Petra might have taught her that denying one's duty and obligation for the sake of love was not such a transgression. She might in fact have changed Astrid's thoughts concerning her mother, made her look at that long-ago night, when her mother had slipped from their townhouse, differently.

Closing her eyes, she sank down onto the bed and saw her mother as she had been that night, standing beneath the streetlamp, her expression both anguished and eager in the muted glow. For the first time in her life, Astrid recognized the doubts that must have plagued her mother to leave all that was familiar . . . to leave Astrid.

And yet she had done it, had walked into the unknown. Despite the risks, she had followed her heart and taken a chance . . . however badly it ended. However wrong it may have been.

Tears blurred her eyes. At last, Astrid understood. Living meant taking chances. Risks. Mistakes even. Better that than running, or hiding as she had been doing.

Opening her eyes, she stared ahead of her, seeing nothing in the still and silent room before her, seeing all.

If only she had spent her time loving Griffin—truly loving him—perhaps he could have loved her back. Instead she had worked so hard at pushing him away, encouraging him to wed another, convincing him nothing existed between them. Nothing worth keeping, at any rate.

No wonder he had decided to wed Petra. If he had felt anything at all for her, she had killed it.

A chill feathered her spine. If she had fought for them, then perhaps the thought of waiting for him at Balfurin, of taking a chance on him—on them—might not have seemed so very impossible.

She shivered, hugging herself as the chamber's coldness seeped into her bones. She glanced at the fire, noting that it still smoldered in the hearth. And yet it felt as though the temperature had dropped.

Rising to her feet, she made her way to the mullioned window, the room's chilliness increasing as she approached the fogged glass. Rubbing her fingertips over the icy surface, she peered out, gasping at the sight of swirling snow in the air. It fell thickly, blanketing the ground. Beyond the lake, blinding white stretched across the countryside. Squinting against its brightness, she strained to locate the road, already buried beneath the snow.

Leaving suddenly posed a new challenge.

Chapter 25

G riffin buried his chin in his coat and pulled the wide brim of his hat low over his eyes in an attempt to ward of the sting of snow and wind. Waya lifted his legs high to pass through rapidly rising drifts. The Reverend Walter's mount trekked behind him, falling in his tracks.

"How goes it, Reverend?" Griffin called over the howling wind.

The man nodded from deep within a scarf of tartan, squinting out at the winter-shrouded landscape, lashes tangled with white frothy flakes. "Told you we should have waited out the storm," he called.

Griffin pressed his lips into a grim line. The reverend had done his best to discourage their departure, but after lacing his palm with coin, the good man quit his warm cottage.

Griffin was eager to return to Balfurin, regretful

of his hasty departure, and impatient to see Astrid's dark eyes again. Ironic that. Especially considering he had only ever sought to escape a similar pair of eyes. Now he longed for the sight of them.

He should have spoken to Astrid before he'd left, but he'd been too damned aggravated to spare a moment for her.

Instead he had left her alone, under the dubious care of his newfound family.

A tightness gripped his chest, an uneasiness he could not shake. He had to get back. Had to see her. Touch her. He would not breathe easy until he did.

Hefting her valise, Astrid made her way downstairs, intent on locating Laird MacFadden and seeing about arranging an escort, storm or no storm.

A mocking smile twisted her lips. At the very least, Osborn would he happy to accommodate. Certainly his carriage could navigate the snow-laden roads, and she knew how badly he wanted her gone before Griffin's return.

Raised voices drifted on the air. Slowing her pace, she advanced cautiously through the dining hall's tall double doors, observing Griffin's family at their breakfast. The smell of sausage pudding rose pungent on the air. No one paid heed to her.

Osborn leaned forward in his chair and shook his head in agitation over his half-eaten plate of food. "We have to go after them! They cannot have gotten far . . ."

Her hand flew to her throat, knowing at once he had discovered Petra missing. It had not surprised her when no one noted the girl's disappearance yesterday. No one noticed when she was in the room, after all. No. All discussion was on Griffin and his sudden departure.

MacFadden opened his mouth to respond to Osborn's histrionics, but his eyes fell on Astrid hovering at the edge of the room. "Lass," he greeted, cool blue eyes dropping to the valise she clutched in her hand. "Going somewhere?"

Striding into the room, she stopped and lowered the valise to her feet. Nodding, she moistened her lips and prepared to voice the request she had rehearsed in her room.

Osborn's sharp voice stopped her cold. "I'd like to know how *you* are involved in all this."

"Me?"

"Aye, you. No doubt you wanted Petra out of the way so you could continue your dalliance with Shaw. What have you done with her?"

"Nothing." She motioned to her valise with a

347

snort. "And would I be leaving if I wanted Griffin for myself?"

"Who knows the workings of the conniving female mind? Perhaps you wanted to stop their marriage out of spite, eh?" He nodded as though satisfied with that conclusion. "Is that it?"

Ignoring him, she addressed MacFadden. "Would you arrange an escort for me to travel as far as Edinburgh, sir? I see no reason to delay my return home any longer."

The request did not fall easily from her lips, still she uttered the words that would take her forever from Griffin.

Rubbing his chin, MacFadden assessed her. "Should we not wait for Griffin—"

"Whatever for? Your grandson and I have no . . ." she paused, groping for the proper word, "ties to speak of."

"Ties," Gallagher muttered, leaning in his seat toward MacFadden. "Call it what you will, but sending her away is going to stir a hornet's nest with Griffin. We'd best keep her here until he returns."

Heat licked her cheeks and her fists knotted at her sides. "I can assure you my comings and goings don't bear Griffin's notice."

"You're not leaving until you tell me where my daughter has absconded." Osborn surged from his chair and rounded the table, a steely light in his eyes.

"I know nothing," she replied, weary at heart.

"You lie," he insisted. "I'll have the truth."

"What do you recommend, Osborn?" Gallagher queried, his heavy beard lifting around the corners of his smirk. "We torture the lass?"

Osborn stopped before her, eyes glittering with malice as they stared down at her. "I can think of ways to make her talk," he answered, clearly missing Gallagher's derisive tone.

Suffering his glower, she did not put such a thing past his capabilities. Lifting her valise, her fingers slick around the handle, her gaze drifted to MacFadden. "I appreciate your hospitality, sir, but I would be grateful if you were to extend it further in the form of an escort."

Osborn snatched hold of her arm, forcing her to look at him again. "You're not going anywhere. Not until you answer for your part in this." He jabbed one finger high on her chest below her collarbone. She fought back a wince.

"Even if I knew where Petra was, I would not tell you."

"See," Osborn blustered, his face blossoming an unbecoming shade of red. "She knows! She knows, I tell you."

"Come, lass," MacFadden demanded, one dark brow arched. "Do you know where Petra has gone?"

She stood stoically before them, thinking of Petra and Andrew making their way south toward Glasgow even now. Toward their life together. Happiness.

Instead of answering, she pressed her lips together. At her mutinous silence, Osborn retorted, "Of course she does."

"I don't know where Petra is," she declared, her temper snapping. "All I know is that I want to leave this place before Griffin returns." Emotion thickened her throat, bringing with it a damnable sob that burned the back of her throat. *She had to.* "I want to go home and forget everything." She swiped a trembling hand through the air. "Forget all of this. This whole bloody journey!" *And Griffin.* She wished to forget Griffin. Forget loving him.

Heavy silence fell.

Osborn shifted his attention, looking over her shoulder.

A tremor skimmed her spine. The tiny hairs at her neck tingled.

Deep awareness settled in the pit of her stomach. Slowly, she turned.

"Griffin," she breathed, heat rushing to her face

as she realized he had her heard her every word.

He stood in the wide threshold, travel-worn, the hem of his cloak sodden from snow and mud, his hat hanging limply in his hand. Her heart ached at the sight of him, her gaze hungrily devouring him—this man she had thought never to see again.

She spared a quick glance for the reed-thin man at his side. The reverend no doubt. Here to wed him to Petra, the bride she had helped escape. Nervousness coursed through her. How would he react to the news that Petra had fled?

"Griffin!" MacFadden rounded the table. "Why did you not tell us you were leaving? With this wretched storm, I was plagued with worry."

Griffin's boots clicked over the stone floor, ringing with quiet command, eyes fixed on her as he removed his gloves. He motioned the reverend into one of the dining table's high-backed chairs even as he remained standing, a dark brow arching as he eyed her.

She flexed her fingers around the handle of her valise, her palms growing slippery with perspiration.

His eyes drilled into her with an intensity she could not decipher, burning a hole straight through her. Surely he was not angry over her words, not when he intended to marry Petra. Why should he care if she left?

"No one seemed to give a damn about what I had to say." Although he addressed his grandfathers, his eyes spoke to her, sharp with accusation, conveying that he thought she shared in that charge.

And he was correct. She had not considered him. Or Petra. Just as she had not considered or trusted Portia all those years ago.

And yet she had changed, had become a different woman in loving him. She helped Petra escape, after all.

Longing seized her, a deep yearning to confide to him that she had awakened at last. As though emerging from a dream. She understood it was not her place to make decisions for Griffin. Or anyone. The only person in the world whose happiness she could control was her own. And for the first time in memory, she actually believed she deserved happiness. Would not settle for less.

"What are you talking about?" Gallagher demanded with a puff of his barrel chest.

"I did not leave to fetch the reverend for me and Petra." His gaze remained trained on her with unswerving focus.

Both his grandfathers exchanged befuddled looks.

"I fetched the reverend so that Petra might marry the man *she* wants to marry."

"You," MacFadden quickly supplied with an impatient wave of his hand. "The lass agreed to marry you."

"*Agreed*," Griffin echoed, nodding. "A bit different from *want*, is it not? She may have agreed to wed me, but she wanted to marry Andrew."

"Andrew?" Gallagher scratched his thick beard. "Who the devil is Andrew?"

"You had no right," Osborn bellowed. "Such a decision falls to me and *I* say my daughter will not marry a servant."

"Who is this Andrew?" MacFadden's confused gaze shot back and forth between Griffin and Osborn.

"A good man who loves and *wants* to marry Petra," Astrid volunteered. "He doesn't care what happened to her," she added, hoping that conveyed just how honorable his intentions ran. Petra's family should be relieved that such a man wanted to marry her, but Astrid knew enough about the ambitions of men to know that it would matter little . . . if at all. No doubt Griffin's revelation would send the entire MacFadden clan thundering after Petra. Her shoulders slumped. She and Andrew would never reach Glasgow.

"I knew you had something to do with this," Osborn exploded, slamming his fist into his palm as if he wished it were her.

Griffin looked at her strangely, head cocked. "You knew about Petra and Andrew?"

Raising her chin, she decided the time had arrived for Griffin to see she wasn't the same woman he had met on a Scottish roadside. Someone afraid to live. Afraid to surrender her heart lest she become as lost and pitiable as her mother.

"I did. And I provided a distraction yesterday so that they could escape."

"You deceitful witch!" Osborn cried.

Griffin watched her, approval glowing in his eyes. An approval she felt deep within herself, a lovely suffusing warmth.

"You knew, too. You fetched the reverend for them?" Her gaze dropped to the reverend, now sitting at the table with a pint of ale before him, watching the scene unfold as if it were a Drury Lane performance.

"Yes. I fetched the reverend for them." Griffin stared at her one long moment before adding, "And for me."

"You?" she asked, confused. "But you said—"

His gaze dropped to her valise. "You're leaving." The statement hung between them, accusatory, and yet a question lingered in his eyes.

He had not fetched the reverend so that he could wed Petra. The bewildered thought tripped through her mind. What did he mean he had fetched the reverend for *him*? Unsure, she took a halting step toward him.

Osborn stepped between them, blocking Griffin from her eyes, filling her vision with his hate-filled countenance.

"I'll know where my daughter has fled this instant."

Griffin spoke, his voice dangerous and low. "Then perhaps you should ask me."

Osborn swung to face him. "You? How would you know? She absconded after you left."

"Yes, but the good reverend and I happened upon Petra and Andrew on our way back here."

"You've seen Petra?"

"Yes."

By now, Osborn's eyes bulged in his flushed face. "And you did not force them to return with you?"

"No," Griffin answered so evenly that even Astrid began to feel exasperated. "In fact," he added, "I wished them Godspeed on their way."

"Where are they?" Osborn growled.

"On their way to Glasgow. Where they will board a ship bound for America."

"America!"

"Yes." Griffin nodded in satisfaction. "I had the good reverend marry them this very morning. And as a wedding gift, I supplied them with the means for passage."

Chapter 26

G riffin watched as all eyes swung to Mr. Walters, seeking confirmation. The reverend raised his tankard in a cheerful salute, his easy smile quickly slipping when he caught so many dark glowers cast his way.

"Griffin," MacFadden began, "how could you aid your own kinswoman in . . . in," his grandfather paused, sputtering for words, waving a broad hand as though he could catch the words on the air. "Do you care so little for the lass that you would aid her in wedding someone so beneath her? And then send her halfway across the world to God knows what fate?"

"Petra and her husband carry signed letters from me granting them management of my lands in Texas for a period of two years. If after that time, they are content with their life there, and I am satisfied with reports of their progress, I will sign over the deed."

"Lands?" Osborn sneered. "You mean a *farm*. You've sentenced my daughter to life as a farmer's wife in some primitive Godforsaken frontier."

"Andrew's accustomed to hard work. And Petra will thrive there . . . a place where people will not judge her for her rape or the mark on her face, but by the merit with which she lives."

Silence met his announcement.

MacFadden's dark brows drew together in an expression of deep contemplation.

Griffin looked to Astrid, the only person, he realized, whose opinion really mattered to him.

Her dark eyes glowed as they looked at him, her approval shining through. The precise look he had missed seeing in his father's eyes. The look in her eyes wiped clean all the guilt he had harbored over the years.

And in that moment, he knew it was worth it. Helping Petra, giving up his lands, everything he had ever worked for, everything he had ever known, in order to remain here . . . it was all worth it. *She was worth it*. They both were.

Griffin cleared his throat. "I will remain here."

MacFadden lifted his head, losing the rather dazed expression on his face. "Aye. Well. That, at the least, is right." He nodded, looking vastly pleased. "This is your home now."

"Well, this is bloody convenient," Osborn hissed, his voice sharp as cut glass. "Petra dispatched, forever lost to me. And Shaw here claims my inheritance as his due. But what of me?" he demanded, pounding his chest. "What am I left with?" His nostrils flared with a harsh release of breath. "Nothing, I tell you. I obtain nothing out of all this!"

"Hell, man," Gallagher snorted. "Quit your bleating. You're hurting my ears."

Osborn flushed as Griffin's grandfathers shared a chuckle.

Griffin said nothing, merely trained his attention on Astrid, wondering what had motivated her to help Petra elope when she had been so vocal about him marrying the girl, when she had been as irksome as everyone else, more so, assuming she knew what was best for him.

"Astrid," he murmured, as if no one else was in the room, as if he spoke to her alone, with no prying ears—or eyes.

Her earlier words played in his mind like a tune he could not quit. *All I know is that I want to leave . . . to go home. I'd like to forget everything.*

Including him?

With his heart pounding fiercely against his chest, he glanced again at her well-worn valise. "You truly mean to leave?"

Something flickered across her face, an emotion he could not name. But emotion nonetheless. Not the inscrutable mask. Not the cool, unaffected expression. No. Her eyes gleamed. A feverish light glinted at the dark centers.

"No," she whispered, shaking her fair head and taking several halting steps toward him.

He nodded, something lifting, easing within him as he gazed into her eyes.

"Reverend," he called, gaze still fixed on her, devouring her. His fingers twitched at his sides, the urge to pull her to him and never let go overwhelming.

The reverend rose from where he sat, dabbing at his mouth, his Adam's apple bobbing as he swallowed his bite of food. "Mr. Shaw?"

His heart swelled, beating fast and hard as a drum against his chest. "I'd like you to perform that other ceremony I mentioned. Now. If you please."

"Certainly." Mr. Walter's gaze shifted to Astrid, along with everyone else's in the hall.

"Lad," MacFadden's voice rumbled gruffly across the air. "You cannot mean to consider this Sassenach for your wife."

"I can. I do." His lips twitched. "I've grown quite fond of this Sassenach," he added, adopting his grandfather's thick burr.

"She's a cold one," Gallagher reminded.

Griffin smiled, recalling that he had thought the precise thing when he first met her. "I've never met a woman who makes my blood run hotter."

Astrid's cheeks pinkened.

"Och," Gallagher mumbled, sagging back in his chair and clapping a hand over his brow. "She's bewitched him."

Osborn thrust his face near Astrid's. "You're naught but a troublesome harpy sent to wreak havoc in my life."

"Indeed," she retorted before Griffin had a chance. "I *planned* for you to murder my husband so that I might be free to wed another. All to vex you."

Osborn's face burned a vivid red, lips working feverishly as if searching for words foul enough to hurl.

Dismissing the man, Astrid's gaze sought Griffin's. "Now step aside," she commanded. "I've important matters to attend."

MacFadden made a slight noise in his throat, a cross between a laugh and a cough. "Perhaps she has the making of a MacFadden after all."

"More like a Gallagher," Griffin's other grandfather chimed with a lift of his chin. "But I already suspected there was mettle to the lass. No grandson of mine would pine after a woman without a fair dose of spirit."

"As pleased as I am that you both approve, allow me to say that I don't give a damn." Striding forward, he took Astrid's hand in his.

"Nay!" Osborn protested, childlike in his pique. Shoving between Griffin and Astrid, he charged Griffin. "*You've* done this! Ruined everything! I shall not stand for it!"

Like a thread stretched overly tight, the last of Griffin's patience snapped. He grabbed Osborn by the vest with both hands. "Do you really wish to make an enemy of me?"

Osborn's mouth sagged open and he issued forth a slight squeak of sound.

"I'm not your daughter to be cowed and manipulated . . . or someone who's going to die so easily at your hands." He tightened his grip and lifted the man to the balls of his feet. "Care to test *me*? Because I've learned many things from growing up in . . ." He cocked his head to the side. "What was it? *A primitive Godforsaken frontier?* I've learned useful things. Like how to make a man suffer for every rotten thing he has ever done."

After a long moment, Osborn spit out in a thread-thin voice, "That's unnecessary."

He flung Osborn from him with a growl of

disgust. "I think you've outlived your welcome here."

Osborn looked at MacFadden, appealing with a small, pitiable, "Cousin."

Griffin's grandfather lifted his large shoulders in an apathetic shrug. "What can I say, Thomas? You've been a trial. Best take yourself home. And don't return unless invited."

Flushing, Osborn tugged his rumpled jacket into some semblance of order before striding away.

Griffin reclaimed Astrid's hand. With a quick glance at the reverend, he promised, "We'll be back."

Pulling her after him, he led her past wide-eyed servants and up the stairs to their chamber. *Their* chamber. Before she packed her belongings and thought she could leave his life as suddenly and unexpectedly as she entered it. And that, he vowed, would never happen.

Standing before Griffin, Astrid opened her mouth to speak, but he hauled her into his arms and smothered her lips with the hot brand of his kiss.

She managed a garbled squeak. "Griffin! What are you doing?"

"Punishing you," he said against her lips, "for *thinking* about leaving me." His warm palms slid along her cheeks, rasping her tender skin and trapping her for his kiss.

With a moan of pleasure, she wound her arms around his neck and stood on her tiptoes, returning the kiss. A metallic clank trembled distantly in her head, similar to the sound of her back garden gate opening and shutting the night her mother had left . . . fleeing Astrid for a chance at her heart's desire.

The sound reverberated through her now, the discordant clank marking the crumbling of her defenses, her willing departure from the known and familiar, the cold and lifeless, into a world of heat and fire, an uncertain life fraught with risk.

For the first time, Astrid willingly placed her trust and heart into the hands of another. Stepped from the shadows into the light. Despite the risk. Or perhaps because of the risk—the exhilaration of living.

"Astrid," he broke away to mutter, planting several small kisses to her lips, her chin, her cheeks. "My love."

A rough sound rose from her throat, half sob, half laugh. Her fingers clutched his biceps. She sagged against him, convinced her weak knees couldn't support her. "You brought the reverend for *us*?" she asked between kisses.

"You don't think I would marry anyone else. It's been you. Only you since I first saw you on that road. An angel sent to rescue me."

Astrid pulled back to look deeply into his eyes. Her fingers came up to cover his on her cheeks. "Rescue *you*?" She shook her head. "You rescued me," she whispered starkly. "In every way. You've given me life, Griffin. Breathed it into my very soul, my heart."

"We'll call it a draw, then. We rescued each other." His thumbs shifted, tracing small circles on her cheeks. "Marry me, Astrid. Marry me today."

She smiled.

What he was suggesting was absurd, terrifying. The unknown. Stark and real. And she had never been happier, more thrilled at the prospect.

"I love you, Astrid," he said, his voice hoarse and deep, reverberating through her.

She closed her eyes, the words squeezing at her heart. "I can't recall the last time I heard anyone say those words to me." And until now, she had not known she wanted to hear them. Needed to hear them.

His hands tightened on her face, his blue eyes glittering with deep intensity. "You're going to hear those words every day. As you deserve. So much you'll learn to take them for granted. I promise you that."

"I love you." Turning her face into his hand, she kissed his palm, thinking she would never tire of those words, never take for granted words she had heard so little in her life. "I love you, Griffin."

He pulled her hard against him, responding with a kiss. His hands slid from her face to the tiny buttons at the top of her dress. "Love me, Astrid."

She laughed lightly against his lips, lodging a half-hearted complaint as he plied his fingers through her hair, loosening the pins.

"The reverend is waiting," she reminded, gasping when his hand closed over one breast.

"He can wait. All damn night if need be," Griffin muttered.

Astrid gave a small yelp as he swung her up into his arms and carried her to the bed. "I, however," he added, "can't wait another moment. You love me." His blue eyes glinted down at her. "As far as I'm concerned, you're my wife."

Running a hand along his square jaw, she waited for the whispers in her head, the ones that had always been there, calling for duty and restraint, to remind her that people waited downstairs, no doubt talking about them, speculating . . .

And yet nothing. Nothing could be heard save the beating of her heart, the hum of her blood rushing in her ears. All for love. For Griffin. For living and loving freely for the first time in her life.

Griffin stopped at the bed, his arms cradling her tightly against him. She could feel the thud of his heart against her side, matching the rhythm of her own.

"Astrid?" he murmured and her gaze slid up to his, reading the silent question there . . . the patience and understanding in the pale blue depths.

He would do whatever she wished. *Restrain* himself, save his passion, deny spontaneity, and stow away his desire for later. He would pull away, take her downstairs and properly wed her before he touched her again. For her. Because he loved her.

The old Astrid would have taken the offer. And felt the correct, respectable lady for it. Whether true or not, she would have cloaked herself in the façade and never surrendered to passion, to him, herself.

Glancing down, she slid her fingers beneath his vest, caressing the firm chest through his shirt. "Are we *still* wearing our clothes?"

Grinning, he dropped her on the bed. "Not for long. Not for long."

Epilogue

"**H**ow long are we going to sit here?" Griffin asked, his voice warm as a summer breeze sweeping through her. Especially welcome considering that Yorkshire was almost as cold as the Highlands this early in spring.

Griffin glanced out the window. "The servants are likely wondering at the carriage sitting in the drive."

"Hmmm," Astrid murmured with a nervous tilt of her head, fingers tapping her lips anxiously as she glanced out the part in the curtain and considered the impressive home of the Earl of Moreton.

"Forever, then?" he asked at her continued silence.

Astrid shook her head vigorously, smoothing gloved hands over her muslin skirts. "Just a bit longer."

She had taken great pains with her wardrobe this morning. Rising early, she had left Griffin asleep, naked and tangled enticingly in the bed linens at the nearby inn where they had taken lodgings.

Griffin smiled indulgently and moved across the carriage to sit beside her. He plucked her hand from her lap and ran his thumb over the back of her glove. "You don't have to do this."

"Yes. I do." With a deep, bracing breath, she nodded and allowed him to escort her from the carriage. The front door opened before they knocked, the butler's ready gaze telling them that their presence had long been known.

Moments later, they found themselves led into a well-appointed drawing room. Astrid glanced around, contented to see that Portia lived in such comfort.

"I will inform Lady Moreton of your presence." Bowing, the butler left them. The moment the door clicked shut, she sagged against a chintz-covered sofa.

Griffin sank down beside her, his eyes meeting hers in concern. "You're certain you want to do this?"

"It's long overdue."

"I don't think you have anything to be sorry

about." He tapped her nose fondly. "As far as I'm concerned, you couldn't be more perfect."

She snorted and shook her head. "You must really love me."

He leaned over her, lips brushing hers in several nibbling bites. "I *must*."

Her fingers curled into his jacket as he deepened their kiss, their tongues mating in a feverish kiss.

The click of the drawing room doors registered dimly. Shoving at his broad shoulders, she wiggled out from beneath him and rose to greet her sister-in-law.

"Astrid," Portia murmured, blue eyes blinking in astonishment.

Bertram's sister had matured into every inch the elegant lady, her once waifish appearance long gone. With her jet tresses arranged elegantly atop her head and her gown of deep blue, she looked the perfect countess.

"Hello, Portia," she murmured, resting a hand on Griffin's arm. "This is my husband, Griffin Shaw MacFadden."

Griffin stood tall at her side, inclining his head ever so slightly, a polite smile on his lips, but in his eyes lurked a wariness, a readiness to pounce and defend if Astrid were in any way affronted.

She slid her fingers down his arm to lightly encircle his wrist, letting the simple touch stay his impulse to shield her.

"Your husband?"

Flushing, Astrid realized she had not even shared the news of Bertram's demise. With fumbling fingers, she pulled Bertram's signet ring from her reticule and handed it to Portia.

Portia accepted the ring, studying it.

"I'm sorry, Portia." She fought to swallow down the sudden lump in her throat. "Your brother is dead. Buried in a churchyard in Dubhlagan, Scotland."

A deep sigh rattled loose from Portia's chest. "I can't say I'm surprised. If anything, I would have thought Bertram met his end long ago. He certainly did nothing to promote a long, prosperous life."

"No," Astrid murmured, thinking of how Bertram had died. How he had lived. "He did not."

Portia lifted her gaze from the ring. "And you've remarried."

"Yes."

She nodded slowly. "If Bertram's death brought nothing else, I'm glad it gave you your freedom." She glanced once at Griffin before settling her gaze back on Astrid. "And love."

Astrid's face warmed. She reached for Griffin's

hand. He laced his fingers through hers in a reassuring grip.

"Thank you for bringing the news in person. You didn't need to do that."

"Yes. I did." -

Portia's slight smile slipped. "Don't tell me you've harbored some sense of guilt or responsibility all these years."

"I did you a disservice—"

"No harm done." Portia cut in with a wave of her hand. "I'm happy. I have a doting husband and two lovely children. Don't waste another moment fretting over the past."

Astrid blinked.

With a rueful shake of her head, Portia stepped close and embraced Astrid. Stunned, Astrid could hardly breathe, much less move within the circle of arms.

"It happened a long time ago," Portia murmured near her ear. "I'm simply relieved to see you happy." Pulling back, she dropped her arms and gave an encouraging wink. "Now return home. Enjoy your life."

With a single nod, Astrid met Griffin's devoted gaze, a great lightness sweeping through her at the love she saw reflected there, the same love she felt within her. "I already am. I already am."

Unforgettable, enthralling love stories,
sparkling with passion and adventure
from Romance's bestselling authors